LAWSON

Cerberus MC Book 6
By Marie James

Copyright

Lawson: Cerberus MC Book 6
Copyright © 2017 Marie James & JA Essen
Editing by Marie James Betas
EBooks are not transferrable. All rights are reserved. No part of this book may be used or reproduced in any manner without written permission, except in the case of brief quotations embodied in critical articles and reviews. The unauthorized reproduction or distribution of this copyrighted work is illegal. No part of this book may be scanned, uploaded, or distributed via the Internet or any other means, electronic or print, without the publisher's permission.

This book is a work of fiction. The names, characters, places, and incidents are products of the writer's imagination or have been used fictitiously and are not to be construed as real. Any resemblance to persons, living or dead, actual events, locale, or organizations is entirely coincidental.

Extras:
Cover design by: Essen~tial Designs

Synopsis:

My plan was as simple as they come... in theory. Show up at the Cerberus clubhouse and give dear old Dad a piece of my mind. What I didn't expect was being welcomed into the open arms of a father who had no idea I existed.

More importantly, I didn't anticipate HER. Delilah Donovan was a breath of fresh air. She would soon become my reason for wanting to become a better man, my reason for getting out of bed with a smile on my normally sneering face. But no matter how much I changed, she'd always be too good for a man like me.

It was over before it could even begin.

Acknowledgments

Firstly, if it weren't for the dedicated fans of my original Cerberus MC Series, this book and the ones to follow would not be written. So thank you, my glorious readers, for urging me (sometimes aggressively) to continue the books!

My amazing husband, you are first and foremost my biggest fan, and for that, I'm so incredibly blessed.

Laura Watson... seriously you are the peanut butter to my jelly... the sugar to my Kool-Aid... the peas to my carrots. Without you, Marie James wouldn't even be a possibility! Thank you for your dedication to my brand, which you've committed to 100% and do so with an amazing Canadian smile on your gorgeous face!

Brittney... my boo. What can I say? I miss you every day. I wish we lived closer and could see each other more than twice a year. Thank you for your support and the ear to bend when I'm frustrated and just not feeling very PC.

Speaking of PC, Linda, you amazing southern woman you. I didn't make the mean girls list. (Of which was filled with amazing, far from mean, brilliant women) and I'm nearly certain you have a huge hand in that! You keep me in line when my inner demon child wants to come out and play, and it has been nothing short of incredible working with you and Foreward PR.

Steph and MaRanda... two amazing women from Wyoming... I never thought I'd find such an incredible friendship in the middle of a fly-over state, yet here we are. Many thanks and boob squeezes for your continued support, laughs, and advice! I truly treasure you both.

My amazing BETAS: Laurs, MaRanda, Jaime, Rachel B, Brenda, Sally, Crystal , Shannon, Margaret, Katie, Rachael Y, Louise, you gals keep me sane and I'm forever grateful for the help, suggestions, and edits for this book. A special shoutout to Erin T and Cecilia for taking an extra look at this manuscript!!

Shout out to Give Me Books. Kylie and the girls, you've helped me with almost every release, and I'm grateful for your support!

Bloggers. You keep the Indie world running smoothly, and I'm awed by the support you give each and every one of my books. If it weren't for you, no one would even know who Marie James is!

Readers!! ARC Team!! You amazing Stalkers!! Thank you for reading, sharing, and recommending! Thank you for reviewing and promoting! I appreciate each and every tag, like, and comment!

If you enjoy this book, please, leave a review and tell a friend. The book is loanable so send it to someone who's interested in reading! Discuss it. Speak to one another about what you loved and what you hated, but more importantly, grab the next one!

Peace, love, and Southern sweet tea!   ~Marie James

Prologue
Lawson

"Please don't say that," I beg the only parent I've ever known.

Is that possible? Can you plead death away?

"You need to listen." She gives me a weak smile, the action barely tugging up the corners of her mouth. "You're so stubborn. Just like your father."

My ears perk. She hasn't mentioned the male DNA donor in years. The last time I caught her talking about him, she refused to give me details, citing she'd tell me everything when I was old enough to understand. All I knew was my father was dead, long before I was born.

Drew whimpers from the other side of her hospital bed, clinging to one hand while I hold on to the other.

"My time is up, beautiful boys."

I don't chastise her this time. I don't insist that I'm a man and beautiful is never a word I want describing me.

This time, I let the tear roll down my cheek unchecked.

"No, momma," Drew says through his sobs. "We're not ready."

"We'll never be ready," I murmur.

"Come here," she says to me. "I have so much to tell you."

We both position ourselves closer, fitting easily beside her cancer-ridden, frail body on the single bed.

"Promise me you'll listen to all I have to say." Drew vows, quick to agree even when he doesn't know what he's signing on for. I hesitate. Nothing good comes from that type of intro. "Promise me."

I nod my head in agreement. Ten minutes later, I'm broken, shattered. My mother is gone, my world is imploding, and the new information I've been given is enough to drive me mad.

Chapter 1
Lawson

"This is possibly the worst idea you've ever had," my younger brother Drew complains as we walk down an ill-maintained gravel road. "What do you expect? For him to just answer the door and welcome us with open arms?"

"That's the last fucking thing I want," I sneer. "I want some damn questions answered. We'll probably be out of there in an hour."

"Sure is a long ass trip for an hour of time," he grumbles.

"Watch your mouth," I warn.

"You cuss," he whines. "I should be able to cuss now, too."

I look over my shoulder at him, nearly tripping on yet another pothole in the road. How anyone on a bike navigates this road without ruining their suspension is beyond me. That realization makes me pull my phone from my pocket, checking the map for the hundredth time since we got off the Greyhound bus.

"I'm a man. When you're grown, then you can use whatever language you want."

He laughs at me, sputtering "a man?" in a way that makes my already simmering anger bubble to the top.

"I'm eighteen," I argue. "Legal in every way."

"Not drinking," he challenges.

"I have a fake ID for that," I mutter as my eyes catch the sight of a compound with numerous houses gathered behind it.

"I want one," he says excitedly.

"You wouldn't pass for twenty-one, idiot. I bet you don't even have hair on your nuts yet."

I smile, facing forward so he can't see me.

"I do, too." He mumbles something under his breath two steps behind me.

My fifteen-year-old brother has always tried to keep up with me despite our three year age difference.

"Wow," he hisses as our destination comes into view.

"Yeah," I agree. "The assholes in life always seem to have more than everyone else."

A half dozen houses are the backdrop for a more industrial type building. It pisses me off more, even as a part of me hopes this is the wrong place. Facing my past isn't something I ever thought I'd have to do.

I don't break stride as we head through the open gate and onto the porch. I press the doorbell as Drew, visibly uncomfortable, shifts from one foot to the other.

I look over my shoulder, making sure he's behind me and safe as the door swings open.

Unfamiliar brown eyes stare back at me. This man has auburn hair with gray sprinkled in at his temples.

"You'll know him when you see him," Mom says, using one of her final breaths.

As if he's seeing a ghost, he just stares at me. My eyes narrow at his scrutiny.

He breaks the eye contact first, turning his head to speak over his shoulder. "Babe, can you come here?"

I watch as the most tatted up motherfucker I've ever laid eyes on walks up to join us. His hand makes contact with the man who opened the door before his eyes even look toward me.

Recognition marks his face also. I stare back at him for a brief second. His ice blue eyes, the same color as mine, fight for understanding.

"You must be my dad," I sneer.

"What the fuck?" the blue-eyed fucker hisses, earning a slap to the chest from the other man.

"Please come in." The untatted man offers his hand. "I'm Robert."

I side saddle past him, finding more than a dozen pairs of eyes staring back at me while my younger brother apologizes for my rudeness and introduces himself. Regret swims in my gut at the sight of all of these spectators. The bravado I mustered on the walk here, dwindles away quickly as I take in the tough-looking grown men scattered around the room. I don't miss the handful of gorgeous girls in the room, either.

Just as I'd suspected, these old fucking bikers are still doing what bikers do; fucking young girls while throwing the used-up ones out like trash. Several older women, gorgeous in their own right, stare back wide-eyed and confused. They must be the ones training the new ones as their replacements.

"Time to clear out," a bald man with sleeves of tats peeking out from his t-shirt booms.

Groans and complaints echo around the room, but everyone begins to stand, gather their things, and disappear down the hallway at the back of the room.

The man barking orders must be Kincaid, the club president. The soft look he gives to the two assholes behind me isn't in character with what you'd expect from the leader of an MC. Information on the club was limited during my research over the last couple of weeks since Mom passed, but the internet had plenty of information on other clubs.

A pair of teenagers gawk at me. Clearly twins, or very close in age, they linger, eyes darting from the intruders in their world and back to the guys standing at my back.

"Go," one of them insists.

The boy moves quickly, but the ice blue eyes of the girl hold mine, the delicate column of her throat working on a rough swallow under my attention. It's clear she's attracted to me when her tongue swipes at her bottom lip. I'll fuck that mouth later, given a chance, but I have other shit to deal with right now.

"Dad?" she whispers.

"Go," the booming voice comes again.

She scurries away as disgust sends goosebumps down my arms.

Dad? I can't decipher which pisses me off more, that I may have just envisioned my sister on her knees deep throating me or that my father has other children he stuck around for when my mom, pregnant with me, was tossed to the curb.

I spin, my eyes first searching for Drew, something I've done my whole life until they land on the other two.

"How do you want to do this?" I ask the man who looks like an older version of the guy I see in the mirror each morning. He has tats on nearly every part of his body, stars on his pierced cheeks, and despite his age, it's still working for him. A look into my future doesn't seem so bleak, even if vanity is the only thing I honestly want to focus on right now. All of the other things that need to be said come with a pain in my chest that's difficult to get rid of.

"However you want," the brown-eyed man says. He motions to the vacated couch across the room. "We can sit."

Drew, always obedient, follows him while I stand locked in place staring at the man who ruined my mom's life. It isn't until I see the pleading in my brother's eyes as he looks at me after sweeping his attention around the room, that I cave and move to sit beside him. I didn't miss the pool table, arcade games, or the TV too big for any person to own when I first walked in. Those materialistic things don't mean shit to me, but Drew is easily impressed

"Nice place you have here." I avoid eye contact as I look around the open area of the room. "It begs me to wonder just how many pregnant women you forced out after they got used to such luxury."

Drew trembles beside me, and I hate having this conversation in front of him. I haven't given him the gory details of what Mom whispered in my ear on her last day in this world.

"None," Robert says.

I huff a laugh. "Funny, that's not what happened to my mother."

"And who is your mother?"

The gall of this motherfucker.

"What's wrong, Snatch?" I hiss. "Can't remember the last time you fucked a woman?"

He narrows his eyes at me but keeps his mouth shut.

"I'll give you a hint. I just turned eighteen."

Robert's eyes widen as my sperm donor hisses. "Darby."

I hear Drew sniffle at the sound of our mother's name and it pisses me off coming from his lips more than I ever thought it would.

"Don't speak her name, ever again," I growl.

The men across from us share a private look before turning their attention back to us, making my blood pump harder, thicker in my veins. It's taking everything I have to stay seated and not attack both of them.

"Are you sure?"

I glare at him. "Are you kidding me? I would tell you to take a long, hard look in the mirror," I point at my face, one I'd been proud of until seeing him. "But you're kind of looking in one, don't you think?"

Tattooed fingers sweep over his head as he soaks all of this in. Minutes drag by before he speaks again. "I'd like to speak with your mother. There seems to be a lot of things we need to discuss."

My eyes sting at the possibility of speaking to my mother again. "Like what? You want to bitch her out for telling me how to find you? Reject her one more time since I'm interfering in your life again?"

He shakes his head, but I continue.

"Tell me, Snatch, what was it about her or me for that matter that would make you reject us but have two more children with some other woman? Did we not fit into your life or was it her specifically that you couldn't stomach?"

"That's not what—" Snatch holds his hand up to stop Robert from speaking.

"One," he says with no anger or agitation in his voice. Cool, calm, collected, and more than a little infuriating. "You can call me Jaxon. I haven't gone by Snatch in over fifteen years. Your mother wouldn't know that because I haven't seen her in over eighteen years. She never knew my real name."

I bristle at the implication of my mother being the type of woman who would sleep with men before getting to know even their names. It's Drew's hand on my forearm that keeps me from knocking this asshole out.

"Two," he continues, not bothered by my restrained anger. "Your mother never told me she was pregnant. She disappeared one night, and we never heard from her again."

"Bull—" I get the same hand he held up at Robert. Even enraged, I silence my words, which pisses me off even more.

"Three, even though it doesn't make any difference, Samson and Delilah are adopted, so there was never another woman."

"Law," Drew whispers drawing my stunned eyes to him. "Just hear them out."

I shake my head, but words are impossible to form.

"Please," he begs, exhausted from traveling through numerous states to get here. He leans closer and whispers. "I'm tired and hungry."

Protecting Drew has been my focus since I was old enough to understand that my mother's continued bad decisions left him fending for himself many times. This time is no different.

I stand from my place on the couch. "We shouldn't have come here. Come on, Drew."

He hesitates at first, but I feel his presence at my back as I grab my duffel bag from where I dropped it on the floor when I'd first walked in.

"We'll find a hotel or something," I mutter to him as my hand encircles the doorknob.

"We don't have the money for that," he adds.

"I'll figure it out."

"Like last time," he whispers just as Jaxon calls out, "Don't go."

"Please stay," Robert says walking closer than Jaxon is willing to at this point. "We have plenty of room in the house."

I ignore him and look down into the pleading eyes of my baby brother.

"What will happen if you go to jail?"

"I won't," I promise and turn back to the front porch.

"You said that last time," he persists.

Guilt and a flood of memories hit me all at once. They're troublesome enough to make me turn in the direction of the two men I never wanted to see longer than to say my peace.

"I'm not calling either one of you dad."

Relief at my concession is clear on Robert's face. Jaxon looks like he could puke any minute.

Chapter 2
Delilah

"Who was that?" I ask my brother.

Nervous energy has me pacing my room as he sits on the bed, uninterested in the two boys that just showed up at the clubhouse. He's only able to focus on a way to convince Dad and Pop to let him go on the senior trip to Mexico when he's not even a senior until fall. I'm grateful for the lack of attention and the inspection my response would bring if he bothered to notice me.

"No clue," he says in a dismissive tone.

"Diego and Morrison seemed to recognize the older one," I add.

"Guys looking for work?" he offers even though it's a ridiculous notion.

"The dark-haired kid is younger than us, Sam. So I doubt that."

He doesn't even bother to pull his eyes from his cell phone as he types furiously on the screen.

"Does it matter?"

"Of course it matters," I hiss at him, the self-absorbed response has me stopping in my tracks. "He has Dad's eyes."

He huffs. "We have Dad's eyes."

"And we're blonde. How many guys do you know that have black hair and piercing blue eyes?"

His gaze pulls from his phone and meets mine. "Piercing? Really, Delilah?"

"What?" I shrug and continue walking across the room. With my back to him, I fiddle with things on my dresser.

"Maybe it's a long-lost son," he offers with no enthusiasm.

"Don't even say that," I squeal turning back to him. "That would be disgusting."

Dammit.

His phone drops to the turquoise duvet covering my bed, and I have his full attention now. The one thing I was hoping not to draw. I can handle a distracted Samson, but when his twin eyes stare into mine, all of my secrets spill out with minimal effort on his part.

"Disgusting? Tell me, Delilah, what would be so gross about Dad having a blood-related child with *piercing* blue eyes?"

"N-nothing," I mumble. "I misspoke."

"You're the smartest girl in our school, so I highly doubt that."

I turn away from him without a word. I can feel the heat of my embarrassment flushing my cheeks.

"They had duffel bags with them," he says as if I didn't notice them, too. "They're probably moving in with us."

I turn, fast enough to knock a few books off of my dresser, only to find his back at my door and his laughter echoing down the hall as he heads to his room.

Moving in?

There's no way the beautiful stranger will end up here.

I let it sink in as I pick up the things I knocked down. Neither one of my dads would turn away a kid in need, and even though the older one looked one hundred percent grown, the younger one isn't.

Sticking my head out of my room, I listen for my brother. I'm met with silence and knowing him, he's locked away in his room on his phone or he's masturbating.

I shudder at the memory of forgetting to knock before entering his room last week. As I try to force bile back down, I head to the spare bedroom. It's clean, but I'm not sure who slept in the bunk beds last, so I strip them and grab fresh, clean sheets to remake them. Sometimes Dustin and Khloe's little boy stays in here and sometimes it's friends from school or others from next door.

Satisfied that the beds are ready to go, I scoop up the dirty linens and run them down to the laundry room. From the small window, I see Gigi sitting on her front porch painting her nails. Her body is angled so she can keep an eye on the back door of the clubhouse. Seems the handsome, blue-eyed stranger caught her attention too. There's no other reason for her to be battling the late May heat, and I know for a fact she hates to sweat.

Disgusted with myself at finding him so handsome and the possibility that he could be my brother, I head back upstairs and keep the door cracked so I can hear them if they come home with my dads.

I don't wait long before the sound of the front door opening and closing makes it up the stairs. Sticking my ear to the crack in the door, I listen for movement and conversation from below. Unable to decipher the voices, I step out on the landing just as my dad, Jaxon, is coming toward me. Both boys, the younger one with excited anticipation in his eyes, the other with more anger on his face than any guy his age should suffer, follow behind him.

"I changed the sheets on the bunk beds," I inform him.

"Thanks, sweetheart," Jaxon says with a quick kiss on my temple as he walks past to the spare room.

"Perfect little ass kisser aren't you?" the older boy sneers as he walks past.

I recoil at his rudeness but follow them into the room.

"You guys have free run of the house except for the bedrooms. Stick to your own so personal boundaries aren't broken," my dad explains as Drew bounds up the bunk bed stairs and plops down on the mattress. "Hopefully you'll be comfortable."

"Are you kidding?" Drew yips. "This is better than anything we've ever had."

My heart clenches. A bunk bed is better than anything? That's both sad and pitiful.

"Drew," the tall guy beside me chastises with a frown.

I see my dad's eyes soften as he looks up at Drew who's crossed his legs at his ankles and positioned his hands behind his head. The kid is truly in hog heaven right now.

"Which room is yours?" The gruff whisper from beside me has more effect than it ever should.

I take a step back and to the side, creating some distance between us. Bumping into the door and causing it to knock against the bump stop garners my dad's attention and he turns to face us. First, his eyes assess the boy, and then they turn to me.

"Lawson, this is my daughter, Delilah. Delilah, this is—"

"His bastard son," Lawson interrupts holding his hand out to me as my eyes flash to my dad.

His lips flatten, but the slight nod of his head tells me to shake his hand, and that he's handling a difficult situation the best he can.

When he wraps his hand around my smaller one, there's no burst of electricity, no zing up my arm predicting my future obsession with this man. The only thing I feel is the cold sweat on his palm betraying his anxiety over this whole situation. It's almost worse than that burst of adrenaline I've read about so many times in books. His somatic reaction to this situation makes me feel sorry for him, pity the life he may have had up until this point. It pushes away the anger I felt with his snide comment in the hall and makes me want to pull him against my chest and tell him everything will be fine.

"Nice to meet you," I manage after an awkwardly long handshake.

"I can't wait to get to know you better," he says as I jerk my hand away.

In a rude gesture, I rub my hand against the fabric of my cut-off shorts, a way to let him know I feel his discomfort. It's mean and something out of character for me, but he needs to know I can read him like a book. Let him act macho and pissed off with everyone else, but his secrets were revealed in a simple handshake.

"This is Drew," my dad says interrupting the stare off Lawson and I are having.

I divert my eyes to the younger boy, closing the space between us with an outstretched hand. "Nice to meet you, Drew."

He shakes my hand over the rail of the top bunk and due to my height, or lack thereof, I have to stretch to reach it.

I pop back down on the heels of my bare feet when an appreciative grunt echoes around the room. Embarrassed, I pull down the hem of my tank top that had shifted up on my back.

Turning and not making eye contact with anyone but my dad, I direct my words at him. "I'll be in my room until supper."

He nods as I reach up on my tiptoes and kiss his cheek. "Maybe change your clothes."

A suggestion I plan on following the second I get back to my room. "Yes, sir."

Lawson is chuckling as I scurry past him and make it to the safety of my bedroom. Closing the door, I twist the lock for good measure.

With no time to ask my dad questions, my mind races with what putting Lawson and Drew up in the spare room means. Are they living here? Is it only for a few nights?

Bastard son?

Samson was right. The worst possible explanation of this situation has just been laid at my feet. I feel sorry for them. Just the small glimpse into their lives with a few spoken words from Drew's lips paints a dreary picture.

The ding of my cell phone pulls me from my selfish thoughts of wondering how them being here is going to affect my life. I'm no better than Samson.

Gigi: *What's going on? I saw them go inside your house*.

"Of course you did," I mutter to the text message.

Ignoring her text, I toss my phone back down on my bed and change my clothes.

Avoiding him without seeming rude will probably be my best bet. He's a grown man, or at least he looks like one so he won't be here long. The rules in the house aren't what I'd call strict, but there are limitations to our choices. Lawson doesn't seem like the guy who's going to stick around after the 'my house-my rules' speech is given to him.

Chapter 3
Lawson

"Dinner is in forty-five minutes," Jaxon says as he steps away from the bunk bed where my brother is acting like Oliver Twist who's climbed into a real bed for the first time.

Way to keep things close to your chest there, Drew.

"Not hungry," I mutter before he reaches the door. I pray my stomach doesn't growl in protest to my lie.

"Kitchen's always open if you get hungry later tonight," he offers, unlike the asshole I made him out to be. Leaning in close and focusing on me after checking to see if Drew's attention is on us. He gets closer than he ever has before. "I'll give you anything you need, money, opportunities, a real chance at life, but don't hurt my family."

My jaw clenches to the point of pain, but I keep my focus across the room.

"That includes my daughter."

Now he has my attention. He read me like an open book, or he saw my cock thicken in my jeans when she reached up and shook Drew's hand. I nearly groan for the second time at the memory.

The door snaps shut before I realize he left.

"They don't want us here," I tell my ecstatic brother as he reaches his hands up to see if he can touch the ceiling while lying flat on his back.

"They seem shocked, but I never got that vibe from them," he counters.

"You wouldn't," I mutter sliding the strap of my duffel off of my shoulder. "You were too busy jizzing in your pants over a goddamned bunk bed."

He chuckles, used to my brashness. "Wait until you lay down, asshole. These mattresses are perfect."

"Language," I warn.

He huffs but doesn't respond. My mother's stubbornness runs through my blood like a living thing. It's the exact reason I choose to sit in the rolling chair in front of the desk on the far side of the room.

Movement outside of the window catches my eye, and the sight of long, golden legs peeking out from the steps leading up to the house next door makes me smile and reminds me of the slew of hot chicks who were in the main building when we'd first arrived.

Maybe living here surrounded by hot chicks won't be so bad.

I shake my head, clearing that thought. I have no desire to spend more than the minimal time needed on this property. I have to get Drew settled, make sure that he'll be safe and they won't just shove him off into the system, and then I'm out of here. The fact that these two men adopted twins helps settle my nerves somehow. Anyone taking the step to welcome non-biological children into their home is an act of compassion many people wouldn't consider.

Drew's slow and steady breathing tells me just how exhausted the kid is. We've been traveling for several days. Add in the emotional stress of losing our mother less than a month ago, and it's no wonder he can fall asleep only minutes after invading some stranger's home.

Dark hair and dark eyes clear the front edge of the porch's roof. The girl sitting there meets my gaze as if she either feels me watching her or she knew exactly where we'd be in this house. I don't turn my head after getting caught. Instead, I smirk at her. Her head dips back, out of view, but less than a minute later, she's wiping lotion or tanning oil down her legs. The motion isn't economical in the least. Her attempt at a sensual rub down makes my eyebrow quirk and my dick jump more from underuse than attraction.

Note to self: avoid the brunette.

Aggressive women aren't my style at all. The last thing I need is a girl trying to take control of any situation we're tossed into together. It's the thrill of the chase that gets my blood pumping, the prospect that I'm convincing an otherwise uninterested party to act a certain way.

I have a feeling that the toy I want to play with most is somewhere in this house. The girl on the porch, performing for some guy she doesn't even know, doesn't hold a candle to the fun I'll have with Delilah.

***

"Hey."

I spent several long minutes looking at Drew sleeping peacefully before waking him. He's the picture of innocence, long dark lashes resting against his cheeks and a slight pucker to his lips. I know different though. This kid has seen more, been forced to endure more heartache than anyone ever should. My only goal in life is to protect him.

He draws in a long breath, stretching his muscles out on the bed. "I told you this bed was awesome."

"You need to go down and eat," I tell him.

"Awesome," he says climbing off of the bed. "I'm fucking starving."

"Seriously, Drew?" I narrow my eyes at him. "You need to watch your mouth. These don't seem like the type of people who are going to tolerate that language from a fifteen-year-old."

He nods, both in understanding and not wanting anything to ruin his chance to sleep in a soft bed rather than a worn out mattress on the floor. The last month has been tough on both of us. Hitchhiking across several states before some sad fucker felt bad enough to give us the money for bus tickets took a lot out of us.

He pauses at the door, looking over his shoulder at me sitting back in the desk chair. "Aren't you coming?"

I shake my head. "Not hungry."

I can tell by the look on his face that he doesn't believe the lie, but he just nods and closes the door behind him when he leaves.

"Drew," I call out a second later.

I spring up from the chair and pull the door open. Both my brother and Delilah are in the hall walking toward the stairs.

"Drew," I say again.

"What's up?" he asks as he turns back to me.

Delilah stops, turning her nosey ass attention to us. "Can I help you with something, Princess?"

Her nose shrivels as she looks at me with disgust, but she takes the hint and disappears down the hall.

"What, Law? I'm hungry."

"Don't tell them anything," I instruct. "Don't give them details about our life. Hell, tell them we came from Utah or something. Feed them anything but the truth."

He frowns. "You want me to lie to your dad?"

"He's not my fucking dad. He's merely a sperm donor who treated Mom like shit."

"Fine," he mutters and walks away again without a backward glance.

I wait, annoyed by the laughter that's flowing up the stairs, for Drew to return to the room. Boredom sets in, and the girl next door is no longer on her porch, but the pull isn't strong enough to get me to leave this room to join the happy little family.

Fifteen minutes after I give up looking at random shit on the internet with my phone, Drew comes back up to the room with a grin on his face. I hate that it falls when he steps through the door.

"What's up?" he asks looking at my phone with apprehension. "Are we leaving?"

We haven't stayed anywhere very long for a while.

"Not just yet," I answer. "Happen to get the Wi-Fi password?"

He shuffles on his feet. "I did, but Samson keyed it into my phone, so I don't know what it is."

I slide my phone back into my pocket.

"I can go back down and get it for you," he offers.

"No thanks," I grumble and sit further back in the desk chair with my arms crossed over my chest. "Sounds like you were having a good time down there."

"I won't next time if you don't want me to."

I'm an asshole.

"It's fine." I want to ask him what they were doing, but I just can't bring myself to, and now that I mentioned it, Drew will avoid telling me anything.

A yawn escapes his mouth before he has time to react and cover his mouth. "I'm so tired."

"You should go to bed," I say without inflection. "I'll keep first watch."

He shakes his head but climbs the stairs on the bunk bed anyway. "I think we can both sleep at the same time, dude. I don't think they're going to bother us."

"What have I always told you?"

"Safety is an illusion, and it's not worth the risk," he mutters before kicking his sneakers over the side of the bed.

Rolling my eyes, I scoop them up and place them under the edge of the bed, all the way to the left just like always. It's just part of the routine, in case we have to get out fast.

"I don't mind staying up with you," he says, sleepiness already clouding his voice.

"I got it." I turn off the bedroom light and sit back down in the chair. "Get some rest."

Soft snores fill the room mere minutes later. I force away the possibility of making a life in New Mexico. The last thing I need is to be in the shadow of a couple of washed-up bikers.

From the darkness of the room, it's easy to look out over the perfect stone-faced homes. Four homes make a semi-circle behind the building we first came into earlier today. Perfect, but not cookie cutter, each one having its own personality to fit the occupants. They're bigger, nicer, more substantial than any home I've ever been inside of before.

I shudder thinking about the last time I was in a house this nice. I wasn't in it long before streaks of red and blue lights filtered through expensive, sheer curtains. I feel as unwanted in this house as I did in that one.

Chapter 4
Delilah

Sighing, I snuggle deeper into the sofa. My happy place. The perfect time of day where everyone heads to their rooms and I can sit and read without being distracted.

There may be no one around, but my focus isn't on the eReader in my lap, but rather the guy upstairs who refused to come down for dinner. Drew showed his face, and pleasantly, although extremely guarded, interacted with the family. I couldn't keep my eyes from the base of the stairs, every second of dinner spent waiting for him to show up.

Noise at my back startles me, but when I look over my shoulder, I find myself alone.

I turn from having my back against the arm of the couch to facing the direction the noise came from. It doesn't take long before an unfamiliar figure clears the bottom of the stairs.

Lawson.

Of course, he would show his face after everyone disappeared for the night.

Sitting in the shadows, I watch in silence as he stops and looks around. I can't tell if he's familiarizing himself with the layout of the downstairs or if he's casing the place.

"Can I help you find something?"

He doesn't jump like I expect, or even turn his head in my direction. He knew I was here the entire time. Under the dim light at the base of the stairs, I watch his hands clench, closing and opening twice before he finally acknowledges me.

"What do you have in mind?" His throaty voice is more seductive than I'd like.

I swallow, the growing lump in my throat. "I-I can make you a sandwich. You must be hungry."

"You don't know a fucking thing about me," he sneers, his anger an overreaction to my simple offer.

"I know you didn't come down for dinner. I know Drew ate three plates of lasagna before he was full enough to stop shoveling it in."

The sadness I felt earlier creeps back up at the defensiveness he feels he has to exert at me.

"I just figured you'd be hungry, too." I set my eReader on the low coffee table. "If you don't want to eat, that's fine, but if you're planning on sneaking out, you can't use the doors. My dad has already set the alarm."

"Which one?" he asks.

"Huh? Which door? All of them," I inform him.

He chuckles, the sarcastic tone grating over my sensibilities.

"Which dad?" he corrects in a way that makes my eyes narrow.

I can get behind him having a crappy attitude because of the life he's had up until now, but having a problem with my dads because of their sexuality isn't going to fly.

"Does it matter?" He stays silent, staring in my direction as if he has night vision. "Do you have a problem with gay men?"

He shakes his head, but I can't tell which question he's answering.

"They aren't the first gay couple I've encountered, Princess. Which one has you on lockdown?"

My lip twitches in agitation. "We aren't on lockdown. It's for our own protection."

"Protection?" He huffs and turns his head away from my direction. I sag, finally relaxing a little from being under his hard eyes. "Sounds like something Jaxon would do. He seems like a control freak."

I stand from the sofa, angry at this jerk coming into our home and questioning the way we live. He doesn't have a damn clue the trouble that could find us from the years my dads spent battling bad guys all over the world. If he could find us so can others. It's not like we advertise where the Cerberus' hub of operation is, but it only takes a simple web search to find it.

"Listen, asshole," I growl closing the distance between us but not getting close enough that he can reach out and touch me. "If you don't want me to question your life, where you came from, why your brother ate dinner like he hadn't eaten in days and was terrified he wouldn't eat again for a week, then you need to stop making hasty judgments where my family is concerned."

"I think I like you feisty," he teases with a smirk.

I hate that damn smirk.

"How about you stay away from me and I'll stay away from you."

He shakes his head again. "That's the last thing I want."

Crossing my arms over my chest, I gawk at him, hating the confusion this entire conversation is causing. "Well, you're rude, and the last thing I want is some boy with a chip the size of Texas on his shoulder ruining my summer."

He steps a foot closer, and warning bells go off in my head. Immediately, I question my safety in my own home.

"I promise you, I'm all man. There's not one part of me that's still a boy."

I tense, unsure of how to take his blatantly sexual comment. I stand my ground but remain quiet.

"Besides, how will you suck my cock if we're avoiding each other?" He draws another foot closer, so close I can feel the energy flowing off of his body. "Maybe I can sneak in your room at night? I won't mind coming to you as long as you stay quiet."

With wide eyes, I stare up at him, but he's not finished speaking. For the life of me, I don't know why I want to hear everything he has to say.

"But don't worry, Princess. When I'm pressing against the back of your throat, you won't even be able to whimper."

"I'd never," I hiss, taking a step back and finally coming to my senses. "That's never going to happen between us."

He shrugs, nonchalant as if he hasn't just said the filthiest thing I've heard directed at me.

"Does that usually work for women? Or is it just another defense mechanism?"

"Women?" He snorts. "You're far from a woman."

I want to argue with him, but proclaiming adulthood right now doesn't seem like the best course of action.

"I normally don't go after *girls*, but you'll do in a pinch."

"I can assure you, you're wasting your time."

"You'll suck me off eventually," he predicts.

"I'd rather drink bleach," I hiss, giving him a wide berth as I walk past him toward the stairs.

"Bleach won't pull your hair and make your pussy wet," he calls after me.

Taking the stairs two at a time, I get away from him as quickly as I can. When I realize my eReader is still on the table, I debate going back down to get it. I shake my head at the idea.

"Not even worth it," I mutter. "I can read on my laptop."

I click the door lock in place, hoping he can hear it echo in the quiet house. Hopefully, he'll take a hint and won't even try to get in here tonight. I war with myself as I climb into bed and grab my phone from my nightstand, wondering if I should tell my dad about what he said.

I decide that he's just an asshole, all talk and no follow through. He wouldn't hurt me, especially not in my own home. I know my dads to be teddy bears, but they're more than a little intimidating. Rob is muscled and fit similar to a college linebacker, and Jaxon is covered with so much ink and piercings only an idiot would challenge him.

The vibration of my cell phone is just the distraction I need. Gigi's name flashes on the screen, full-on duck lips and a peace sign. She demanded I use the picture.

"Hello," I answer.

"So?" she hisses.

I don't answer. I know what she wants, but making Gigi wait for answers is always fun since most everyone in her life gives her what she wants, be it attention from the boys at school, the teachers who think she's perfect, or her mom and dad who have no clue just how wild their daughter is.

"I saw your light come on, Delilah. I know you're alone so spill." I smile at her insistence. "Tell me about the hottie."

"He's a jerk."

"Hmm. He looked like a bad boy." I hear rustling in the background as if she's settling in for some serious gossip. "Tell me more."

"Not much to tell. He's rude, crude, and egotistical."

She laughs. "So you hit on him, and he turned you down?"

I roll my eyes at her assumptions.

"That's gross. He's Jaxon's biological son."

"And?" she says. "I know that part. I heard Mom and Dad whispering about it in the kitchen earlier."

"That makes him like my brother. So no I didn't hit on him."

More like he offered or expected me to do devilish things to him.

"Not even close," she responds.

"What?" Shaking my head, I try to focus on the conversation rather than wondering where in the house Lawson is.

"He's not your brother, not by a long shot. You're adopted, he's blood. You've been there your whole life. From the looks on everyone's faces at the clubhouse earlier, they'd never seen those boys before in their life. It's different, but it isn't gross," she explains.

"No thanks," I mutter.

"Give him my phone number," she urges.

"What? No, I'm not doing that."

"If you're not staking a claim, then I should have a shot."

"He's not some uncharted territory you can claim, Gigi."

"Why are you arguing about it?" I shift on my bed, uncomfortable with her questions.

"I'm not," I finally answer. "He's all yours."

"Good." I can hear her grin through the phone. "Now just let him know."

"Sure," I tell her and hang up the phone.

Like I'll ever have an intentional conversation with Lawson again. Avoiding him at all costs seems to be the best way to survive his and Drew's intrusion into our lives.

Chapter 5
Lawson

A genuine smile, the first in a very long time, is on my face as I watch Delilah scurry up the stairs. Toying with her is going to be more fun than I ever thought possible. I'd judged her wrong, thinking she'd cower or cry, run to daddy when faced with my teasing. She challenged me. Stood her ground like she was invincible. It's stupid on her part, but more than a little entertaining for me.

I hear the lock turn on her bedroom door, and my smile grows bigger. If she thinks a simple door lock will keep me out of her room, she's got another think coming.

Standing still, I listen for the sounds every house makes as it begins to calm from the day's events. I familiarize myself with each one, the low rumble of the AC, the quiet murmurs coming from the master suite, and the New Mexico wind rustling the trees outside of the dining room window. Feeling sure that no one other than Delilah knows I'm down here, I slink into the kitchen.

The mention of lasagna from my earlier conversation with the blonde bombshell has my mouth watering and the hunger pains from my stomach setting into my bones. As silent as possible, I pull open the door to the fridge, and I'm met with the most organized shelves I've ever faced before. This has to be Delilah's doing. She seems like the OCD, anal-retentive type.

I almost want to cry when I see that even though Drew ate his weight in the meal, there is still lasagna left over on the shelf. Not bothering with the microwave or a plate, I grab a fork and begin shoveling the food into my mouth. The flavors explode on my tongue, but I can't be bothered to savor the best meal I've had in weeks. My only goal, satisfying the hunger in my gut, doesn't allow me to even pause in between bites much less appreciate the effort that had to have gone into preparing it.

After getting my fill, I replace the lid and place it back on the shelf. It's only then that I consider the fact that this meal was prepared, time was taken, from the looks of it, to be made from scratch. No store-bought Stouffers for this family. Even as happy as my stomach is, it angers me even further.

Contemplating just leaving the dirty fork in the otherwise spotless sink, I hold it in my hand and look around the kitchen. Sleek stainless steel appliances with every cooking gadget known to man, down to the canisters labeled with flour and sugar take up space on the counter. Perfect little kitchen for a perfect little family.

I shake my head, thinking of ways to knock them down a notch or two and wash the damn fork. After drying it, I place it back in the silverware drawer, upside down and backward of course. This asshole act is the only thing that comes to mind at the moment.

My hand shakes as I push the drawer closed, the urge to destroy this entire house a physical being in my body. I won't. I can't bring any more trouble down on me. I won't do anything to compromise Drew's future. Jaxon seems like a big enough asshole to get rid of him the second the cops would slap cuffs on my wrists.

No. Fucking with Delilah and making Samson's life a living hell seem like a much more fitting task. Every day, they live the life I should've had. Every day, they wake up in a perfect home not having to worry about their safety, where their next meal is coming from. Those two have no idea just how good they have it, how lucky they are. It's my job to make them realize what an imperfect world is really like.

With my belly full and a sinister smile on my face, I push off of the counter and make my way back to the stairs. My plans can start first thing in the morning. Right now, I need to catch a few hours of sleep and rejuvenate my body.

The low murmurs I'd heard after Delilah shook her ass all the way up the stairs are louder than before. I creep along, getting closer to the door to what I can only assume is the master bedroom. Keeping my feet over a foot away, I angle my head so I can hear better.

"I can't fucking believe her," Jaxon hisses. "She just leaves, pregnant with my son, and doesn't bother to tell anyone?"

"It's pretty fucked up," Rob responds.

"Eighteen years!" Jaxon hisses. "Eighteen fucking years and not so much as a letter? A phone call?"

"She was mad you rejected her," Rob interjects.

My fists clench, the words my mother whispered in my ear on her deathbed showing up, unwanted, at this moment.

Your father isn't dead. Find the Cerberus MC when I'm gone. He didn't want us. You'll recognize him when you see him.

This asshole has the nerve to pretend he didn't know about me?

Maybe he knew and never told Rob?

"She was a club girl for Christ's sake," Jaxon bellows.

"Keep your voice down."

I hear him huff but his next words, although coming out on a hiss of breath are quieter. "She was fucking everyone in the club, Itchy."

Itchy?

"Not just you and me," he continues. "Ace. Snake. Snapper. She knew where you and I were heading. She pushed us together. She had to have known she didn't factor into the equation."

"Feelings are messy," Rob cajoles. "You know neither one of us had a damn clue this is where we'd end up when we started the whole group sex scene."

"And Drew? Do you think she told that poor kid's dad?" Jaxon has no damn clue about Drew's asshole father. "She probably lied about him also. Hell, knowing Darby she doesn't have a clue who his father is. She probably didn't know Lawson was mine until he got older."

I'm seething, angry enough at the shitty way he's talking about my mom to reach for the door handle.

I don't consider that he's right. I don't let the memories of all of the men that filtered in and out of our lives figure into the equation of my anger. I won't concede to his way of thinking, even if it is so fucking close to the truth that it's eerie.

I pull up short when he starts speaking again.

"He spent his entire life, living God knows what way, no father when he had two perfectly good men here willing to give him everything he could ever want. Who does that to a child? Who is so damned prideful that they stew in their stubbornness and let their son suffer for almost two decades?"

"I'm sure she did what she thought was best at the time," Jaxon growls, but Rob keeps going. "We told her we didn't want children. Do you remember the numerous conversations we had, lying in bed after Misty showed up with Griffin? She was only reacting to what we had said."

I wasn't the only product of some quick fuck by a biker? This club is more fucked up than I thought.

"What the hell are we going to do now?" Defeat fills Jaxon's voice.

"He needs us now," Rob says softly.

"He doesn't want a fucking thing to do with us," Jaxon counters.

Damn right I don't.

"He doesn't have many other choices. We give them a place to land, provide both boys with what they need." Rustling of bed covers can be heard before Rob continues. "It's all we can do. Provide that and hope they're smart enough to take it."

"That's doubtful," Jaxon interrupts. "Did you see the look in Lawson's eyes? I had that same look in mine. Coming from a shitty home, living the way I had to, the things I had to do just to survive. I was pissed at the world, ready to take any motherfucker on that challenged me. Hell, I was willing to destroy my own life for just the smallest taste of revenge."

"I remember the angry fucker you were when you showed up at boot camp," Rob recalls. "I don't think you spoke a word to anyone until at least Swim Week."

"Exactly," Jaxon mutters. "It took the Marine Corps for me to realize that I could have a different life than the one I'd thought I was destined to all my life."

"Maybe that's exactly what he needs, too."

My hands shake, the trembling damn near bone-deep, as I step away from the door.

Marine Corps?

Fuck those two if they think even for a second that I'm going to sign up or participate in that shit. Taking the stairs two at a time, I head to the bedroom they were pitied into giving us. I keep in mind that Drew is sleeping, oblivious to the pain he's going to feel tomorrow when he wakes up to find me gone. Leaving is the only option. If they ship me off, I won't be able to help Drew at all.

Silently, the door opens, and I lock us both inside. His soft breathing fills the room, and I envy the peace he's found in sleep. Sitting down on the desk chair, I give myself a few moments for my nerves to settle.

"The doors have alarms on them."

Delilah didn't mention the windows, but is it a risk I should take? This house is out in the middle of nowhere. I don't have a clue about the terrain, and navigating it in the dark will be almost impossible. I flex my neck, leaning my head over the back of the chair, trying to think of the best course of action.

I'm eighteen. They can't force me to go into the military, but they can use Drew as a bargaining chip.

I can't allow that to happen, but leaving right now seems impossible. I close my eyes as the exhaustion from the day, fuck, the last several years, begins to weigh me down. Stomach full of lasagna, I don't stand a chance. My eyes flutter closed before I have the ability to realize I'm falling asleep.

Chapter 6
Delilah

A thump outside of my room wedges its way between sleep and conscious thought. Rolling over, I ignore the intrusion. I tossed and turned all night, and Sunday mornings are made for sleeping late.

"I don't want to leave." The unfamiliar whining filters through my door, and I sit up in bed.

"We can't fucking stay," Lawson snaps at his younger brother. "Hurry before you wake everyone in the house."

I didn't figure that they would stay long. Lawson isn't the type to abide by rules, and my dad isn't one to cave or bend his rules for anyone, much less an angry boy who's mad at the world.

I find nothing but their retreating backs when I pull open my door. Each with the duffel bag they arrived with, they slowly make their way down the stairs.

That's when all hell breaks loose.

"And where do you think you two are going?" The anger and irritation in Jaxon's voice are palpable.

I creep down the stairs, finding the boys in a standoff with my dad in the living room.

"Leaving," Lawson hisses. "And you can't fucking stop us."

I believe him, and the surety in his tone tells me he believes it too. The only problem is when my dads, Jaxon specifically, make their minds up about something, it's as good as written in stone. He's not one to be pushed around, but I fear digging in will only make Lawson push back more.

"Not going to happen," Rob says with quiet authority.

"Try and keep us from leaving," Lawson challenges.

Jaxon takes a step closer, and the tension in Lawson's back is visible.

"You're eighteen, Lawson. I can't keep you from leaving this house. I won't even attempt to, but Drew is not leaving with you."

"He's my brother," Lawson sneers.

Chill bumps race over my arms at the menace in his voice.

"What's going on?" I jump, startled when Samson speaks over my shoulder.

I turn back to the cluster of people ten feet away, praying they don't notice our intrusion. Of course, my dads know we're here, but the other two seem oblivious to our eavesdropping.

"Lawson is trying to leave," I explain not taking my eyes from the altercation that seems to be seconds away from turning physically violent.

"Let 'em leave," he whispers. "I have no idea why they showed up in the first place."

It appears my brother's goal of distraction for my dads isn't going to work the way he wants. I can tell by the tone of his voice that he anticipates Dad being too angry to change his mind on the senior trip.

"He's a minor," Jaxon interjects. "You're not leaving here with him to end up God knows where."

"The world is a scary place, Lawson." Rob is doing his best to de-escalate the situation.

Lawson's maniacal laugh makes my skin crawl.

"Scary? You have no fucking idea what we've been through. We'll be fine."

"That's the fucking point," Jaxon rages. "You shouldn't have to face the awful things you've been challenged with for as long as you have."

"Don't start caring now, *Daddy*."

Uncomfortable with the direction everything is heading, Drew shifts from one foot to the other before deciding to take a step back from his brother.

"Who do you think will win?" I roll my eyes at my brother even though he can't see me do it.

"Let's hope it doesn't come to that," I whisper.

"Dad's pretty strong, but Lawson seems like a psycho. It'd be an awesome fight to watch, but I think he'd win because dad's old."

"Dad's not old. Now shut up so I can listen."

I must speak too loudly because Jaxon's eyes lift to meet mine. I can tell he wants us to leave, to let this be just between the four below, but I can't turn away.

Noticing the direction of his eyes, Lawson turns his head enough so he can look over his shoulder at us. Anger, animosity, and hostility fill his bright blue eyes, but I also don't miss the twinge of fear in them either. I beg him with my eyes to calm down. There may even be a hint of pleading, asking him to stay, but his lip turns up in a sneer, either unable to read my expression or not caring how I feel.

"Looks like the whole family is here," he spits before turning back to Jaxon.

"Would you like to go into the office and speak privately?" Rob offers.

"Talking is the last thing I want," Lawson says. "We're leaving."

He goes to walk around Jaxon but surprisingly stops when Dad holds his hand up. "Feel free to leave, but Drew stays here. You can ruin your life all you want, but I won't stand by and watch you ruin his."

"Fuck you," Lawson barks. "Let's go, Drew."

Lawson grabs his younger brother by the arm. The wince on Drew's face makes it clear that the grip Lawson has on his arm is painful.

"You're hurting him," I say, unable to watch the tear rolling down Drew's cheek.

"Mind your own fucking business, Princess. This doesn't concern you."

Lawson's command doesn't surprise me. He's pissed and practically cornered. I would expect nothing less.

"No," Drew yells, yanking his arm out of his brother's grasp. "I'm not going anywhere."

Confusion swarms Lawson's face. It's apparent he's never gone against his brother's orders before.

"Now," Lawson commands.

"I'm staying," Drew says in refusal, crossing his arms in defiance.

Lawson remains silent, mulling over his options as he glares at his younger brother.

"What would Mom say right now? What would she tell you about choosing these people over family?"

Another tear rolls down Drew's cheek, and his throat works on a hard swallow before he speaks. "She would tell you to stop being stubborn. She would tell you that Rob and Jaxon are offering a chance at a real life. She would tell us to be grateful and take every opportunity we were handed."

Lawson shakes his head. "You'll regret being here with them."

Jaxon steps out of his way this time when Lawson heads to the front door. "You're always welcome here, son."

"Don't fucking call me that," Lawson mutters before disappearing out the front door and into the cool, morning air.

Drew all but collapses. Thankfully Rob anticipated it and catches him on his way. Drew shies away from Pop but doesn't make a move to get off his knees.

"Go get dressed," Jaxon instructs as Rob consoles Drew.

Looking down, I realize I'm only in my sleep shorts and a thin tank. "Yes, sir."

After changing in my room, I head back downstairs, finding Samson, both of my dads, and Drew around the kitchen table. Sunday morning breakfast is going on like the blow up didn't just happen ten minutes ago.

Jaxon is at the stove making an array of different pancakes just like he's done for as long as I can remember.

"Samson?" he asks as he flips a pancake over with the spatula.

"Simple is fine," he responds without looking up from his phone.

"Delilah?"

"I think banana and blueberry would be perfect."

"Drew?"

I look over at the young man. His face is still red, but the tear streaks have been wiped away. He looks uncomfortable and out of place.

"Apple cinnamon is the absolute best," I tell him with a gentle smile.

"I'm allergic to cinnamon," he answers weakly.

"Noted," Jaxon says from across the kitchen as he throws the bottle of cinnamon in the trash. I have a peanut allergy, and no form of them are allowed in the house. Watching what my dad just did makes my heart swell. He'll make sure Drew is safe here as well.

"The mint chip is excellent," Samson offers, and my eyes sting at his generosity.

Drew's eyes light up. "I love mint chip ice cream."

Jaxon chuckles from the stove. "These pancakes will be so much better. I promise."

"Babe?" Jaxon prompts.

"Simple works for me today," Rob answers.

I grab the seat next to Drew, so he's not left alone on this side of the table. He moves his phone closer, and I don't miss the protective edge to the action, but I understand it.

"Has he called? Texted?"

Drew shakes his head. "He'll be back." He tries to sound hopeful, but the skepticism in his voice betrays the front he's putting on.

"Of course he will," I agree.

"He gets mad sometimes. He comes back after he walks it off."

"Our door is always open to him," Jaxon says as he slides pancakes onto Samson's plate. "If he texts or calls, remind him of that."

Drew meets Dad's eyes, seeming to analyze if he's being genuine.

"He said some pretty awful things," Drew reminds my father.

Jaxon shrugs, as if having arguments in the living room at nine in the morning is nothing to worry about. "It's an adjustment, Drew. We're allowed to get angry. Could he have handled it better? Of course. But, I get the feeling your brother has been fighting and clawing to keep you guys safe for a long time. He'll come around once he realizes we're not out to hurt you or him."

Drew nods. "He'll be back."

Only this time there's more confidence in his words.

Chapter 7
Lawson

"Stupid motherfuckers," I mutter as I jump off of the front porch and leave all five of those assholes in my dust.

If Drew wants to live in some swanky ass house that's fine. So much for fucking loyalty. All he gives a shit about is his damn stomach.

Mine growls at the thought of more of that lasagna from last night.

Voices draw me to the front of the metal building we entered for the first time yesterday. Moving my duffel to my other shoulder, I peek around the house. Paranoia is vital in every situation. I can't believe Jaxon and Rob just let me leave. I was so sure after last night there would be a Marine recruiter standing in the living room first thing this morning. It wouldn't surprise me if the voices were coming from a group of guys heading my way to get me to step in line.

Instead of a mob coming after me, I find a group of guys, mostly in their twenties it seems, hovering over a motorcycle.

One guy, with his back to me, is struggling with the rear tire.

"He'll never get it," a tall guy mutters.

"This is fucking hard, you asshole," the guy working on the bike hisses. "Harley's are completely different from dirt bikes."

"Rocker can do it in a couple minutes, and he started with dirt bikes," a blond guy taunts.

"He's been doing this shit for years," the crouched guy complains.

"You don't get to wear the cut until you can change a fucking tire," the tall guy responds.

With my head down but still peeking over at them, I step away from the corner of the building. The crunch of my boots on the gravel draws the attention of several of the guys.

"Hey kid," one calls out.

I bristle but keep walking with a firmer grip on the strap of my duffel bag.

"He may look like his daddy, but he sure as hell doesn't have his personality," someone taunts with a southern drawl.

I spin around, facing them but not knowing which asshole is bringing Jaxon up right now.

"Kid acts like he's got the weight of the world on his shoulders," a dark headed guy working on the bike adds.

"You got a fucking problem?" I ask the group in general.

"Enough," a booming voice commands from the front porch of the metal building. The bald tatted-up guy, thick with muscles, looks ominous as he looms above us. "Scooter, you got that damn tire on yet?"

"No, Prez," he mutters.

I chuckle, and several of the guys look at me.

"Think you can do better, Lawson?" Why in the hell does the Cerberus MC President even know my name?

"I wouldn't be bitching and complaining. It's a simple fucking tire, not a goddamned flat."

Kincaid steps down from the front porch and gets closer to me. I don't miss the fact that he keeps several feet of distance between us, and I appreciate the space.

He angles his head to Scooter who's now standing, glaring at me. "Give it a try."

I look at the curious group of guys. They watch our interaction with interest.

I take a step back, holding my hands up. "No thanks. He's got that so fucked up, the next person riding it will end up as road kill."

Scooter growls at me, but Kincaid stops his advancement with a hand on his chest. "That one then."

I follow his finger to a magnificent bike, albeit a little dirty.

"Prez," one guy mutters. "Surely you're not going to let some punk work on your bike."

"Shadow's gonna be pissed if he has to fix something that kid breaks," another adds.

All it takes is a quick look from Kincaid to make the heckling stop.

"Go ahead," he urges when he sees the hesitation in my eyes.

Challenges like this I can take. The cockiness that has been forming all my life may be half false bravado, but my skills around anything mechanical are nothing but pure talent.

With a grumble, Scooter rolls over another jack, and I situate it under the bike. Once it's suspended, I take a step back, envying not only the money a bike like this costs, but also the care that has been taken to maintain it. I shouldn't expect anything less from bike lovers though.

All the tools I need are readily available which makes this even easier.

Less than ten minutes later, I stand, having taken Kincaid's rear tire off and put it back.

"I'd suggest a power wrench for those bolts on the exhaust before you ride." I swipe at the sweat trailing down my face with the bottom of my shirt. "The roads around here are complete shit. That tire's liable to roll out from underneath you."

"They are," Kincaid agrees with a smile.

"He didn't even take the caliper off," Scooter mutters.

I cough, clearing my throat to keep from laughing at the awe in his voice. Growing uncomfortable with everyone shifting their attention between the bike, Kincaid, and me, I grab my duffel and start to walk away.

"A word, Lawson?" I stop but don't turn around. He may have expressed it as a question, but the command in his voice is still there.

I hear his boots crunch on the gravel, but when I turn my head to look back at him, he's walking toward the door he came out of a bit ago, not walking toward me.

"Can someone teach Scooter how to change a tire?" Kincaid says as he walks past the group. "It's dangerous for him not to know how."

"Lawson seems to be the perfect teacher," the tall biker answers.

"Fuck that," I mutter, as I follow behind Kincaid. "He's unteachable."

I chuckle when Scooter growls as I walk past.

A fellow biker claps him on the shoulder. "You can't get pissed that the kid schooled you today."

"This is the clubhouse," Kincaid explains when we walk into the wide open front room of the building we arrived at last night. "Looks a lot different now than it did when your mom was around."

I remain silent, not wanting to know if, as club president, he took advantage of what my mom was offering while she was here.

"Knocked that wall out." He points to the area to the left. "Still have rooms down the hall to the right. That's where the guys outside stay."

"Where was my mom's room?"

His steps falter, but he turns and faces me like I'm a man and not a child. I can tell by the clouded look in his eyes that I'm not going to like what he has to say, so I steel my spine. "Darby didn't exactly have a room. She, umm... she stayed in different rooms while she was here. Same as all of the other women. Khloe was the only female who had her own room for a while, and that was only because she was underage when she arrived."

I nod, trying to act like the man he's expecting me to be. "I understand."

And I do. My mother was always a giving person, be it the shirt off of her back, the last piece of bread in the cabinet, *her body* to any man that smiled her way. Realization is painful, but it's no less the truth because of the pain in my chest.

"It's the same now?"

Kincaid chuckles, but I can tell he's not laughing at me. I suspect he thinks I'm wondering about the women for personal use.

"There aren't any women around much these days. Original members have gotten married and built their houses out back, like your d-, like Snatch... I mean like Jaxon and Rob have."

I follow him as he heads into the surprisingly clean kitchen off to the right and accept a bottle of water from the fridge.

"Thanks."

"Anytime," he says with another smile.

"Back to your question. It's not unheard of for one of the guys to bring a chick home, but they entertain in their rooms. We gather here sometimes. It's the only place on the property big enough to house us all and summertime in New Mexico is brutal. We were having a Saturday lunch yesterday when you and your brother showed up."

I appreciate the explanation, even more so since I don't have to ask for information. I know he can tell I need it but would rather die than ask Jaxon.

"My girls Gigi and Ivy rarely come over here unless I'm here. Delilah keeps to herself mostly. The guys come over. Sam mostly. The younger kids tend to stick around the pool, especially this time of year."

"There's a pool?" I hadn't seen one since showing up.

"Two actually. We have an indoor one. It's in the building to the far right. That's the one the kids use." He points in the opposite direction as if I can see through walls. "The other one has a fence around it, but it's for Cerberus members only."

"Don't want the dirty bikers around your kids?" I clarify.

He laughs. "Spot on, kid." I frown even though I don't think he's using it in a derogatory way. "I have two teenage daughters, Lawson. Ivy, I don't have to worry about so much. I'm sure she'll find the love of her life at the library. Gigi?" He shakes his head. "She's a handful. The more I can keep her away from the guys the less chance of me having to kill one of them."

He narrows his eyes at me, and I don't miss his warning. Gigi has to be the one that put on the show with her tanning oil yesterday.

"Hands off," I say with a grin. "Got it."

After a long chug from his own bottle of water, Kincaid speaks again. "Where were you headed just now?"

"I don't have a fucking clue," I confide.

"Strong language," he chides.

"I'm a man," I say standing from my leaning position against the counter.

"Men don't run from their problems," he counters. "Where were you running off to?"

"I—" I shake my head and clear my throat. "I was trying to cool off."

"In the summer heat with a heavy duffel bag? You were sure to fail just because you were attempting the impossible."

"I manage just fine," I hiss.

He holds his hand up. "Calm down. Life is about preparation. You have to be prepared for everything."

"I've managed this far," I mutter. "I'm prepared for anything life can throw at me."

"You're wrong." The soft tone of his voice makes me uncomfortable. "You're prepared for the bad, the ugly. You're prepared to survive things no man your age should be faced with."

"Damn straight," I agree.

"But." He holds a finger up, pointing it to the ceiling for emphasis. "You're nowhere near prepared to accept help from Jaxon and Rob. You're not prepared to understand that even though none of us knew you existed until sixteen hours ago, every one of us is here for you."

"I don't—"

"You do," he interrupts. "You do need us. Drew needs us. There's no reason for you to fight every day, to scrape for food, to get arrested for just trying to survive."

Silence falls over the room as his words sink in.

"Did Jaxon tell you about his own youth?" I narrow my eyes at him. "Of course not. With that chip on your shoulder, you wouldn't have given him the time of day."

I shake my head. Why? I'm not sure. I don't want to listen to him, no matter how much sense he's making.

"No shame in just going back over there." He hitches his thumb over his shoulder in the direction of the house I never wanted to enter in the first place.

I knew less than a minute after slamming the door that I wouldn't be able to walk away from my brother. I was afraid that they would use him as a bargaining chip to control me, but it seems Drew has found his own voice. It makes me both irritated as hell, as well as proud he's finally growing into his own person.

"Jaxon makes like twenty different pancakes. You don't want to miss it." He begins to walk away. Stopping at the threshold, he turns back. "Your father is one of the most loyal men I know. If he seems agitated, frustrated, or unhappy it's because of the years he's missed with you in his life. His anger is with your mother, where it belongs. Not one bit of it is because of you."

My heart pounds a rhythm matching his boots as he heads back out the front door of the clubhouse, no doubt to do whatever it was he'd planned before finding me facing off with his members.

I don't want to stay, but I'm terrified to leave. Cupping my head in my hands, I crouch on the floor, trying to clear my mind enough to make the right choice.

Chapter 8
Delilah

"This is so freaking awesome," Drew says as his hands manipulate the controller in his hands.

"You ever play this one before?" Samson asks, not taking his eyes from the racing cars on the screen.

"Not this version. The one before this I played a little at a friend's house last year." He smiles wide. "But it wasn't on a TV this damn big."

"Makes all the difference," I chime in even though I don't play video games or have a clue about what's better and what isn't.

I want Drew to feel welcome in our home, and if I'm being honest with myself, I want the same for Lawson.

"So," Drew begins, but pauses as if he's thought better of what he was going to say.

"What's up?" I go for nonchalant, but I wonder if he can hear the curiosity in my voice.

"Jaxon and Rob make Sunday breakfast every week?"

"Awesome, right?" Sam says before grumbling when his car spins out and crashes down a steep embankment on the screen. "Taco Tuesday is even more epic."

"I wouldn't call it Taco Tuesday," I say.

Drew's eyes turn over to mine. "No?"

Samson chuckles when I smile. "The kitchen pretty much turns into a Mexican restaurant. Tacos, fajitas, enchiladas, you name it, and we will probably have it."

The look on Drew's face is almost euphoric. "You like Mexican food, dude?"

Drew looks over at Sam and nods. "Love it, but if you guys are feasting every day how do you keep from getting fat."

"Swimming," I answer when Sam blurts, "Sex."

I kick at him with my foot when Drew's cheeks heat and turn pink in embarrassment.

"Don't let him fool you, Drew." I stick my tongue out at my sneering brother. "There's not a girl in Farmington who will give him the time of day."

Drew laughs as Sam's scowl deepens. "Bullshit. Rachel is going to come around. You'll see."

"Of course she will," I assure Samson when I realize I may have taken it too far. I'm not one to hurt people's feelings just to get a laugh. "I think a serious love connection will happen at our birthday party."

"When is your birth—?"

The front door opens, and we all fall silent as Lawson walks inside. He's been gone for over an hour, but just as Drew predicted, he's back.

The blank look on his face and the fierceness in his eyes are still present, but I no longer feel the vibrations of anger rolling off his shoulders.

First, his eyes find his brother, and I commend him for his loyalty. When his eyes sweep to me, I feel his hot gaze like a physical thing. His blue stare rolls slowly over my bare feet, up my calves, and to the hem of my cutoff shorts. By the time they scroll over my stomach, I'm panting.

You'll suck me off eventually.

Lips parting to accommodate my harsh breathing, I find that I can't look away from him.

"Dude," I register Samson saying from the other side of the room. "Quit eye-fucking my sister."

Lawson's eyes narrow, but he doesn't say anything as he leaves the room, heading toward the stairs. I sag deeper into the couch as if him walking away was the relief I needed to have control over my own body again.

I look down at my eReader, but my fingers are trembling too much to type in the PIN to open the screen. Calming breaths help some, but each time I close my eyes to regain composure, I feel his hot eyes on my body again.

Clearing my throat, I turn and place my feet on the floor. The motion sends a ripple of awareness up my spine.

"Wanna go again?" I look over at Sam and find him pointing his controller at the screen.

"Umm." Hesitation is in Drew's voice as he swipes his eyes from Sam to the direction his brother disappeared. "I need to go talk to him."

His voice cracks and I sit up straighter.

"Are you afraid of him? Will he hurt you?"

Drew gives his head a vehement shake. "Never. Lawson wouldn't lay a hand on me in that way."

He shudders and stands from his spot on the floor. Placing his controller on the low coffee table, he looks back at both of us. "My brother is an asshole on his best day, but he loves me. He'd never hurt me."

"I didn't," I begin, but he cuts me off.

"He's the only family I have. He'd protect me with his life."

Before I can respond, he's flying up the stairs.

"What was that about?" Samson mutters tossing his controller on the table with a clatter.

"Loyalty," I whisper with my eyes on the empty staircase. "Family."

"Well, I can tell you Drew is pretty cool until that asshole is around. He's just dragging him down if you ask me." Samson shifts and sits beside me on the couch.

"They're a package deal," I tell him.

"Too bad." He scoops his phone up and activates the screen, sighing loudly when he doesn't have any notifications. "Life would be much better if it were only Drew here."

"How can you even say that?" I turn my eyes to his. "They're brothers. Would life be better around here if I wasn't in the picture?"

He shakes his head, frustrated. "This isn't about you. Lawson is a grown man."

"And? Next year when you hit eighteen, you just want to be thrown out?"

He rolls his eyes. "That's not what I'm saying. My point is he doesn't have to be here if he doesn't want to be. I just get the feeling he's going to make everyone's life miserable on purpose."

I remain silent because I'm pretty sure those are Lawson's exact intentions.

"Have you talked to Dad?" I raise an eyebrow at him. "About the senior trip?"

"One, when have I had time in the last twenty-hours? Two, he's already made up his mind."

"If you get Pop on board, I don't think it will take much to get him to agree."

I shake my head. "Why do you keep worrying about it? You'll get to go next year."

"You can't be serious." He's snarky. "Next year? That's like a lifetime from now. Rachel could fall in love with someone else. This may be the only chance I get."

He has to know that he doesn't have a chance with Rachel right? Every guy she's dated is a dark-haired, all-around bad boy. The girl loves danger, and she definitely has a type. Samson comes nowhere near it. After inserting herself into our lives at a few parties over the years, I realized that she comes in hopes of catching the eye of one of the Cerberus guys. High school boys are the last thing she'll consider.

"Isn't she dating Tristen?"

"For now," he insists.

"And isn't Tristen going on the senior trip?"

"That's the rumor." He frowns when I raise my eyebrow at him again. "The relationships never last very long."

"Exactly." He stares at me, clearly not connecting the dots. "What makes you think you will last longer?"

"I just," he stares down at his hands, and I hate the vulnerability he's showing while talking about a girl who wouldn't even consider him a friend. "Things feel different with her."

"I'm sorry." I sympathize with him. I really do, but he needs to manage his expectations.

Wanting to hook up or date Rachel is a lofty goal. The equivalent would be me driving to Ireland with mapped-out plans to catch Jamie Dornan's eye.

"If you agree to go, they will let me go." A smile spreads across his face and makes his dimples pop out.

"You don't know that. Dad is pretty set on you staying home this summer."

"Only because they've cooked up all these dangers. Mexico isn't all that bad."

I glare at him. "Cooked them up? You've heard their stories. You're well aware of the things Cerberus has done, the missions they still get called out on."

"Girls get abducted. I'm in no danger," he counters.

"Guys have been taken as well." I sigh. "But you want me to come along and risk that chance?"

"You're ridiculous," he huffs. "I'll be there. You'd have nothing to worry about."

"You'll be following Rachel around like a lost puppy."

"And?" He's getting angrier which has happened all the times we've had this conversation over the last couple of weeks. "You'll be in the hotel room, reading a damn book. You'll be safe."

"Right," I say. "Your loser sister has no life."

"You're so fucking selfish."

"Enough," Dad says walking into the living room. I wonder how much of our conversation he's heard.

I look up at him, smiling and relieved for the intervention.

Samson looks up at Dad with resolve in his eyes.

"You don't have the money to go on the senior trip, so there's no point in even arguing about it."

"We have plenty of money," Sam counters.

"I have money," Dad corrects. "You've done nothing but sit on your ass all summer."

I do my best to hide the smile I feel tugging at my lips.

"But if I come up with the money, I can go?" Hope fills my brother's voice. We both know Dad is changing his mind, and he's elated.

"And how do you plan to do that?" Dad looks at him, waiting for a response.

"I'll do anything. Pick up cans, work in the shop. I'll sell plasma if it means I can go."

I shove his shoulder. "You're not old enough to sell plasma."

Dad laughs at Samson's eagerness. "Well? No time like the present."

Samson is on his feet and out of the room so fast he doesn't even realize he's left his cell phone on the cushion where he was sitting.

We both laugh as he hightails it out of the room.

"How are you, baby girl?" Dad brushes his lips across my forehead. "I hope the drama that unfolded this morning hasn't upset you."

"I'm good, Dad. Worried about them." I see nothing but compassion in his eyes. Why can't Lawson see that he's a good man and only wants to help? "They seem to have had a rough start."

"I imagine they have," he agrees. "We'll do anything we can to help them, but you may want to stay away from Lawson. He seems the type to self-destruct. I don't want you in the middle of that."

"Yes, sir," I say as his phone starts to ring.

He pulls it from his jeans pocket and looks down at the screen. "I have to take this."

I nod, watching his back as he walks out of the room.

"Blade, tell me how bad it is."

I figure the conversation is about the boys upstairs, but he walks out the back door, and I'm unable to get the full scoop.

Chapter 9
Lawson

"So you decided to stay?" Drew asks as he closes the door to the bedroom.

I brood, knowing it's not his fault, but feeling pissed off regardless.

"I couldn't leave you, could I?"

He gives me a small smile.

"I wasn't choosing them over you," he says softly. "I was choosing me over the unknown. If there's a chance for me to have a different life than the one we've had, I feel like I need to jump at that opportunity."

I bristle, knowing I've done the best I fucking can for the both of us.

"Sorry for providing such a shitty life, man."

I turn my back to him. The view outside, although empty, is better than seeing the disappointment he has for me in his eyes.

He huffs, agitated with my response. "You didn't give me a shitty life. We had shitty circumstances."

"So it's Mom's fault?" I round on him and sneer. "She did the best she could, also."

I ignore the clenching of his fists. He hasn't tried to punch me in over a year, but I know he has as much anger in him as I do. I blame his abusive father for both of us responding with fists rather than words. We learned from the best after all.

"Really? Her best?" I hate the indignant tone in his voice. My own knuckles pop when I roll my fingers into my palms. "You seem to have forgotten the parties, booze, drugs, and a revolving door of men."

"I haven't forgotten," I hiss, hating that I couldn't protect him from all of it. "She wasn't perfect, but she's our mother."

"Was," he spits.

"I'm well aware that she's gone." My words are pushed past closed teeth, my jaw clenched so hard it hurts.

"What you seem to forget is it was her choices, her lifestyle that put her in that hospital bed."

I shake my head, even though I know he's telling the truth. You don't live the life we have and not think of all of the things that could've made it better.

"She chose cancer?"

He swallows before speaking, and I already know his voice is going to tremble. No matter how upset he is or who he blames, he loved our mom as much as I did, maybe more than me since I had to endure that life longer than he did.

"She chose to drink and party. She chose a lifestyle that would make her body prone to disease."

My anger falls away as the tears roll down my brother's cheeks.

"Listen," I rush out.

My hands scrape over the top of my head. I want to reach out to him, pull him against my chest and vow to protect him from the world, but I know I can't protect him from the pain of losing our mother and the disappointment he feels toward her. I'm unable to placate him because deep down, I feel exactly the same way.

"We'll stay here. Things will get better."

"Y-you don't want to leave?" Longing fills his eyes as he waits for me to answer.

"I'll stay," I assure him.

The knock at the door has me instantly wanting to take my words back. I knew I couldn't just waltz back into this house without at least having a conversation with Jaxon, but I'd hoped for a longer reprieve.

Drew turns and opens the door.

"Hey, Jaxon," he says as he hastily wipes the back of his hands over his damp cheeks.

"Drew," he says looking over my brother's shoulder. "May I have a minute alone with Lawson?"

Drew looks over his shoulder at me. He's both asking if it's okay and begging me not to fuck things up at the same time. I give a slight nod and watch as he steps past Jaxon and closes the door behind him.

He stands near the door, not stiff but not inviting either. I can't get a clear read on how this is going to go down. That alone makes me want to puff my chest and act like a bulldog. Defensiveness has always been my go-to response for most situations.

Silence fills the room, and I can sense his eyes on me. Although my phone is lit in my hands, I'm not seeing a damn thing on the screen. Yet, I refuse to give into the pressure to speak. It feels like an interrogation tactic.

When I look up, I don't find anger on his face, but the pity is full-blown, and it enrages me. Remembering the begging in Drew's face, I do my best to keep my calm.

"If you're here for an apology about earlier, you're wasting your time."

He clears his throat as he tries to fight a smile. Maybe staying calm is the last thing this asshole fucking needs.

I make to stand from the chair.

"Don't," he says. He's not loud, but the warning is clear in his voice.

"I don't like being mocked," I hiss, but my ass stays in the desk chair.

"I'm not mocking you." His eyes light up. "The resemblance, the reaction, the anger and draw to a violent response is very familiar to me."

"I'm nothing like you." He raises an eyebrow. "We may look similar, but that's it."

"You want me to prove that you're wrong?" I shake my head. I don't need some long life story from my sperm donor, but fuck if I don't want to know everything about him. "I don't mind. I'll answer any question you have."

"Father/son bonding?" I chuckle at the absurdity of the concept.

"You're a man, Lawson. You don't need some guy acting like your father, but you can't deny that you need help."

"I don't do fucking handouts. I'm not some charity case."

A smile spreads across his face, and my lip twitches in anger.

He holds his hand up and walks across the room. My blood simmers from boiling when he takes a seat on the last step of the bunk bed stairs.

"I don't know if you're aware of what Cerberus actually does," he says.

"Drugs, guns, and women," I say filling in the rest.

His eyes widen. "The only thing in this house that can be considered a drug is Delilah's EpiPen because she's allergic to peanuts. She's only a *girl*, so no women."

He emphasizes the word as if I haven't noticed how fucking sexy she is, and I don't miss the warning either.

"There are plenty of guns, but those are locked up and safely put away."

"And?" What kind of MC did my mom get involved in?

"We're getting off course," he says but doesn't seem irritated with the diversion. "Cerberus is hired out for missions. We specialize in recovery and extraction. Rescuing people who have been abducted, mostly women who've been sold into the sex trade."

It's time for my eyes to widen in shock.

"With that responsibility comes the need to know everything we can about a situation. Most everything is digital these days and tracking information is child's play."

The hairs on my arms stand on end because I'm beginning to understand where he's going.

"You researched me?" That spot above my eye begins to twitch in annoyance.

"Blade did. He's our main intel guy." He watches my face for a reaction. "So I know all about what happened in Texas. I know you still have time to serve and there's an active directive to apprehend you."

Unconsciously, my eyes dart to my duffel bag near the door.

"Don't even think about it," Jaxon says already anticipating my response. "Running will only make everything worse."

"I won't go back to detention." He nods as if he knew I'd say that.

"I'll do everything in my power to make sure you don't even have to step foot back in Texas to resolve this issue."

"You have dirty cops in your pocket? I mean my PO was pretty cool, but his boss is something else."

"We're the good guys, Lawson. I don't have anyone in my pocket, but we're well known and have a lot of connections."

There isn't a hint of malice or threat in his voice. He's going to what? Take care of my situation the legal way? That never works, but when I look at him and see the confidence in his eyes, I can't help but wonder if it's a possibility. I knew Texas would come after me eventually, I'd just hoped I could run long enough for Drew to be grown before my past caught up with me.

"Tell me what happened," Jaxon urges.

"Don't you already know?" I can't help the anger that rushes out. I may take his offer to help me get out of this, but I don't have to spill my guts about what went down.

"I've been given the summarized version, but I want the truth from you. I'm well aware the police reports are swayed by opinions and personal bias."

I fold my arms over my chest, keeping my lips tight.

"Okay," he says with a nod. "Some other time."

"What do you want me to do?" I ask, hating that I even have to.

"What do you mean?"

"To stay here? What do I need to do to earn my keep?"

"You work, go to school, and finish whatever obligation you have to probation. After that, we can go from there."

"I'm not going to school. It's a waste of time."

He smirks, but not in a way I feel like he's going to give me pushback.

"GED?" he offers.

"I can do that," I compromise and don't feel as angry about giving in part way as I should be. "And Drew?"

"What about him?" Jaxon stands from the bunk bed and walks across the room toward the door.

"I do that, and he's safe?"

Jaxon shakes his head. "He's safe whether you hold up your end of the bargain or not."

"No strings?"

"None," he says twisting the doorknob. His back is to me, but he doesn't make to leave. "I'm glad you're here, Lawson."

His words take some of the sting out, but it doesn't fix a damn thing. Drew may be able to blame our mom for everything, but I can't help but place some of that on Jaxon's shoulders as well. He didn't love my mother the way she deserved. He used her and tossed her away. It's something I'll never be able to forgive him for.

Chapter 10
Delilah

"What's he like?" Gigi asks as she looks down at her bikini top. Finding that it's revealing enough, she turns her eyes to me.

I shrug. "I don't really know. We haven't talked much."

Other than grunts and thigh clenching growling when I walk by, Lawson hasn't said a word to me in the last week. It's like we coexist without any actual interaction.

"Really?" She looks across the pool at him. Sitting with Drew on the edge, Lawson swishes his feet through the water. "He seems like he has a lot to say."

"Not to me," I mutter.

I'd imagined how my life was going to be after the first twenty-four hours, and how it actually ended up is nothing like I thought. I'd prepared myself for sexual harassment, and sickly find myself disappointed that he hasn't continued what he'd started the first night he was here. If he didn't watch me, lick his lips when I walk by, and groan when I reach for stuff in the top cabinet, I'd question if he even knew I existed.

"Does he talk to Sam?"

I shake my head. "Drew is pretty personable, but Lawson has kept to himself. I'm surprised he's actually out here this afternoon."

"I'm not complaining," Gigi says with a small wave of her fingers in his direction when he looks over at us. "He's got a body most boys would die for."

Ivy snorts. "There is nothing *boy* about him."

I laugh, remembering that he told me the same thing not long ago.

"They seem to be settling in fine," I say to change the subject from his muscular arms and ridged stomach.

Why can't he and Drew look alike? I can handle his younger brother's gangly frame, but knowing now what's under his clothes is its own type of torture.

"Is he a senior this year also?" Ivy asks as she adjusts her eReader on her lap.

"No clue. I was serious when I said we haven't talked." I steal a glance in his direction finding his eyes burning in my direction. His hands run up and down his thighs, and I can feel the echo of his touch on my own skin. I should've opted for a one piece.

"I'm sure your dad would know." She stares, unabashedly in his direction. "All you have to do is ask."

"I'm not that interested," I say, making Gigi laugh.

"Yeah, okay." The corner of her mouth tugs up. "Hot guy living in your house and you're not interested. Lie to someone who doesn't know any better."

"Not everyone is a walking sex fiend," Ivy says in my defense.

"Yes," she says pulling her eyes from Lawson. "They are."

Ivy shakes her head in disbelief.

"Seriously, everyone between the ages of thirteen and thirty thinks about sex constantly. It's a statistical fact."

Ivy and I both laugh before Ivy mumbles, "Like you know anything about statistics."

"Hey, Lawson."

My eyes dart to the entrance leading into the pool. My dad is standing there looking at the guys.

"We have an hour before we have to take off."

Lawson nods, but the look on his face isn't as tight as it was days ago. It seems my dad and he have settled into some sort of truce.

"Why is your dad dressed up?" Ivy whispers as he turns around and leaves the pool.

"I wouldn't consider a polo shirt and nice jeans dressed up," Gigi says. "But he's fine as hell."

"Gross," I grumble. "That's my Dad."

"Who's a total DILF," Gigi continues. "My dream guy looks exactly like him."

I watch as her eyes track Lawson as he stands from the edge of the pool. Leaning over, he whispers something in his brother's ear. I try to swallow past the lump in my throat at the sight of the sun reflecting on his glistening skin.

"I wish you wouldn't say stuff like that about my father," I say ducking my head as Lawson rounds the pool.

"He can't seem to get enough," Gigi says absently, but she must not be able to tell that even though she's on full display in a bikini her dad would never approve of, Lawson isn't looking at her.

His admiring eyes run the length of my body, hand adjusting his package as he walks past.

"Bye," Gigi says with a tone she seems to catch tons of boys with. "Always great seeing you."

As hard as it is, I pull my eyes from his body, refusing to watch him walk away. When I look across the pool, I find Drew looking over at us with a wide smile on his lips. He shakes his head and slides off of the edge of the pool into the cool water. The look Drew just gave us makes me wonder what Lawson told him before his epic exit.

"Where are they going?" Ivy asks as Lawson closes the door to the indoor pool.

"No clue," I answer.

"I think I need to stay the night tonight," Gigi says almost absently. "I don't mind digging deeper as far as Lawson is concerned."

I roll my eyes. Gigi never wants to stay unless it's because she thinks she can sneak out of my house easier than her own.

"Speaking of staying the night, Rachel texted yesterday and asked if the party was going to be a sleepover this year."

Ivy snorts and Gigi looks put out. Rachel Grant is the only girl in school she sees as competition. They both like the boys that will undoubtedly break their hearts. They go in with eyes wide open but act surprised when they put out and then are told to get out, each one thinking they'll be able to tame the bad boys they manage to cage for the night.

"Why would she ask you that?" Gigi practically spits. "You're not friends with her are you?"

"Not really," I answer.

"Then why?" Ivy is confused as well.

"Samson?" Gigi asks.

I shake my head. Samson's obsession with the blonde bombshell isn't even close to being secret. "I doubt it. Much to his disbelief, I don't think the girl really knows he exists."

Gigi narrows her eyes. "Has she seen Lawson? Does she know he's living here?"

"Ohhh," Ivy responds dragging the word out.

"I know Sam came home the other day excited like a little Chihuahua. He ran into her at the store, invited her, and she said yes."

"Was Lawson with them?"

I shrug again. "No clue. Maybe?"

"It's the only reason."

"That's not true. She came last year," I argue.

"That's because she found out it was in the clubhouse. She was here for Cerberus, not Samson," Ivy says.

"Exactly," Gigi says pointing at her twin.

"Cerberus wasn't even in town that night," I counter.

"She didn't know that, but didn't she leave after like twenty minutes?" Gigi searches my face for the answer.

"Come to think of it, she did. Samson was devastated." Pissed was more like it. I think he punched a hole in the wall that my dads made him patch the next day.

"She's going to go after Lawson. I just know it." Gigi sits back with a huff and crosses her arms over her chest. "That bitch."

The realization makes my skin crawl. I've never been attracted to anyone Rachel would consider hooking up with, but the thought of her coming onto Lawson makes me territorial.

"RBF much?" Gigi asks with a stupid grin.

"Huh?" I turn my head toward her.

"Just the mention of Rachel and Lawson and your claws are ready to come out."

"No." I do my best to relax. My resting bitch face is usually enough to deter anyone, but Gigi calls me out on it every time it shows up.

"You know I hate to agree with Gigi," Ivy says. "But I could feel the tension rolling off of you, and I'm two feet away."

"I just don't want Samson to be hurt. We all know he likes her, yet he's invisible to her." I hope they buy what I'm selling, but it doesn't sound convincing even to my own ears.

"Samson deserves better," Ivy agrees.

"You can't tell him that though." I frown in Sam's direction as he tries to teach Drew how to do a backflip off the diving board without belly-flopping into the water.

"Kids," Gigi says with a soft voice like she's older than my brother. "They have to get burned a couple times before they learn."

Ivy and I shake our heads as Gigi slides her sunglasses down over her eyes and lies back on the lounger.

"You about ready to go?" My dad stands in front of us, blocking the sun.

"Hey, Pop," I say looking up at my dad. "Where are we going?"

He shakes his head, his beard full enough to almost hide his soft smile. "I thought you wanted to do the shopping for the party."

I sit up on my lounger. "Of course I do."

"Might as well knock it out today." I nod, excited to get away from the house. "You gals won't be able to decorate the clubhouse until the morning of. I don't want the guys to have to live in a teenage hell, or worse, ruin what you decorate."

"You want to go?" I look over at Ivy.

She smiles, always willing to help with stuff like this. "Of course. Have you decided on a theme?"

"Not really," I say and look over at Gigi. "You coming?"

She waves me off as Ivy, and I stand to go get changed. "Not interested."

We begin to walk away when Gigi calls my name. "Just not weird stuff this year."

"Ignore her," Ivy says as we exit. "I loved the hippie theme last year."

"She acts like it's her party," I mutter as we part ways at the branch in the sidewalk. "See you in a few."

I straighten my spine and put a smile on my face. I won't let the thought of Rachel going after Lawson, or Gigi implying I'm a baby, ruin my party planning.

Chapter 11
Lawson

"It's less than twenty miles away, but traffic can be difficult to get through this time of day," Jaxon explains as we stop at yet another red light.

I fucking hate small talk, so I look out the window without engaging.

"The kids are having a party a week from Saturday," he continues, either ignoring my silence or refusing to tolerate it.

I grunt. That's all he's getting.

I don't give a shit about some teenage party. It'll be nothing like the ones I've attended before, so I'm not interested. Well, I try to be uninterested, but the prospect of getting my dick sucked interests me a little. I don't pay attention to him until the unbidden thought of Delilah in that damn simple bikini hits me like a weight in my chest. Black and covering more than some one-piece bathing suits do, it made my cock hard the second her flip-flop clad feet hit the concrete inside the pool room.

"Their birthday is actually on the Monday after," he says hitting the accelerator only to tap the brakes as the next light turns red. "Same as yours."

That gets my attention, and I turn my head toward him. "You know my birthday?"

He chuckles like it's a ridiculous notion that he wouldn't. "Of course."

"More online stalking?" I grumble.

"I had to get copies of everything from Texas, for both you and Drew. We can't register him for school or get you signed up for a GED test without."

"And you what? Studied and memorized it?"

"No, Lawson," he says turning his head toward me and meeting my eyes. "I've been celebrating that day for the last fifteen years. I noticed it, that's all."

I turn and look out the windshield.

"I was a lot like you not too long ago," he says as we make it through what appears to be the last red light before hitting the open road.

"Can we not take a trip down memory lane?" I don't know why I say it. I want to know everything there is to know about him, but doing that while trapped in his SUV on the way to the probation department is the last place I want to find out about dear old Dad.

"I'm in a shit mood," I explain after a long silence. "All I can think is that they're going to cuff me and drag me away."

I steal a glance in his direction. "Promise me you'll take care of Drew if they ship me back to Texas."

"That's not going to happen, son." The sincerity in his eyes eases the anger that normally rises when he calls me that.

"Promise me."

"Promise," he says with enough surety that I almost believe him.

***

"You're going to shake yourself right out of your seat," Jaxon says as we wait to be called back by the San Juan County Juvenile Probation Officer.

I try to stop the up and down hitch of my leg, but give up after a minute of sitting still.

The door to the back opens and an angry mother, along with her crying daughter exit. I pray that whoever made that chick cry isn't the one to call me back.

We wait a few minutes longer before the door opens again.

"Jaxon Donovan?" A lady says after stepping through the door. "Margie Gleason."

She holds her hand out to shake, and Jaxon reaches for it.

"My son, Lawson O'Neil." I shake her hand, refusing to apologize for the sweat that's coating it.

"Follow me," she says turning and typing in a code to reopen the door.

My throat dries as we follow her down a short hallway to her office. The space isn't very big, but it's decorated with a menagerie of random shit she's obviously collected over the years.

We take the seats offered in front of her desk, and my knee begins to bounce again.

"Navajo County wasn't very shocked when I called and told them you were in New Mexico," she says as she settles into her chair.

I don't say anything. She didn't ask a question, and less is always more in these types of situations.

"There's an active directive to apprehend you, Mr. O'Neil."

I want to look over my shoulder, to prepare myself for the cops coming in to put me in cuffs, but I don't want to show weakness.

"Yes, ma'am," I say, but don't explain why I haven't reported to my PO in several months.

"It says here." She drops her eyes to the thin file on her desk. "That your mother passed about a month ago."

"Yes, ma'am," I grit out. I know how to be respectful, and I always try my best when someone holds my freedom in their hands, but talking about my mother isn't going to happen.

"I've spoken with Mr. Garrett in Texas, and he assures me that we only have a few things that need to be done to take care of all of this."

She looks up at Jaxon, eyes narrowing suspiciously. It makes me question his power and the connections he spoke of last week.

"There are procedures we have to follow, Mr. Donovan." She closes the folder and clasps her hands together on top of it. "I'm already suspicious of how quickly we were contacted by the New Mexico Interstate Compact officer."

"He's nineteen on Monday," Jaxon says.

"I understand that's the oldest a youth can be on probation in Texas, but New Mexico allows juvenile probation to extend until a youth's twenty-first birthday in some instances."

Twenty-one? There's no damn way.

"It's my understanding that Navajo County has no desire to file a violation and extend his probation. His adjudication is in that state. They have no plans to transfer a new disposition to New Mexico."

She clears her throat. "Texas has no business speaking with you directly. Interstate Compact dictates that their department works with their state who then works with our state. We then receive information from Santa Fe and proceed accordingly."

"As I've said," Jaxon leans in closer, but not in a threatening way. "Time is limited. I, as well as Navajo County, see no need to drag this out any longer. Lawson is regretful for what he's done, and we're all trying to move past it."

He has no damn clue how I feel about the situation. We haven't talked about it, but now is not the time to argue.

"He broke into a house. The babysitter watching over the two kids was so terrified she ended up in counseling," Ms. Gleason clarifies.

"The house was supposed to be empty," I hiss.

She raises an eyebrow as if she'd been waiting this whole time to prove her idea of me right. "The report says she was terrified you were going to rape her."

I bristle. It's not the first time I've heard the babysitter's side of the story. "I was going after the jewelry," I hiss. "Little girls do nothing for me. I would've hit the house next door had I known anyone was in the house."

"Regretful you say?" Ms. Gleason says with a twisted smile on her face.

Jaxon glares at me until I fall back in my seat.

"Are we able to get Mr. Garrett on the phone? I'm certain he'll be able to clear all of this up."

She shakes her head. "That's not how the process works."

Jaxon leans forward again, but this time pulls his cell phone from his back pocket. Swiping to activate the screen he looks back up to her. "There is no process, Ms. Gleason. Navajo County isn't going through Interstate Compact, as I'm sure you've been told. I'm certain that's the reason you're wound so tight. The phone call your department got from Texas was a courtesy."

The phone begins to ring on speaker and Jaxon places it on her desk.

"Hey, Mr. Donovan." My old PO's voice can be heard clearly on the phone. "How's that kiddo doing?"

Kiddo... It's the one thing I hated about the guy.

"He's great Alan. Listen, I'm at San Juan County with Ms. Gleason, and you're on speaker phone."

"Ms. Gleason," Mr. Garrett says in acknowledgment. I can tell by the tone of his voice that he's spoken with her before and isn't impressed. I get the feeling she isn't well received very often.

"Mr. Garrett," she mutters.

"I told you, Jaxon has no responsibility to San Juan County."

I smile at the PO sitting in front of me, but Jaxon smacks the side of my leg with the back of his hand. I clear my throat and sit up straighter in my seat, relief a tangible thing in my blood.

"What exactly is required for us to put this past us?" Jaxon asks, speaking to Mr. Garrett but keeping his eyes on the woman in front of us. She looks like she could spit nails.

"He has forty hours of community service to satisfy, five hundred and eighty dollars in fees to pay, and there's also the requirement that he be actively enrolled in school." I nod because all of that sounds about right.

"Would your county consider a GED rather than public school enrollment?" I watch as a smile spreads across Ms. Gleason's face and her head begins to shake back and forth.

"He would have to complete the actual GED. Enrollment in GED classes won't satisfy the judge."

"He turns nineteen on Monday," Jaxon shares as if Mr. Garrett hasn't been counting down the days until I age out of the system.

"I'm aware," he says. "We can give him a month. The paperwork for his violation has already been filed with the court."

I freeze as Mr. Garrett continues to speak.

"If he's able to knock out the community service, fees, and get that test passed, we'll just dismiss the modified petition."

Jaxon looks over at me, his eyes analyzing whether he believes I can get it all done. The community service and test are not a problem, but five hundred and eighty dollars is a lot of money. If I had that kind of money, I never would've broken into that house to begin with.

"Consider it done," Jaxon says.

"Thanks for calling, Mr. Donovan. Keep in touch."

Jaxon's phone lights up showing that Mr. Garrett has ended the call. When he stands from the chair and holds out his hand to Ms. Gleason, I stand right along beside him.

"Thank you for your time, Ms. Gleason. I think we'll be dealing with Navajo County directly from now on."

I turn my back on her, needing to get out of there as quick as possible. I'm shaking by the time we make it back to the SUV.

"That could've gone better," Jaxon mutters as we climb inside.

"How am I going to come up with that money?" I mutter to myself.

"You work for it," Jaxon says, and I realize I said it out loud. "You can knock out your community service with Delilah. She volunteers at the animal shelter three days a week."

"Perfect." I can't even hide the bitterness in my voice.

Like it hasn't been hard enough staying away from that girl? As much as this summer is going to suck, I can't deny that resisting Delilah is the lesser of the two evils. Juvenile detention is no joke, and the last thing I want is to end up behind bars again in Texas.

Chapter 12
Delilah

"Wait up," I hear from behind me.

I stop, turn around, and face Gigi who's jogging toward her sister and me.

"No," Ivy grumbles as her twin bounces up with a smile on her face.

"What's up?" I ask even though I know why she's standing here.

"I'm going with you," she beams. "Samson insisted that I come and make sure you don't end up with some stupid birthday theme."

I bite the tip of my tongue until a faint coppery taste fills my mouth.

"We're not going to pick anything stupid," Ivy defends with her arms crossed over her chest.

"Of course not, especially with me tagging along."

Gigi slides past us and climbs into the front seat of the SUV. Pop raises his eyebrow at me as he walks up with the keys swirling around his finger.

"Leave it alone," I mutter to him and climb into the back with Ivy.

The trip to the store is filled with Gigi chattering about what supplies we'll need as she plans *my* birthday party. My anger increases, my mood teetering on not even wanting to have a party anymore.

"You have to stand up to her," Ivy mutters as we watch Gigi's animated arms twirl around.

"Yeah?" I turn my gaze toward her. "You first."

She frowns but doesn't say another word.

"Exactly," I mutter.

I keep my eyes straight ahead, calming breaths passing through my lips as we pull into the parking lot at the party store. Pop meets my eyes in the rearview mirror before he opens his door. Giving him a slight nod, I let him once again take the reins, and I hate myself for it.

"We'll need everything that glitters, but nothing too girly." Gigi takes a breath then continues. "But nothing pink or purple. If you want turquoise, show it to me first before you put it in the cart."

"Gigi," Pop begins, looking over at her. "Feel free to dictate how your party will be in a couple of months, but you're not running this show."

Gigi huffs, disappointment clear on her face. "But Samson—"

Pop holds his hand up. "If Samson cared about decorations he should've come with us."

She turns around, the pink on her cheeks betraying her embarrassment. She isn't reeled in very often, but when she is things get better for a while.

Gigi isn't a mean person on purpose. She just has tunnel vision and is so self-involved that she doesn't pay much attention to others' feelings. Inconsiderate would be the perfect word to describe her.

"Thanks, Pop," I whisper as I walk past my rescuer.

"We'll talk about this later," he says with a smacking kiss on my forehead.

It's a warning of sorts. He tells me all the time to stand up for myself, to not let her take control over the things that are mine. He's reiterated more than once, that doing it now will give me the courage and strength to do the same when I'm on my own in the world and faced with the same type of people.

I hate confrontation, but I know Gigi's lack of consideration for others is coming to a head, and I won't be able to avoid the altercation that's been building for years for much longer.

"What are you thinking," Ivy asks as she loops her arm through mine.

She ignores her sister as Gigi grabs a shopping cart. There's less pep in her step, and her shoulders are hunched noticeably. Ivy, used to being treated poorly by her twin, gets almost jubilant when Gigi is chastened. I, on the other hand, hate seeing anyone upset, even if her own actions brought on the castigation in the first place.

"Dark," I tell Ivy, pulling my eyes away from her sister. "Black lights and neon."

A smile spreads across Ivy's pretty face. "I think that's a perfect idea."

Pop trails along behind us as we make our way around the store. He points out several things that would go great with the theme we're working on, and I'm grateful for his input. Unlike Dad, he loves to shop and get involved in things like this.

"Glow sticks?" he asks holding up a huge package of multicolored sticks.

"Of course," Ivy says and takes it from his hands. She grabs a second package and adds it to the pile growing in the cart. "Did you see any necklaces or bracelets?"

"Down the other aisle," he answers and leaves to go find them.

"What the hell is he staring at?" Gigi mutters, speaking for the first time since we arrived.

I look in the direction of her eyes and see Clay, a guy I shared homeroom with last year. He grins when we make eye contact, and I feel my lips turning up in a smile in return. Gigi sighs when he begins to make his way over to us.

"Such a creeper," Gigi says under her breath.

"Be nice," I tell her. I may allow her to be a certain way with me, but I won't sit idle while she's mean to others.

"Hey," Clay says as he gets within a few feet of us. "How's your summer been?"

"Good," I answer. "Yours?"

"Hot, boring," he responds as his eyes dart to the shopping cart. "Getting ready for your birthday party?"

"Of course. Did you get your invite?" Summer birthdays are tough, but Samson uses social media to let everyone know the details of it each year.

"I did." The smile never leaves his lips.

The silence between us grows awkward as I fully take him in. He's no longer the skinny boy from class. His shoulders have gotten wider. His once thin, wiry arms have filled out, stretching the fabric of his t-shirt. It's almost as if he's gone from boy to man in a matter of months.

Gigi must have noticed his transition as well because she takes a step closer, admiration of his body clear in her eyes.

"Hey, Clay," she all but purrs.

"Hey," he says with quick acknowledgment before his eyes find mine again. "Wanna trade?"

"I'm sorry," I say, confused.

"I go to your party, you come to mine?"

I clear my throat, unsure of what to say. I've always found Clay handsome, but chasing boys or even having the nerve to speak to one I find attractive has never been my strong suit. Now that he looks different, more like the type of guy I'd never engage with in fear of rejection and less like the nerdy boy who would've been a perfect match to my equally awkward personality, I'm not sure how to act.

"When's your party?" Gigi asks, sliding even closer to Clay's elbow. "I think one last awesome party is just what I need."

His eyes dart to her, and as if realizing for the first time that Gigi is flirting with him, a slow, seductive smile slides across his face. All of his attention is directed at her. I hear Ivy huff as we watch her sister trail her finger over Clay's muscled arm.

"Good to see you, Clay." He doesn't even acknowledge me as Ivy and I turn away to continue our shopping.

"Well that didn't take her long," Ivy hisses when we're two aisles over.

"Never does." I grab a package of green, glow-in-the-dark mustaches. "What do you think about a photo booth with all kinds of props?"

I turn to find Ivy grinning and holding a package of lime green and hot pink face masks. "It's like you're in my brain."

"Here are the bracelets and necklaces," Pop says emptying his arms into the cart. "I also grabbed plates, cups, straws, and these little bags for party favors."

I frown and Ivy giggles at Pop's cluelessness. "I think we're past party bags."

"What?" He looks at the package pinched between his fingers. "You're never too old for party favors."

"Never," Gigi says bounding up, back to her old self after having been doted on by a boy. "We can put the jello shots in them."

"Like hell," Pop says looking at the package of small, lidded containers she's waving in her hand. He tosses the neon colored package back on the shelf. "Okay. No party favors."

Gigi frowns when he snatches the package out of her hand and tosses it next to his discarded item on the shelf.

"Food shopping next?" Ivy asks as we make our way to the front of the store to check out.

"Catered," Pop answers. "Delilah didn't want to have to worry about cooking."

"Awesome," Ivy says with genuine happiness.

"Can we start the car?" Gigi holds her hands out for the keys.

Pop's eyes go from Gigi to Ivy. Unspoken conversation flows between them. With a small nod of her head, Pop hands over the keys. Ivy follows her twin out of the store, knowing he would never let Gigi go alone. It's not only a safety measure, but we can never guarantee Gigi won't get a wild hair and take off. Impulsive isn't a strong enough word to describe her.

"D," Pop begins as we wait for the lady in front of us to load her luau items on the counter.

"Please," I beg, holding my hand up to stop him. "I know what you're going to say, but you don't see her like I do."

"Enlighten me," he says, a smirk playing at the corner of his mouth.

"It's all a front for her. I honestly think Gigi is more insecure than any of us."

"I can agree with that," he says pushing the cart to the counter as the luau lady rolls her cart away. "But you shouldn't allow her to treat you poorly."

I hand him several more items from the cart so the cashier can ring them up. "I seriously don't even think she realizes she's being rude."

"Even still," he says. "You have to stand up for yourself, especially with the people you're closest to. Feeling taken advantage of and disrespected by the ones we love does more damage than when it happens with strangers."

I nod, knowing he's right but also unsure of how to proceed from here.

Half an hour later, we're pulling up to the front of the clubhouse. There's no sense in carting our purchases to the house, so we opt to just store them in the front entry closet until Saturday morning. Ivy is carrying an armload, and surprisingly Gigi has offered to help as well, when Dad and Lawson pull in, parking beside us.

Lawson, never making eye contact or offering to help with our bags storms past, taking the sidewalk toward our house rather than cutting through the clubhouse.

"What's his deal?" I mutter, startled to the point of jumping when Dad's hand lands on my shoulder.

"He's had a rough life," Dad whispers in my ear. "Just treat him with kindness."

I watch his back as he disappears around the corner, but my thoughts stay with him as we get all of the purchases stowed away in the closet.

Chapter 13
Lawson

"Community service," I grumble as I run a soft towel over my wet body. "Fucking probation."

Working for my money has never been a problem. The burglary was out of necessity when the work around the small town we lived in dried up. Jaxon's offer to let me pay off my probation fees in the shop working on the motorcycles is like a dream come true. I'd do that shit for free just to fill my time.

After wrapping the towel around my hips, I swipe my hand over the condensation on the mirror. Empty, ice-blue eyes stare back at me. It's strange finding their familiarity in those of my long lost father. The compassion he's shown since mine and Drew's arrival has never faltered. That type of humanity is a foreign concept to me. I can see, feel even, the love he has for me. It's been there since realization struck him in the chest the day we showed up at the clubhouse.

Pissed about the things I've missed, the opportunities that have been lost by not knowing this family, it takes all the strength I have to not punch a hole in the wall. My anger isn't dissipating by any means, but the blame is beginning to shift, and it makes me sick to my stomach that I'm starting to have ill feelings toward my deceased mother.

"So fucked up," I say to myself, stepping out into the hallway.

A squeak and a hiss register in my ears, but it's the hands on my bare stomach that have my undivided attention. Warmth, flowing from the lime green tipped fingers against my skin, spreads from the point of contact all over my body, my cock getting the message first. Twitching against the softness of the towel brings a smirk to my face, as I watch Delilah jump back a step.

"I'm so sorry," she apologizes quickly and bends at the waist to grab a stack of laundry I'm just noticing must have fallen to the floor.

The top of her head grazes my already straining cock when she stands upright.

"Oh, God." Her cheeks flush the most amazing shade of pink when she realizes what she's done. "Did I just head-butt your... your... penis?"

Rolling my bottom lip between my teeth to keep from laughing at her, I remain silent, letting the awkwardness seep a little further in. I love the color on her face. It means she's not unaffected by me even though she's avoided me for the better part of a week.

"Gives a whole new meaning to giving head," I whisper, noticing the huskiness in my own voice.

Her eyes dart from mine to below my waist, pausing long enough to understand exactly how I feel about the situation.

"Oh." I don't even know if she realizes that she's staring at my towel-covered cock, but he's received the memo loud and clear.

Betting on a shy reaction, I flex, making it jump behind the towel. She only gawks harder. Her perusal only serves to make me harder, the tip growing wet with desire.

"It's yours if you want," I tell her palming my length.

She may see it as taunting her, but relief from the pressure exerted by my hand is immediate. A groan rumbles in my chest as she continues to stand, staring as if she anticipates it revealing itself to her.

God, I wish.

"Is your mouth watering to taste my cock, Princess?" Her eyes snap up to mine, the trance she was in broken by my filthy words. "I'll return the favor. I bet your pussy will be the best-tasting thing I've ever put my mouth on."

Heat overrules the agitation in her eyes when she looks up at me, but she remains silent. My cock screams in protest when I release it from my grip. A second later, the same hand is reaching for her, running my thumb over the fullness of her bottom lip.

"I don't fuck very often," I whisper taking another step closer to her. "But I'll make an exception for that tight virgin pussy of yours."

She blinks up at me. Once, twice. Then searing pain radiates from my foot and up my calf. She's already down the hall and inside her room before realization hits. She just stomped on my fucking foot with her sneakers on.

"Goddammit," I hiss, hopping on my uninjured foot while I try to soothe the pain she's just inflicted.

"What happened?" Jaxon is the last person I want to interact with tonight.

"Stubbed my toe," I lie and place the throbbing foot back down on the carpet.

His eyes narrow, dart down the hall toward Delilah's room, and back at me, but he doesn't say anything about his suspicions.

"I was coming up to give you this." He offers a piece of paper, and I take it.

"You already paid my fees?" I ask looking down at the printed receipt.

He shrugs. "I was just waiting for the receipt. I paid them as soon as I found out about them. Navajo County is a little old school, so I had to wait for snail mail for the receipt."

"Thanks." The word tastes like shit in my mouth, but the man did me a favor, and I refuse to just brush that off.

"No big deal," he responds, but to me, five hundred and eighty dollars is a fuck ton of money. "You'll work it off."

"Yes, sir."

"Delilah leaves at nine in the morning to head to the animal shelter. Knock out the community service first then you can worry about working the money off."

"I'll be ready," I tell him and turn toward the bedroom.

"Lawson?" I face him again. "There's a lady in the house. Please don't roam around in only a towel."

I nod, acknowledging him and leave him standing in the hallway.

I can't shake the image of Delilah's chest rising and falling with her harsh breaths when she was touching me. My skin still burns from the contact, even though it's been several long minutes since she pulled away from me.

"What's up?" Drew asks from the top bunk of the bed.

His eyes never leave his cell phone to look over at me as I drop my towel, of which I'm thankful because just the thought of Delilah's soft lips is making me thicken again.

I tug on the tightest pair of boxer briefs I own in an effort to constrict my cock and then a pair of athletic pants. "Not much," I finally answer. "Just that I'm now at the mercy of this fucking family because Jaxon paid my fucking probation fees without even bothering to consult me on it."

He laughs before speaking. "You're the most ungrateful asshole I've met."

"Don't cuss," I mutter as I sling myself on to the bottom bunk. "And it isn't about gratitude. He shouldn't just do shit without speaking to me. I could handle the money without his fucking help."

"Now you're just lying to yourself."

I glare at him through the bottom of his mattress.

"You wouldn't be able to get that much money without breaking the law, and you know it."

"Whatever." I roll over and face the wall.

Silence fills the room, and just as I'm sure he's fallen asleep, he speaks again. "Gigi was eating you alive this morning at the pool."

"Who?" I ask refusing to play into whatever game he's trying to start.

"The twin with the dark hair?" I don't answer. "The wild one in the barely-there bikini?"

I grunt a noncommittal sound. Of course, I noticed her. With her tits on full display and a devious smile, she's kind of hard to miss. Man-eaters aren't my style at all though. Now, the gorgeous blonde in the navy suit beside her? That's a whole other story.

"You planning on going to the party next weekend?"

"Probably not," I lie, knowing even though I shouldn't, I want to be wherever Delilah is. Even if that means some lame ass teenager party.

"I'm going to go," he says, and I can hear the smile in his voice. "There are going to be tons of fine ass girls there. I bet I can convince one of them to get on their knees for me."

I laugh, so deep in my gut, I get a cramp.

"Dude, seriously?" I hear him huff in agitation.

"Asshole," he mutters as I feel him turn over above me.

He doesn't say another word. I hate that he feels like he has to act like a badass all the time. I've done it for years for self-preservation, but he should be able to live worry-free.

"You have plenty of time to worry about shit like that," I say to him. "Don't try to grow up any faster than you have to. Being grown fucking sucks."

Especially when you're not grown at all and have to depend on your absentee father to foot the bills for crimes you committed because your mother lied to you about his existence.

I sprawl out on my back and relegate myself to another sleepless night of thinking about Delilah until my balls ache so bad I want to scream.

Chapter 14
Delilah

"Perfect," I whisper with a quick pop of my lips.

I could lie to myself, claim dry lips as the reason I've slicked on tinted gloss rather than my normal chapstick, but it would do no good. Lawson hasn't left my brain since the minute he showed up. Last night, after feeling his hot skin against my fingers, I tossed and turned, the interaction on repeat in my brain. There's nothing I can do about the redness in my eyes from lack of sleep, but he doesn't really pay me any attention, so maybe I'll get lucky, and he'll not even notice.

But, I want him to notice me.

Shaking my head at the ridiculousness of it all, I grab my keys and cell phone from my desk. I don't get boy crazy. Yeah, I've found guys at school good-looking, but getting to the point I want to doodle their names on my notebook never entered my mind.

Making sure I pulled my door closed behind me, I make my way down the stairs with a grin on my face. I know most teens spend their summers vacationing in the sun, going to parties, and sleeping late, but I've enjoyed going to the animal shelter four to five days a week. Even though summer is coming to a close, and I've been busy with the animals, I still get excited about my volunteer work. There's nothing greater than the smiles on the dogs' faces when I show up.

In the kitchen, I find Dad, Pop, and Drew at the breakfast nook, each eating breakfast. Over the last week, Drew has stopped shoveling food into his mouth like someone is going to take it away from him. He's growing comfortable in his skin here, acclimating better than I thought he would, after witnessing his first meal with us.

"Hey, Delilah," Drew says with a quick smile before taking another bite of chocolate cereal.

"Morning," I respond and head to the coffee pot.

"Coffee?" Pop asks noticing my change in routine.

"Yeah," I mutter pulling two cups from the cabinet. Being nice, I decide to make a cup for Lawson. He hasn't gotten out of bed before noon since his first night here, so I know these early days are going to be brutal for him. "I didn't sleep very well last night."

"Too excited about the party to sleep, huh?" Dad smiles over his own steaming cup of java.

"Something like that," I answer. "Where's Lawson? You told him nine, right?"

"He's still sleeping," Drew answers before Dad can respond to my question.

"I'm sure he's awake," Dad says. "Run up and grab him. You don't have a set time to be there, but I know you hate being late, even if the schedule you're keeping is your own."

I grumble to myself as I finish fixing my cup and refuse to be nice any longer. His cup sits empty when I turn and head back up the stairs. It's rude to keep people waiting, and rudeness is a pet peeve of mine.

Knocking on his bedroom door goes unanswered. I look over my shoulder, noticing the bathroom door is open, and the light is off. Last night's scene runs through my head again, and I do my best to ignore the full body shiver that runs up my spine and out of my fingertips.

Agitated, I turn the doorknob and swing open the door. The bang as it swings wide and hits the wall startles the sleeping boy on the bottom bunk. He jerks, his large hand shooting straight to his dick as if protecting it at all costs is priority number one. The sheets are tangled around his legs as if he got too warm in the night and kicked them off.

Unbidden, a small sigh escapes my lips at the sight of his straining penis, large and thick, behind his sweats. I swallow around the lump that is forming in my throat until his husky chuckle makes the lean muscles on his stomach jump.

Unable to pull my eyes away from his body quickly, my eyes take long seconds to meet his. White teeth clamp onto his bottom lip, and his eyes hold mine in challenge.

"Wanna help me take care of my little problem?" If I thought he had a sexy voice before, I can vouch that his early morning, throaty words nearly make me breathless.

"Little?" I squeak before catching myself.

Now is not the time to get all weird and awkward, spouting the words that have no place out in the open.

"I'll be gentle," he assures me, the playful smile never leaving his lips. "Unless you like being gagged until tears run down your beautiful cheeks? I'm more than willing to give you what you need to have those rosy lips wrapped around my cock."

Cock.

Such a dirty word, but for some reason, it has that shiver reigniting over my skin.

"You look terrified," he husks out, shifting, so his body is angled more in my direction. "Sweet really. The little virgin girl scared of me. The thought of you choking on my cock makes my nuts ache. Take care of it for me, Princess."

My eyes are once again pulled to his hand gripping his length.

"No thanks," I finally manage to say. "You disgust me."

He really doesn't, but the blatant sexual innuendo is being taken too far. I hate him for calling me Princess. I hate him for thinking he can say such awful things to me. But more so, I hate myself for wanting to open my mouth to a boy for the first time in my life.

"You'll have me in your mouth eventually," he promises.

I shake my head and turn back to the door. "You have five minutes to be downstairs, or I'm leaving without you."

I turn right, heading to my room and into my en-suite rather than left to join the rest of the family in the kitchen. My cheeks are burning and much to my dismay, my mouth is watering.

"Vulgar, disgusting asshole," I hiss as I splash water on my face. Next up is the wad of tissue paper that swipes the color from my lips. "This is never going to work.

I contemplate telling Dad that he's going to have to find something else for Lawson to do, but I know that means explaining why I have an issue driving him to the animal shelter. Even though he acts like a total jerk every time we speak, I don't want him to get into trouble. The last thing I want is to put my dad in a position where he feels like he has to choose between the two of us.

"I'm doing it for Drew," I remind myself in the bathroom mirror.

I don't know the specifics, but I've overheard enough to know that Lawson is on probation for something that happened a while back in Texas. He has community service hours, and if he doesn't complete them, he'll be in more trouble. If he is arrested, Drew will suffer, and I'm not petty enough to do something to compromise that. Drew's nice to me, respectful and actually a pleasure to be around.

"For Drew," I say with more conviction before turning around and making my way to the front door.

"Been waiting for you, Princess," Lawson says as I descend the stairs. He glances at the screen of the phone to check the time.

"Have fun you guys," Pop calls from the kitchen. "See you at dinner time."

We walk outside, heading around the clubhouse to my car.

"Did you have to change your panties?" Lawson whispers, leaning in so close I can feel the warmth of his breath on my bare shoulder.

"Stop," I warn.

"Personally," he says with an audible smile in his voice. "I've never gotten off so fast."

I glare at him. "You can't be serious?"

I climb inside of my gently used Corolla and hit the unlock button for him. Cranking it, I blast the AC immediately. Even at nine in the morning, New Mexico is hot as hell.

"I can't wait to get to New England," I mutter and crack the windows to allow some of the heat to pour out.

"What's that, Princess?"

"One," I turn to glare at him. "Stop calling me Princess. Two, quit making sexual advances toward me."

"You like it," he counters as I put the car in gear.

"I don't."

"I bet if I slide my hand in your panties, you'll be wet for me."

I snap my head in his direction, pissed, less about his words and more so because he'd be right. "Try it, and I'll break your fucking hand."

In mock surrender, he holds his hands up by his ears. "Damn, Delilah. Chill the fuck out."

"Please, just stop."

"I'm just joking with you, giving you a hard time."

I crinkle my nose oddly annoyed that maybe he doesn't find me attractive enough to want to do dirty things with. It makes no sense, but I have no control over the emotions.

The trip to the animal shelter remains silent until I speak as we pull in and park in the employee lot. "You'll be meeting with Dana. She's the day supervisor. I know Dad spoke with her, but I'm certain he didn't give her details of why you're here."

He nods, the only clue I have that he's even heard what I said. With anxious energy, his fingers drum on his jean-clad legs. For reasons I don't even understand, I reach over and calm his left hand by placing mine over it, the contact no less heated than it was last night in the hallway.

"Don't be nervous," I say when his eyes meet mine. I pull my hand away when his lip twitches.

"I'm not," he assures me. "Just ready to pet some dogs."

I laugh and climb out of the car. When he meets me at the front, I just smile over at him.

"What?" he asks, voice tinted with the agitation I've come to associate with him.

"There won't be much petting for you today."

"The hell does that mean?"

"You'll see," I tell him, the bounce in my step growing with the knowledge that he's about to have an eye-opening experience.

***

The grumbling meets my ears before I round the corner to the kennels. We've been here for four hours already, and I haven't seen Lawson since I dropped him off with Dana in reception. I went about my day walking the dogs and sitting on the floor while the cats surrounded me to get their ears scratched.

"How does something so little and cute make so much shit?"

I can't help the grin that spreads across my face. Lawson thought he'd be doing what I come here to do every day, but the community service hours given by the shelter are a little more interactive than the ones of the volunteers. Dana's take on the situation is that if probationers have to get down and dirty with the less shiny part of the job, then maybe they won't re-offend. I've done my fair share of kennel cleaning when there wasn't someone else here to do it, so I don't feel sorry for him at all.

Rounding the corner, I find Lawson crouched low to the ground, coveralls doing nothing to make him any less appealing. He's scratching at the head of a mid-sized dog of questionable breeding. The dog revels in the attention it's getting, flopping to his back for a tummy rub when he's had enough attention paid to his head.

"You didn't deserve to be left to fend for yourself, did you, Buddy?" The dog yips in excitement. "I know exactly how you feel. Life sucks sometimes."

My heart begins to thunder in my chest. The pain and understanding in Lawson's voice are enough to make me take a faltering step back.

"He's had a rough life. Treat him with kindness," Dad's voice rings in my ears.

He stands abruptly, the classic Lawson sneer marring his gorgeous face. He can't even be real with himself. The thought saddens me.

"You gonna help me tomorrow?" The dog yips and turns in a quick circle. "You can't spray a hose so maybe just shit a little less?"

He grins when the dog yips again and tries to bite at the spray coming from the end of the hose as he begins to clean the kennel.

I back away, giving him the time he needs, but knowing just how much it sucks to be stuck in your own head. He needs a friend, someone he can speak to without judgment, but his mouth ruins everything. His defenses are up so high he'll destroy any form of friendship I try to offer.

Chapter 15
Lawson

"Another day, another pile of shit to clean."

At the stoplight we have managed to get caught at the last three days we've been going to the shelter together, she looks over at me. I grin at her, and she returns it. I haven't said anything off-color since that first drive in. It makes her uncomfortable, and for some fucked up reason, I find myself giving her what she wants. As much as I love the color of her tongue and the way she licks her lips when I talk dirty, I hate the distance it puts between us. She avoids me, either in repulsion or because she's tempted, so I've refrained the last two days.

We've chatted about our futures. She has everything planned out as much as possible. Rhode Island for college, where she'll major in Sociology. She explained her need to understand how her mother was drawn into a cult, giving up her entire life for an eccentric megalomaniac. I can relate, even though I'd never admit it to her. My mom may have never been in a cult, but drugs and the party life were just as detrimental to her family and her health.

Personally, I have no long-term goals. Getting off of probation and finding a job is my only immediate concern. I can work off the money that Jaxon fronted me, but that doesn't mean I have a paid job once it's repaid.

"Those dogs love you," she tells me as she hits the gas when the light turns green.

"I don't know how you manage not to bring them all home." I grin at her again. "Buddy is seriously hard to leave every day."

Buddy, the name I gave the dog I connected with on the first day, greets me with a smile every morning.

"I tried," she confesses. "Pop put the brakes on it the first day he came to pick me up."

I laugh, imagining her standing there pouting when he rejected the idea. "You mean those pretty blue eyes of yours didn't work that time?"

Her fingers grip the steering wheel tighter. "I don't get everything I want."

"You will." My voice sobers when she turns to look at me. "The entire world will open up for you. I'm certain of it."

"The world?" She huffs. "I'm terrified to leave the little bubble my dads have created. Moving clear across the country to go to school? I must be crazy."

"What are you running from then?" Why I'm so interested in the trajectory of her life, I have no idea. Maybe it keeps me from thinking about my own, a simple distraction to my own limited options.

"I'm not running," she assures me with a frown. "Gigi? She'll end up being the runner. I doubt she'll make it through senior year before she hits the road. The grass is always greener and all that."

"She's the wild twin?" Her eyes follow me wherever I go. If Delilah thinks I'm suggestive, she should hear the shit that comes out of that chick's mouth.

She nods. "Like you haven't noticed her."

"Oh, I've noticed her." I scrub my hand over the stubble growing on my jawline. "She's kind of hard to miss."

Delilah's lips form a flat line as she studiously looks ahead, suddenly distracted by the traffic around us.

"Everyone wants her. The boys fall at her feet. The *world*," she says with disdainful agitation, "is at her feet, not mine."

"Not everyone," I whisper barely loud enough for her to hear.

***

One thing I didn't inherit from my mother is my work ethic. Day three cleaning kennels and I've managed to cut my time from the first day by almost half. Granted, I spent most of the first day bitching and bemoaning my position on the animal shelter ladder.

"Jesus, your breath stinks," I tell Buddy as he puts his wet paws on the coveralls covering my legs and tries to lick my face. "What do they feed you?"

He yips in my face and I recoil at the disgusting smell.

"I'm going to bring you some gum or something, dude. You have a serious problem."

"We have dental sticks in the back closet."

I look up, hands still rubbing at Buddy's ears to see Dana smiling on the other side of the kennel.

"Perfect," I say looking back down at my furry companion.

"You should get him a treat and then take him for a walk."

"Really? I have three more kennels to clean, and that Doberman takes bigger shits than a horse."

She shakes her head, but her smile never falters. My first day here, Delilah noticed how nervous I was. I'm sure she thought it was because it was a new place, but it had more to do with getting treated like shit at the place in Texas I was supposed to work my hours at. Being in trouble for breaking into a house to steal so you and your brother could eat for the month was a low point in my life, but being made to feel like the scum of the earth for being hungry only pissed me off. That attempt at community service lasted fifteen minutes and ended with the supervisor clutching his bloody nose.

"Okay. Clean the last couple of stalls then head out and help Delilah. She's taken it upon herself to walk five dogs at the same time, and I know they're only going to end up dragging her through the pasture."

I clean the stalls in record time, grab Buddy a treat for his god-awful breath, and head out to find the girl I can't get out of my head no matter how hard I try.

"You're going to break my leg," she screeches.

My smile turns into wide eyes as I sprint toward her. On the ground, with several leashes wrapped around her legs, she bats one dog away. The opportunistic motherfucker has jumped on her back. I manage to push him away before he starts hip thrusting at her.

The laugh spills out and is met with glaring blue eyes. "Really? You find this fucking funny?"

I shake my head no, but the laugh still rolls through me. "Upsetting more than anything. You were just batting him away. If I tried to mount you, you'd probably break my dick off."

I grin down at her as she bites her lip trying to hide a smile. "A little help, please?"

"Yeah. Shit, sorry."

I detangle the leashes from around her ankles, my heart thudding when I realize I dropped Buddy's leash and he's probably halfway to Colorado by now. I look over my shoulder, relieved to find him bouncing playfully near a terrier. Bored, the smaller dog lies in the grass with his head on his paws, waiting for us to get back to his walk. Being ignored doesn't stop Buddy from entertaining the idea.

She takes my outstretched hand and lets me pull her back to her feet.

"Thanks," she mutters. "They normally aren't such jerks. That new one has them all riled up."

I look over at the solid white dog. "She's probably in heat. Would explain Blackie over there trying to take a ride on your back."

"Gross," she laughs and smacks my chest with the back of her hand. "Help me?"

Regretfully, I pull my eyes from her face and look down at the tangle of leashes in her hands. We spend the next ten minutes getting them back in order.

When she looks up smiling as the last one is pulled free, I notice the smear of dirt. God, I hope it's dirt smeared on her cheek.

I take a step closer, my hand instinctively reaching for her face.

"Dirt," I whisper as my thumb brushes the softness of her face.

Her eyes find mine, innocent and filled with a need I'm certain she doesn't understand.

"You're gorgeous," I pant. "Your mouth—"

Her face shifts, leaning into my hand.

Buddy barks just as I'm leaning in, refusing to let this moment pass us by. She jumps, startled by the intrusion into our moment. With lips parted, I read her face. Trust, desire, and compassion fill her soft blue eyes. An unfamiliar rush washes over me, heating my skin and making me uncomfortable. In true form, I ruin the moment the only way I know how.

"Your mouth would feel amazing wrapped around my cock."

She blinks, unsure if she heard me right. I can see the anger flash across her face before she just turns and walks off. I'm left, standing in a field holding leashes to six rambunctious as fuck dogs, watching her walk away because intimacy, even on the simplest level, isn't something I can tolerate.

When the walk is over, my arms are killing me. Fighting half a dozen dogs is better than any day I've spent at the gym.

"After you get them kenneled can you come out and help me?" Dana says as I pass by the rolled up door outside of the large animal shelter. It's empty now, but I've heard that they sometimes have farm animals and horses that have been recovered by animal control. "I need your muscles."

"Sure," I say with a smile and a wink.

"One big flirt just like your daddy," she mutters with a quick laugh.

For some reason, the comparison doesn't even bother me this time. I want to go find Delilah, but I figure keeping my distance is best. I don't have a damn thing to offer her. I ruin everything I touch, and the last thing she needs is some horny fucker like me taking everything she has with nothing to offer in return.

"What's up?" I ask Dana as I make it back to reception after caging the now tired dogs.

"This is Rachel Grant," Dana says pointing to the wet dream of a teen standing near the desk. "She brought a truckload of dog food. Can you unload it for her?"

I smile at her, and she doesn't even notice that it doesn't reach my eyes. Who in the world delivers dog food in a bikini top and shorts so short the bottom curve of her ass hangs out?

Man-eaters that's who. No thanks.

I follow her out, ignoring the blatant shake of her ass.

"Truckload?" I ask opening the tailgate of a newer Chevy pickup. "It's four bags."

"Big bags," she counters.

"Your muscles," she says as her fire engine red fingernail drags down my arm from shoulder to wrist, "are so big, you shouldn't have any problem."

My eyes narrow, but her smile only grows bigger. "Maybe next time spend less on your truck and buy more dog food. We can use more donations."

"Oh," she says with a flip of her hair as I reach for the first bag. "My family can afford loads more dog food. If I bring more will you unload it?"

"Of course," I answer and toss the dog food to the ground and reach in for another. The sooner I get them off her truck the sooner she can get the fuck out of here.

"I may bring so much you'd have to take your shirt off to keep cool."

I smile and grab the last bag, refusing to explain that the blazing ass sun would do more damage than sweating with a shirt on.

"You about ready to go home?" A genuine smile crosses my lips at the sound of Delilah's voice. Fuck, at least she's talking to me even though the derision can't be ignored in her voice.

"Yep," I say over my shoulder. "Anything else you need Ms. Grant."

The blonde in front of me smiles while the blonde at my back huffs. Jealousy. I love it. It means I still may have a chance even though Delilah Donovan is probably the only thing that can complicate my life even more than it already is.

"Nothing today." She rolls her bottom lip through her teeth. The sight is more off-putting than the sexiness she's clearly trying to exude. "What else do you need, Lawson?"

"Really?" Delilah mutters loud enough for me to hear.

"Leashes and dental sticks." Rachel recoils. "Seriously, those dogs have some of the nastiest fucking breath."

I turn my back to her to scoop two of the four bags of food.

"See you at the party on Saturday!" Rachel says either to my turned back or Delilah. "I'll bring my overnight bag."

"Can't fucking wait," Delilah mutters as I walk past her to the storage room.

I feel her presence behind me. After dropping the bags on the empty pallet in the corner, I turn to her.

"What I said earlier—" I sigh and run my hand over the top of my head.

"Is it that difficult?" Her words sting, but at least there's a smile on her face and no sharp tools in her hands.

I quirk an eyebrow at her.

"Apologizing? Is it that difficult?"

I grin, my eyes lingering on her lips before meeting her gaze.

"I don't do it very often. Will you forgive me?"

"For what?" she prods, insisting I actually say it.

"For saying those awful things. I'm sorry." Well, that wasn't as painful as I imagined it would be.

"You didn't mean them?" Her throat works on a swallow, the action drawing me closer to her.

It's my turn to bite my lip, trying not to lie to her because fuck if I didn't mean every word out in that field. I release it immediately, wondering if I look as stupid as the chick from earlier.

"The truth?" I whisper mere inches from her mouth. She nods, eyes focused on my lips. "You sucking my cock, me licking the length of your pussy, the way you're going to feel sliding down my cock when I take you the first time is all I think about. I meant every word."

She swallows again and nods. "Good to know."

My eyes flutter as my mouth reaches out to hers. She deserves more than being Frenched in a storage room that smells like dog food and mothballs, but not everything in life is as glorious as we watch in movies.

My lips meet air, and when I open them, I see her back as she walks away from me. My cock aches at her rejection, but a smile is on my face all the way to her car.

Chapter 16
Delilah

"Can you be any more obvious?" Ivy sneers at her sister's question, but she pulls her eyes from Griffin anyway.

"You can't tell me you didn't miss him while he was away," Ivy says looking down at her clasped hands.

I hate to tell her that while she's had her eyes on Griffin; his eyes have been on her sister. She either doesn't see the way he watches her or she ignores it.

"He's been gone a couple of weeks," Gigi says with a shrug.

"Months," Ivy corrects. "He's been gone for months, and he's fixing to deploy to Germany."

"Okay?" Gigi says but doesn't pull her eyes from whatever guy she's honed in on tonight.

"There's no telling when he'll be back home," Ivy whines. I rub a hand over her shoulders. "Or *if* he'll ever make it home."

"None of that. We're supposed to be having fun." I tell her. I look over at Gigi. "Quit being a bitch."

She turns her head, shock in her eyes and just stares at me as if I've grown three heads in the last five minutes. "Sorry."

It's a half-assed apology, but it's the best she ever has to offer. When she looks across the room, I follow her line of sight. Lawson. I should've guessed.

He's not looking at her, however, his eyes are locked with mine. Drew calls his name from the other side of the room, but he winks at me before turning his attention to his younger brother.

"He seriously likes you," Ivy whispers and I can feel my cheeks flush.

"He likes embarrassing me," I counter.

"You either go after him or I will," Gigi spits before she stands in a huff and walks away.

"She's disgusting," Ivy says. "You don't have to worry though. I don't think he'd touch her. I heard her on the phone with someone bitching because she came on to him and he shot her down. She thinks something's wrong with him."

"Because he didn't accept when she threw herself at him?" Ivy nods. "She's nuts."

"Mom and Dad have been talking about sending her to boarding school."

My eyes widen. "They wouldn't."

I look across the room finding Griffin, Shadow, and Diego huddled together. I wince when Gigi bounces up to them and commands all of Griffin's attention without so much as a glance in his direction. Diego frowns and shakes his head. Gigi walks away, pouting like a reprimanded child. Griffin's eyes follow her until she disappears into the small crowd on the make-shift dance floor. He doesn't stop looking until he takes a punch to the shoulder by Diego. I grin when Shadow tries to hide his laugh behind his beer bottle. Griffin straightens, nearly standing at attention as the MC President rips into him for checking out his underage daughter.

"He doesn't even know I exist."

I turn to find a tear glistening on Ivy's bottom lash.

"Maybe I should be a slut like my sister. He'd have no choice but to notice me then."

God, I feel terrible for her, but I have no experience with guys, so I don't have anything to offer.

"I doubt that's the best course of action. Acting that way just makes them want to use you and toss you away."

"Really?" Ivy asks, her eyes darting to the bare skin of my thighs not covered by my shorter than usual skirt. "Are you wearing half a skirt for Lawson?"

I clear my throat, knowing she's exactly right. I have no defense.

"He gets his jollies by torturing me. I'm sure if I actually challenged him, accepted one of his grotesque offers, he'd back away in a flash."

"I doubt that," she mutters.

"He's an asshole," I assure her.

"Yet you say it with a smile." She returns my grin. "Delilah has a crush on the bad boy. Never thought I'd see the day."

I look at her but refuse to say anything else. It isn't until the light from the neon pink disco ball is blocked that I look away.

"Hey, ladies." I smile up at Griffin, but then wince when Ivy's fingernails dig into my thighs.

Without pulling my eyes from his, I grab her hand and bend a finger back until she releases her death grip on my leg.

"How long do we get the pleasure of your company?" I ask sweetly.

"I have to be back in San Diego tomorrow," he says as he takes the empty spot on the sofa next to Ivy.

She's stiff as a board, but she deflates when he wraps his arm around her shoulder and pulls her to his chest for a hug. "How are you, kiddo?"

I wince. Kiddo? Damn, that's got to hurt.

"Fine," she grumbles but doesn't pull from his embrace.

"Looked like you and Diego were having a heated conversation. What was that all about?"

At least he has the decency to blush, but Ivy glares at me when he pulls his arm away to run his hand over the top of his crop-top. I don't imagine she'll ever wash her shirt again.

"He was…. Ah… giving me some advice that could save my life. Pointers about survival and shit."

"For your deployment? Or the enemy combatants in the clubhouse?"

His eyes dart back to Diego, and the glare in his President's eyes has him putting a little distance between himself and Ivy.

"Stop," she mutters.

"Cut me some slack, D. She's less than two years younger than me."

I tilt my head, taking in his discomfort. He defends his sexual attraction to Gigi, but calls Ivy kiddo?

"Did you tell him that?"

He shakes his head back and forth almost violently. "Fuck no. He'd kill me."

"Hey," Samson says as he walks up. "You said we could use your playlist."

"Yeah, sorry." Griffin stands and walks away with my brother.

"And I thought Gigi was a bitch."

I sigh, hating that teasing Griffin was at her expense.

I slap my hands on my knees, the uncomfortable sting from the impact lighting my nerve endings on fire. "You just need to take your mind off of him."

"Impossible."

"Let's try anyway."

I hate to dance, mainly because I suck at it, but if she needs the distraction, I'll throw myself on the proverbial altar for sacrifice.

"I hate this song," she mutters as Dawin's Dessert begins to fade out.

She perks up the second it transitions into Nelly's The Fix. We both look up to find Griffin grinning at us. Thumb up in the air, he winks at Ivy. She may think she's invisible, but playing her favorite song reveals that it's so far from the truth.

Before the song is over, we're both glistening with sweat, and there's a smile on her face I haven't seen in a very long time.

"And this one!" Ivy squeals when Anaconda by Nicki Minaj blares through the speakers.

I shake my head, fanning my overheated face with my hand. "I have to sit this one out. You want a water?"

She nods and bounces around in a circle with her arms in the air. I can hear her singing the lyrics as I walk away.

"Jesus," Dad mutters when I step up to the refreshment table. "It's like watching mating on Animal Planet."

I grab a water and turn back to the dance floor.

"I hope nobody gets pregnant out there," he grumbles.

I laugh, head thrown back at his complaint. He's smiling when I turn back toward him. "That's not how it happens, Dad."

An eyebrow shoots into his hairline, the star tattoo on his cheek twitching. "And just what do you know about it?"

I smile wider. We've had the birds and bees talk a couple of years ago. It left me broken and disgusted, and it's not a subject we've revisited since.

"Just what I've watched on PornMD." Both eyebrows disappear into his dark hair.

"I'm canceling the data on your phone." I roll my teeth through my lips. "And turning off the Wi-Fi in the house."

"I'm seventeen, Dad. I can't stay a little girl forever."

His eyes narrow in challenge. "Seventeen on Monday," he corrects.

"Old enough to consent," I tease.

"I'll kill any bastard with the balls big enough to touch you."

"So violent," I say as I tilt my water up to my lips.

"We'll talk about it tomorrow," he hisses and storms off.

I watch as he joins Pop on the other side of the room. Pop looks over at me as Dad flails his arms and animatedly tells him about our conversation. He smiles and rubs dad's back to try to calm him, but the look in his eyes tells me to stop torturing the man. I give them both a little wave and head back to the dance floor.

I bite my lip when I pass Lawson stretched out on the sofa. Rachel is practically in his lap. If I thought my skirt was short, it has nothing on Rachel's. I know I'm not the only one who can see her lime green panties glowing between her legs.

"So fucking skanky," I whisper to myself as I walk past them.

Samson is still standing near the stereo system with Griffin, but he's throwing daggers at Lawson. My night just went from playful and fun to disappointing in an instant.

I can't wait for everyone to leave so I can go to bed and just forget about the whole damn thing.

Chapter 17
Lawson

"Where are you going?" Drew asks with a yawn from the top bunk.

I reach for the doorknob. "I need to find Delilah and explain that what she saw earlier with Rachel wasn't what it looked like."

He chuckles. "You're screwed."

"I hope not," I tell him as I pull the door open.

"Why in the world didn't you go find her then?" He shakes his head and looks back at his phone.

"I tried to find her. She just disappeared," I explain.

"If Jaxon finds you in her room at two in the morning he'll rip you to shreds."

"You let me worry about Jaxon," I mutter stepping out into the hallway.

"Famous last words," he says with another laugh as I pull the door closed. I still hear him through the door. "Your funeral."

I tiptoe down the hallway, grateful for the plush carpet under my bare feet. Her door isn't pulled all of the way closed, so I stick my head in. The bed is made, and she's nowhere to be seen.

I turn back and make my way down the stairs. If I'm caught in the common areas by Jaxon or Rob, the fallout will be less intense.

The sight of Delilah, bent over in her short skirt, is worth anything the men of the house can throw at me. I'd gladly spend time in jail so long as they have no way to pull these images from my mind.

Backlit by the light inside the fridge, her golden hair seems to glow in a curtain around her. Resisting the pull her body has on mine would only be in vain, so rather than announcing myself, I close the distance between us and wrap my arms around her middle. She stiffens, frightened at first, but soon settles into my embrace.

"I couldn't keep my eyes off of you tonight," I whisper in her ear, nuzzling into her soft neck.

She whimpers when I pull her closer. I never imagined the warmth of her skin against mine would be life-altering, but here I stand in the dark kitchen of my newly discovered father's house a new man.

"Jesus," I pant into the web of her tangled blonde hair. "I can die a happy man."

"Well isn't this cozy." The kitchen light flips on bathing us in light that leaves nothing to the imagination.

Releasing Delilah, I turn to face a pissed off Samson, only to find the shimmering eyes of—

"Delilah?"

My stunned eyes flash from the devastation on her face to the blonde now standing directly against my side. I recoil, taking a few steps away from Rachel. She bats her eyelashes at me, and I move further away until my hip collides with the counter.

"What the fuck is going on?" Samson seethes through gritted teeth.

"Isn't it obvious?" Rachel's breathy voice makes my skin crawl. The look in her eyes dares me to tell him I've made a mistake.

"We were..." I sigh and drop my hands to my sides. I've got nothing. I can't explain to Samson that I thought Rachel was his sister. The look in his eyes says he's ready to snap me in half, and a week ago I would've welcomed the chance to beat his ass, but things have shifted for me since working with Delilah at the animal shelter.

"We were just getting to the good stuff when you so rudely interrupted," she sneers at Samson. "You need to get over your little obsession with me. It's never going to happen. I'm only interested in real men."

I bite my tongue but stand stock still when her fingernail scrapes down the front of my bare chest.

I can't even look at Samson. His anger is secondary to the pain that's crushing me under Delilah's devastated stare. She just nods, gives me a weak, sad smile, and turns and walks away.

"Don't," Rachel warns catching my arm when I take a step to go after her. "She's upset that her twin is upset. She'll be fine."

I squeeze my eyes shut, only able to hear the soft retreat of her footfalls on the stairs. Even as upset as she is, I don't even hear her door close with a thud.

"Was this your plan all along?" Samson says with fists balled at his sides.

I shake my head.

"You knew I liked her." He jabs his finger in Rachel's direction. She merely rolls her eyes, looking bored.

"Doesn't matter, Sam. There's no mutual attraction. We're only friends." She says it sweetly, but the twinge on his face tells me it doesn't make things any better.

"You're a whore!" Samson yells.

I take a step forward. Rachel may not be an innocent angel, but I wrapped myself around her, and he's out of line. "Enough," I hiss.

"Enough? You've got to be fucking kidding me. You show up out the fucking blue, with some devious agenda and you have the nuts to stand there and tell me enough?"

"What the hell is going on?" Jaxon's booming voice circles around us.

Only now does Rachel step away from me, having closed the distance between us when Sam started ranting.

A menacing grin spreads across Samson's face, and I just know the fallout from this is going to be awful.

"Lawson here is pushing up on my girl. Pretty sure they were about to fuck on the kitchen table."

"She's not your girlfriend."

"I'd never touch you. Gross."

Jaxon and Rachel speak at the same time.

Jaxon holds his hand up when Samson begins his rebuttal. "And watch your mouth."

Samson's eyes narrow as he looks at his dad, but he doesn't make a sound. Jaxon commands respect, and I find myself standing a little straighter, even though what I'm about to face could end up with me on the street.

"Rachel, go get your things. Rob will give you a ride home."

"But I drove?" she argues, stopping short when Jaxon's glare lands on her.

"You can come get your truck in the morning. I'm not sending you out on the road this late at night."

"Yes, sir," she mutters and walks away.

Silence fills the room around us when she leaves. I'm not going to be the first person to speak, but I also haven't been given permission to speak. Why I'm resorting to the things I learned in the probation boot camp last year, I have no idea. Yet, here I stand, waiting to be addressed like I'm still in that hell hole with a drill instructor in my face.

"Calmly," Jaxon says with a warning in his voice. "Tell me what's going on."

He looks at Samson first, who crosses his arms over his chest and pouts for a quick second before he begins to speak.

"D and I came down to cut into our birthday cake early." Sam looks at his father, who smiles at him? The hell? "We—"

"Didn't want to wait for the family." Jaxon grins wider before schooling his face back to impassive seriousness. "Just like every year."

"Right." Even pissed Samson gives his dad a quick smile.

Seems my impromptu need for Delilah has ruined a family tradition. And my night just keeps getting better.

"When we stepped into the kitchen, Lawson and Rachel were all hugged up on each other in front of the fridge."

Jaxon looks toward me. All I can do is shrug in response and pray Jaxon doesn't figure out that it was his gorgeous daughter I'd wanted in my arms instead. I have a feeling though, that if Samson saw my arms wrapped around his twin, he'd lose his shit even more than he is now.

"And they were naked?" Jaxon asks.

"No," Samson cringes at the idea.

"Your yelling woke me up because your brother was hugging some girl in the kitchen?"

"We're not brothers," Samson insists while I say. "Not related at all."

The only thing we can agree on.

"Semantics," Jaxon says as he pinches the bridge of his nose in frustration.

"No," Samson insists. "Not related."

I nod in agreement. Adding, "like at all."

Being related to Samson in any way would be more of a slippery slope with Delilah, and I have enough problems with that situation. More along the lines of needing her more than I should ever feel about any other human other than Drew.

"Fine," Jaxon concedes albeit reluctantly. "Not related, but this is how we're going to settle this mess."

He turns to me. "No messing around with chicks in the house."

I agree even though there's the little issue of Delilah. "No problem."

"Also, I think it's best that you stay away from Rachel Grant," Jaxon adds.

"That's not a problem either."

He turns to Samson. "You don't just get to claim a girl because you think she's pretty."

"But—"

Jaxon holds his hand up, and Sam silences immediately. "It's not right to stake a claim on another person. Besides, it's creepy as hell. You have to let go of the idea of her if she isn't attracted to you."

"This sucks," Samson mutters.

"She told you how she feels, son. Just let it go."

"I've liked her for as long as I can remember, Dad. There's no way I can just walk away from that."

"You are blinded by her." I shift from one foot to the other, not wanting to be anywhere near this little father/son moment. "So much so that you didn't see the way that Kennedy followed your every move tonight."

His eyes widen, a small smile playing at the corner of his mouth. "The girl with pink hair and huge tits?"

Wow, this boy is driven by his hormones. He even cups his hands out in front of him for exaggeration.

"Really?" Jaxon frowns. "Don't talk about women like that. I've taught you better."

"Double D's dad." Samson is full on smiling now.

"Is this over?" Jaxon asks looking back and forth between us.

I nod, the first one to extend my hand to Samson. I don't miss the pride in Jaxon's eyes, but it doesn't exactly give me warm fuzzies.

"Sure," Samson says, his smile faltering as he reaches out to shake my hand. I let him squeeze harder than necessary. He's the one with the bruised ego, so I'll give him the small victory. I have a girl I need to speak to, to explain what actually happened in the dark tonight.

"Kennedy fucking Farmer," Samson sing songs as he leaves us and makes his way to his room.

"Rachel Grant? Really Lawson?" Jaxon's full attention is on me, and I wonder if this is when the calm, cool, collected guy disappears and he slams my head into the cabinet for hurting his son.

I shrug. "What?"

"Nothing," he says with disappointment in his eyes as he turns and walks toward his bedroom. "I just thought your interests were somewhere else."

Rob walks into the room with Rachel right behind him, gives Jaxon a quick kiss, and heads out to take her home. She waggles her fingers and does that unattractive lip and teeth roll again before she disappears out of the door.

When I hear Jaxon's bedroom door, I bound up the stairs, meeting Gigi and her twin on the upper landing.

"I thought you were staying the night?" *Please be going home.*

"She wants to be alone," the bookish twin says. Gigi doesn't even look in my direction. I appreciate the reprieve from her attention.

When Gigi is a few steps ahead of her on the way down the stairs, the other twin turns to look at me. The seriousness in her eyes makes me wish I could remember her name.

"You really hurt her," she whispers before she follows her sister out of the house.

"Hey, Kennedy. It's Samson Donovan." I'm not surprised he ran up the stairs to call her, but it's really putting a damper on the plans I have.

I groan, knowing I can't go to her right now. Leaving her alone, letting her stew in her anger isn't going to happen, but Rob will be back before too long, and there's the possibility that he'll check in on his little girl before calling it a night. Either he or Jaxon has opened our door and peered into our room at least once a night since we arrived. I figure they're either making sure we haven't snuck out, or it's one of those parental safety things I'll never understand.

I close myself into my room. Drew is snoring softly as I settle into the desk chair and hope that it doesn't take the house long to fall into slumber. I have a girl to win back.

Chapter 18
Delilah

"I'm fine, Daddy. Just can't sleep. Too much excitement today," I lie not even bothering to look up from my phone. He or Pop checks on us every night before they turn in. They have for as long as I can remember.

The door clicks closed. No 'night, sweetheart' or 'see ya in the morning.'

I look up to see the dark figure still standing in my room.

"Daddy?" The husky voice sounds pleased. "We can play it like that if you want, Princess, but that's not really my thing."

I sigh, closing out of the casino slots game I'm playing on my cell phone. The last thing Lawson needs as ammunition against me is knowing I can't stop playing those stupid apps.

"What do you want?"

"To talk." His response is quick.

"Find out just how intellectual Rachel isn't?" I pull my eyes from him and stare off into a dark corner of my room. "I don't have the time or patience to deal with you right now."

He chuckles. "I never would've even confused her with someone with brains." He takes a step in my direction, ignoring the second part of my statement.

"Go to bed Lawson. I've had enough of your shit tonight." I grab my headphones from my bedside table. "I'm sure you'll find another way to hurt me tomorrow."

"I didn't know you cared." I can hear the playfulness in his voice, and it does nothing but make me angrier.

"I don't," I argue. "It pissed me off that you pulled that shit with the one girl that Samson will never get over."

He laughs and takes another step forward. He's hesitant and calculating, and I wonder if he's afraid I'm going to attack him. He's got another thing coming if he thinks I'll waste that type of energy on his sorry ass.

"Samson is on the phone with Kennedy Farmer, probably jacking off to her voice while they talk about Pokémon Go or something."

I tilt my head, confused. "The pink-haired girl with the umm..."

"Big tits?" He takes another step closer so his face is now bathed in the light of the moon coming through the window. "Yeah, her."

"He just handed Rachel over to you?"

"Not exactly." He runs his hand over his head. "I need to talk to you about what you saw. I have to explain myself."

"No need," I tell him. "Your silence downstairs said a thousand words."

"What did you want me to say?" He sits on the side of my bed, on top of the blankets so I can hardly move my legs. "Was I supposed to tell your twin brother that I went into that kitchen and wrapped my arms around the girl I've been obsessing over for weeks?"

I huff. "You met her like two days ago."

"You sure are dense for a smart girl."

I could pop him in the eye right now.

"Short skirt, gorgeous blonde hair, legs that go on for days."

"Seriously, Lawson? Do you just enjoy torturing me?"

"I have a mind to tie you to this bed and gag you. Force you to shut the fuck up until I'm finished speaking."

"I don't want to hear a fucking word you have to say." My voice quivers and I hate that he has enough power over me to make me cry. "You could've stayed in your room tonight, but instead you want to rub it in my face? That's cruel, but probably a great decision on your part. I'm sure she's great at giving head. She's sucked off practically every popular guy at school."

His hand covers my mouth. When I try to turn my head to get away from him, his other hand fists the hair on my nape, tilting my head back and forcing me to look in his eyes. They practically sparkle in the dim light, and I feel hypnotized by them.

"Be quiet." Fear and something very similar to heat settles low in my stomach. He notices my reaction and smiles like the devil that he is. "Naughty girl. You like it rough?"

I draw in a hissing breath through my nose.

"I. Thought. She. Was. You."

I try to shake my head, rejecting his words, but my movement is impeded by his grip in my hair.

"If I pull my hand away will you scream?"

"No," I mumble against his palm.

"Promise?"

I nod as best as I can.

I lick my lips the second he pulls his hand away, the tip of my tongue running over his finger. Accidental? Deliberate? At this moment I can't tell.

"Fuck," he mutters. "The things you do to me."

"I'm not her," I finally manage to say. "I will never be like her, throwing myself at your feet, flirting with you until you cave."

"There's nothing about her that appeals to me, Princess." He presses his index finger against my lips, but I turn my head forcing him to pull it away. "Everything about you makes my blood boil, makes me want things I've never wanted before."

"Like my lips around your..." I swallow. "Cock?"

"Damn, Delilah. I love your filthy mouth." I expect a grin to hit his mouth, but it stays in a flat line. "I'd sell my already dark soul to the devil for that, and all in good time, but you're more to me than a blowjob."

I let the sound of my heavy breathing fill the room, grateful that my covers are pulled up so he can't see the quick puckering of my nipples.

"And you'd never have to throw yourself at my feet. Although I get the feeling I may end up doing just that to you."

I search his eyes for deception, finding nothing but wide-open honesty.

"Why now?" My voice is thick with arousal and temptation.

He shakes his head as if he doesn't have an answer, but he finally speaks. "I'm tired of fighting it. Tired of jacking off to thoughts of you, dreaming of you every night knowing you're in here all alone."

"That's... descriptive." His hand finds mine, and I suddenly feel too warm, too open and exposed. "I'm not just going to jump into sex with you. I'm not the type. Rachel maybe—"

His fingers brush against my lips again. They part on a harsh breath at the contact.

"Let's agree to never mention her name again." I agree with a quick jerk of my head. "Tell me you want this too."

"I don't know what you want," I confess.

"I want to spend time together, talk, and get to know each other."

"You don't talk. You grunt and give one-word answers. You're a vault, Law."

He smiles brightly. "I love when you call me that." His finger sweeps over my lips again. Talk about obsessive behavior. "I'll open up."

I frown.

"I'll make an effort to open up to you. I want to."

"What made you change your mind?"

He sighs. "Honestly?"

"No, Lawson," I snip. "Lie to me some more."

"There was this sense of calm that washed over me when I wrapped my arms around Rachel earlier." I jerk my hand from his. He grabs it back immediately. "Don't. I thought she was you. Every spark, every raised hair on my body was yours. It all belonged to you."

"I was jealous of her," I admit.

"And I love that about you." His hand cups my cheek. "Can I replace the warmth of her body with yours?"

I laugh. "Do you know how fucked up that sounds?"

He gives me a sad smile. "I do, but it doesn't make me want to do it any less."

"Over the covers?"

"I'll take anything you're willing to give me."

I stretch out, sliding down to rest my head on my pillow rather than my back against the headboard.

"When did you turn into this softy?"

He chuckles as his body lines up behind mine. "I can try to cop a feel if that makes things more suitable for you."

I laugh but pull the blankets down to my waist. The heat of his bare chest against my thin tank top is absolute bliss. His arm wraps around my stomach, but rather than reaching high or low he settles it palm down on the sheet. Needing just a little more, I intertwine my fingers in his.

"You're so warm," I whisper.

He grumbles incoherently just as my mouth stretches in a yawn.

"Okay, Romeo. You have to go. If we fall asleep, Dad and Pop will kill us both."

"Worth it," he mumbles against my neck.

"Go," I tell him and hitch my shoulder to jolt him.

I roll to my back as he climbs off of the bed.

"Goodnight," he whispers as his lips brush my forehead.

"Nope," I tell him with a hand tugging at the back of his neck.

I press my lips to his, giving his tongue the access it demands when it presses forward.

His strong hands cup my face as he controls the kiss I instigated. Fire shoots all over my body, this kiss nothing remotely similar to Brandon's lips last year at the homecoming game.

Lawson worships me with his tongue, taking the time and care to explore my mouth and allowing me to do the same. When he pulls away, I'm hungry for more. My neck flexes up, lips seeking his. He pecks them like an elderly relative and pulls away.

"Sleep, Princess. I'll see you in the morning."

I'm still smiling, still have fingers pressed to my lips as I drift off to sleep. This year may be the best birthday I'll ever have.

Chapter 19
Lawson

"What are you thinking about?"

I turn to find Delilah watching me as we wait at the red light.

"Your mouth," I answer truthfully.

She grins wider and shakes her head. "And exactly why does that make you smile like a fool?"

"I was thinking about the way the syrup from your waffles yesterday morning clung to your bottom lip." I take her right hand from the steering wheel and close my fingers around it. "The way your tongue peeked out to lick it away."

Fuck, I'm getting hard.

"You're obsessed with my mouth." I nod knowing I'm obsessed with every single thing about her.

She's still staring at me when a horn blares behind us. Her eyes dart to the rearview mirror before she pulls her hand from mine and places it back on the steering wheel as she accelerates. I leave my hand on her thigh, the innocuous touch shooting fire into my blood.

Her throat clears. "How did your test go last week?"

I'd already forgotten that I went in for my GED exam on Thursday.

"Good," I answer. "I passed."

She beams with pride, and it makes me a little uneasy. Did she think I wouldn't?

"What's that look for?"

"What look?" she says but doesn't take her eyes off the road.

"Did you doubt my ability to pass it?" She shakes her head. "I'm a criminal deviant, not an idiot."

I can't even hide the agitation in my voice as I pull my hand from her thigh.

"Really?" she asks looking down at her leg as if the sensation of moving my hand is all that she can focus on. "I can't be proud that you passed your test without you getting upset that I'm happy?"

"Whatever," I mumble and look out the window.

"Don't whatever me," she snaps. "I don't think of you in a negative light at all. What you're struggling with is self-deprecation and shit from your past. Don't deflect that mess on me. I don't deserve it."

I bite the inside of my cheek until the taste of blood fills my mouth. She's right, but admitting that out loud is another character flaw.

Without a word, I put my hand back on her thigh. She doesn't swat it away, but a tension fills her muscles where there was nothing but welcoming calm a few minutes before.

***

My day has gone from bad to worse, I realize as I stand in front of Buddy's empty kennel.

"What happened?" I ask Dana when she walks up.

"He was adopted on Saturday." She's beaming, pride filling her eyes.

"By who?"

"A family with two excited little boys," she answers. "They'll take great care of him."

"How the hell do you know that? They could be budding psychopaths and only adopted a dog so they can torture him."

Far-fetched, but with my luck lately, I can see how it may have rubbed off on Buddy just by association.

A calm hand clasps my shoulder, and even though I want to pull away from her, I remain stock still.

"The preacher at the Baptist church, his wife, and their two very excited little boys will treat Buddy like the king that he is. I guarantee it."

"Did you vet them? Run a background check?"

She only chuckles as she walks away.

"Be careful," I hear Dana say on the other side of the door. "He's crabby today."

My brows are drawn together by the time Delilah comes into view.

"Crabby?" She tilts her head a little to the left. "You're not supposed to be crabby."

I shrug. "Buddy's gone."

I point to the empty kennel.

"Buddy is with a loving family. He's not gone. Now you can direct your attention to another sweet puppy."

She grabs my hand and drags me behind her to the supply closet.

"We're going to clean the kennels, then we'll walk the dogs and pet the kitties."

"You're going to help me clean kennels?" I raise a skeptical eyebrow at her as she pulls down two sets of coveralls.

A smile plays at the corner of her mouth. "Don't make assumptions about me. It's rude."

"Touché," I mutter.

We dress in the coveralls in companionable silence and then get to work on cleaning.

"I passed my test," I confide as we strip out of the soiled coveralls. "All I have left now is wrapping up my community service this week."

"I bet that's a huge relief."

"The biggest," I agree. "I feel lighter. Like I can get on with my life. Make plans for the future."

I hand her a bundle of three leashes and grab the same amount for me.

"What kind of plans?"

I follow her to the kennels all the way at the end. We'll start there and work our way back.

I chuckle. "Couldn't honestly tell you. I'll start in the garage today. Jaxon made me wait until the test was over. He wanted me to study for the test, but it's one of those things that if you don't know it, spending a couple hours a day for a week isn't going to do much good."

"You spent those hours in your room," she says as she clips a leash to the collar of a black dog.

"Yep," I say with a pop of my lips.

"But not studying? Were you hiding out from everyone?"

"At first, but then after a while, I would just lie in bed and think about where I'm heading." She smiles waiting for me to expand. "Don't give me that look. I haven't figured shit out."

"College?"

I shake my head. "I'm not really a classroom kind of guy."

We make our way to the second set of kennels so I can leash my three dogs. She remains silent, but I can tell from the mood surrounding her that she has plenty to say.

"Out with it," I say nudging her shoulder with mine as we begin to make our way across the field.

"It's just..." She looks off into the distance. "I don't want to sound naggy, but you need goals or something to work toward."

"I know." Her telling me this doesn't cause the same agitation as it would if it was Jaxon or Rob. "I think a mechanic would suit me well. Bikes, cars, that sort of thing."

"To be a legit mechanic, you'll have to go to school."

"Yeah," I shrug. "But it's mainly hands-on experience. I can deal with that. I just have no interest in taking government and history."

"The History of the Harley?" she offers.

"Now that I can get behind."

The dogs bounce around, not having been walked by Delilah since Friday. I'd be anxious and full of energy if I had to go two full days without her, so I understand their eagerness.

When we finally have the last of the animals back in their kennels, fed and watered, we make our way to the supply closet to rehang the leashes.

With her back to me, I wrap my arms all the way around her, enjoying the way she relaxes into me.

"I hate that things were so hectic yesterday." My breath whispers past the hairs that have escaped her ponytail. "It's been over twenty-four hours since I've tasted your lips."

"There you go with my mouth again," she says with a sigh, but I can tell she's not agitated by it. If anything, her breathless words reflect the same need I feel.

Turning her in my arms, I look down at her.

"Not just your mouth," I vow against the soft spot below her ear.

Her head tilts, giving my mouth unfettered access to the delicate column of her neck.

"Every inch of you." My hands find the break in the fabric between her tank top and the top band of her jeans. The coolness of her sweat-misted skin is almost more than I can bear.

My mouth seeks hers. When she whimpers at the kiss, I press against her more.

"Dana is going to catch us," she pants against my swollen lips.

I grin and close my mouth over hers again. The world could implode around us, and it still wouldn't be enough to pull me away from her.

As much as I hate it, the soft push against my chest by her small hands is enough to make me back away. I want this girl more than anything on this earth, but she's calling the shots. If things are too heavy for her, if she's pumping the brakes, all I can do is wait until she's ready for everything I want to give her.

And I want to give Delilah Donovan the world.

"It's time to go home." Her breathless warning skates across my mouth, drawing my eyes to the pink of her lips.

I take a step back, my hand reaching up to cup her at the nape.

"Would you throw me out if I snuck into your room tonight?"

I see the war in her eyes as if she wants me there but being able to resist her temptations isn't something she can handle. Her gaze drops to my chin and I miss the gorgeous beauty of her eyes the second they fall away.

"I'll never push you, never pressure you. I'll never expect more than you're willing to give me."

She takes a step back, her back meeting with the rough wood of the outdoor supply building. "My head doesn't work like normal when I'm around you."

"Likewise, Princess." I clasp her hand in mine, uncaring of who sees us walking together to her car.

She's not some dirty secret, some fling I don't want to be questioned about in case things don't work out. She doesn't seem to mind either and only releases my hand long enough to climb behind the driver's seat. Our hands are joined once more after we settle inside and get our seatbelts in place.

"Are you excited about working in the shop this afternoon?"

"More than I probably should be."

"I heard Scooter and Rocker talking about you the other day."

"Really?" I frown. Showing Scooter up with the bike tire my first day here probably didn't make me a friend in his eyes. "I bet they hate me."

She shakes her head and uses our joined hands to put the car in drive. "They were impressed. I know Diego is impressed with your skill level. He wouldn't allow you in the shop if he didn't think you could handle it."

"The vote of confidence is a huge ego boost. I still have lots to learn," I add.

"Make sure you talk to Dad about mechanic school. He knows people all over, and I know he'd love to get you hooked up with someone to make your dreams come true."

"We'll see," I tell her with non-committal wariness.

If only for being the catalyst to meet Delilah, I feel like I owe him everything. I don't know how much more I can give the man without handing over my soul.

Chapter 20
Delilah

"You're hiding," my brother says after the quick knock on my door and enters without me answering.

"You could wait for me to invite you in," I scold as he walks up and sits on the end of my bed.

I shouldn't be snippy with him, but it's the only way to get out my agitation that it's Samson and not Lawson coming in here.

"I feel like we haven't talked in forever." Falling to his back on my bed, he stares up at the ceiling.

I put my novel on my bedside table, shift my body, and lie down beside him.

"We won't ever see each other in a week after football practice starts," I tell him.

He sighs. "I don't even know if I'm going to play this year."

I shake my head, confused. "You've played every year since you were five, Samson. Of course, you're going to play your senior year."

"Kennedy thinks it's dumb."

"Kennedy is dumb for thinking that." I pause when he stiffens beside me. "Okay, maybe she isn't dumb for thinking it, but she sure as hell shouldn't try to change you."

He grunts but doesn't reply.

"So," I begin. "About Rachel."

"What about her?" He doesn't pull his eyes from the ceiling, staring as if it holds the answers to the universe.

"You've switched your focus." Not a question. It's obvious now with his attention on Kennedy. "Does that mean you're not upset with Lawson anymore?"

He grunts again, and I wait in silence, knowing he'll respond if I fill the room with awkward silence. The wait isn't long, and I hate that because it means he's still fired up about Lawson's mistake in the kitchen last week.

"It's like he's purposely trying to destroy us."

"I don't see things that way," I defend.

"Well, you're obsessed with him, so I wouldn't expect you to be on my side."

I recoil at his view of the situation. "I'm not obsessed with him." I totally am, but not for the reasons he thinks. "He made a mistake."

I'm hesitant to explain to him the man I know, the man that Lawson is around me when no one else is around, but with the attitude my brother is tossing my way I know the outcome won't be him understanding but using my feelings for Lawson against me. Samson has such strong opinions about the situation, there's no way to change his mind.

"He's a calculating asshole," he mutters. "And you're all cozy with him."

"He has community service to finish," I explain. "Dad set that up, not me."

"You didn't object."

"Do I ever object to anything Dad tells me to do?"

Another grunt.

"He's not a bad guy. He's done what Dad told him to do and is staying away from Rachel."

His eyes close, the corners crinkling with agitation.

"Only because the damage has been done."

No, because he never wanted her and his fixation is on a different blonde-haired girl.

"What's he got planned next?" he asks. "Is he going to start sneaking in here, trying to fuck you, too?"

I stiffen beside him, my body responding to his words before I can stop it.

"What?" He turns his head in my direction. "Has he already started?"

"No," I answer with incredulity. "Don't be ridiculous."

My voice breaks, causing his eyes to narrow. He can always tell when I'm lying.

"What aren't you telling me?"

"There's nothing to tell," I lie. "We don't even talk. We go separate ways at the animal shelter. He cleans up shit, and I walk dogs and play with the cats. Besides, his last day was today."

I'm going to miss our time together, but he'd mentioned still going to the animal shelter to help a few days a week. Dana likes having some muscle around for the heavy lifting. I love watching his muscles bunch under his t-shirt, and I lose my breath when he gets so hot he pulls it off to wipe sweat from his face. My cheeks flush, but I refuse to look away from Samson.

He studies my face, and his scrutiny makes tears burn the backs of my eyes. I'm upset that he would hate me if he knew about the private moments Lawson and I shared. I'm hurt that the feelings I have for him have to be kept secret. I hate that I can't profess how I feel and have everyone around me be happy.

"You'd tell me if he tried anything, right?"

"Of course." Another lie. "He won't though. He seems pretty focused on getting done with probation and maybe going to school to be a mechanic."

I realize my mistake the second the words are out of my mouth.

"Don't talk, huh?"

I shrug. "I mean. Sometimes we chat to and from the shelter, but nothing like what you're thinking."

He turns his eyes back toward the ceiling. I know he knows I'm lying, but it's still not enough to lay it all out and confess the things I so desperately want him to hear and be okay with hearing.

"I texted Rachel," he says after several long minutes.

"Since the party?"

"Yeah. She told me she doesn't date boys." I watch him as his left eye twitches. "She implied that Lawson was a man and she didn't have time to waste on me."

"That's Rachel's hang-up. I don't think it's an honest reflection of who you are."

"He's only two years older than us," he spits. "And he's a fucking criminal."

"Hey," I chide. "That's not fair. He did what he thought was best while taking care of Drew while his mom partied all the time. She didn't care that she was supposed to be raising two boys. He had to be the man of the house, and that led to some decisions he now regrets. He didn't see any other way out."

Samson's huff as he gets off of the bed makes my skin crawl.

"Sure do know a lot from just chatting."

I flinch when the door slams shut behind him. Calming breaths don't help to ease the tremble in my fingers. I wish I had a Magic 8 Ball. Looking into my future, knowing how Dad and Pop would respond to the news of what Lawson and I are building, would be amazing. Living in fear that Samson will say something, and they hate me for it is my worst nightmare.

I need someone to talk to, but confiding in Ivy is tricky when Gigi seems to find out everything we say. I know being honest is best, but the fallout could be monumental, disastrous even. Dad and Pop could insist we stop, which would be impossible. They'd know how hard it would be and could make him leave. Distance from him is the last thing I want. Being separated from Drew isn't an option, and I could never put myself between Lawson and his brother.

"It's just a stupid crush," I mumble to myself.

The tears rolling down my cheeks tell a different story.

He's forbidden, so that makes him more appealing.

I can stop what we've been doing. Lie.

I can go back to ignoring him, wanting him in private without him even knowing I'm hurting to touch him. Lie.

I can get over him as quickly as I became attracted to him. Lie.

Destroying my family is worth my temporary happiness. I waver on this one. I'm not a martyr, but the pain I could potentially cause those I care for isn't something I can handle as easily as suffering in silence.

Determined, mind made up, I head downstairs.

"Hey, sweetheart," Dad says with a quick kiss on my forehead.

I fall unceremoniously into a chair at the breakfast table.

"What's wrong?" he asks as he pulls the lid from the saucepan and stirs its contents.

"Not feeling so well."

Seeing Lawson today while my decision is so fresh will only have me doubting it. I have to create distance between us, even if it means pretending to be sick and missing supper. My stomach growls at the thought, and the amazing aroma of alfredo sauce only makes it worse.

"Hungry?"

"No. I can't even think about eating."

"About to start? You always get like this around that time."

I groan. "Seriously, Dad? I'm not talking to you about my cycle."

He shrugs.

I want to tell him. The words are right on the tip of my tongue, but a cheer from Drew as he plays Xbox makes my mouth snap shut.

"I think I'm going to skip dinner and go to bed early."

He replaces the lid and drops the spatula on the spoon rest. He walks across the room, his warm lips meeting my forehead. I nearly cave again.

"You don't feel warm."

He pulls back, studying my face with hands cupped on both cheeks.

"I think I got too hot at the shelter today. New Mexico summers suck."

He releases me, believing my lies and takes a step back.

"Well you only have one more, then you have the choice of whether you want to stay in Rhode Island or come home to visit."

The reminder about college helps. It keeps me focused, and forces me to focus on the light at the end of the tunnel. A couple of kisses and a few kind words isn't enough to take the chance of ruining a family.

I don't feel like what Lawson and I are feeling for each other is wrong, but my opinions aren't the only ones to consider.

"Get some rest, sweetheart." He heads back to the cabinet to pull out pasta. "Maybe consider missing tomorrow at the shelter."

"Night, Dad."

I head up the stairs, thankful I have a few snacks up there. Maybe once everyone is asleep, I'll sneak down and grab some leftovers.

Avoiding Lawson may be easier than I thought. I lock my bedroom door behind me and settle in for a long, boring night alone.

Chapter 21
Lawson

"Damn, you're quick."

I find myself at ease with Jaxon's fatherly clap on my shoulder.

"Quick?" Diego snorts from the other side of the garage. "The boy's a natural around these machines."

"He sure as hell didn't leave much work for tomorrow," Shadow adds.

I frown. Knowing I need more work to pay Jaxon back, but going slow just for the sake of wasting time isn't something I'll do either.

"There's plenty more where that came from," Diego says with a nod before walking out of the garage.

"Not easy to impress Prez," Shadow says with a quick nod before heading out of the garage.

"Not easy to impress Shadow either," Jaxon says in a low voice. "Finished up community service this morning. GED test is taken and passed. Fees are paid. You're finished."

"Not yet," I mutter, sure there are still hoops to jump through.

"Sign this," he says pulling a small stack of rolled paper from his back pocket.

I look down, recognizing the probation discharge from Navajo County. The PO back in Texas had shown it to me when I was first placed at the boot camp.

"Your light at the end of the tunnel," he'd told me. "Something to work toward."

I take the pen he offers. "I'll FedEx it to them, and they'll send official copies signed by the judge no later than two weeks from now."

I sign and hand it back to him. He signs it and puts it back in his pocket.

"Relieved?" He slaps me on the back again.

"More than you could ever know," I confess.

He shakes his head. "I know exactly how it feels to cut those kinds of chains off."

I tilt my head, but he just smiles and walks away. Juvenile probation? Maybe we're more alike than I want to admit.

"Oh, I forgot," he says sticking his head back around the door. "Dinner is in an hour. Be quiet when you head up, Delilah isn't feeling well, so she's napping."

I nod but rush to the house. She didn't mention feeling unwell earlier. I couldn't keep my mouth off of her today at the animal shelter, and I feel fine.

Jaxon is already back in the house talking to Rob in the kitchen. Bolting up the stairs, I find her door locked. My light tap goes unanswered, so I decide to take a shower. If she's sick, I want to hold her, but ruining her sheets with grease stains won't go over very well.

By the time I get out of the shower, I'm met with glares from Samson in the hallway. He may be messing around with Kennedy now, but the sting of rejection from Rachel will hurt for a while.

"You need to stay the fuck away from my sister," he seethes but doesn't push himself away from the wall and into my path.

I huff, annoyed, but not wanting to engage with him. I have other plans for my evening, and it doesn't include beating his ass. That would put a damper on my life here.

"I don't need some boy telling me what to do." I walk past him toward my bedroom. The former softness of my towel becomes a harsh scrape on my head as I do my best to calm down. Backing down from confrontation isn't easy for me.

"I'm a fucking man." I snort and continue to my room, but think better of walking away without saying my piece.

"If you're a man then that makes Delilah a woman."

He shakes his head.

"So that means," I continue. "That she can make her own decisions."

I hear his fist slam against the wall as I close myself in my bedroom. A sense of calming relief washes over me from all but admitting that there's something building between Samson's twin and me. I want everyone to know, but she hasn't mentioned bringing our feelings to light. I have to defer to her in this situation because she knows her family better than I do. I'm ready when she's ready.

Samson is gone from the hall when I step out. Delilah's door is still locked, but the sun is just now going down. Even a locked bedroom door isn't going to keep me from comforting her while she's ill.

I head downstairs, just in time to see everyone sitting down at the table for dinner. Jaxon may be a hardened biker covered from head to toe in tattoos, but he's the best fucking cook I've ever encountered.

"Chicken alfredo," Drew says with a lopsided grin. "Your favorite."

I smile wide, ignoring the glare from Samson on the other side of the table. "Looks great."

Jaxon nods, the delight of my praise is barely hidden behind his eyes.

"Where's D?" Rob asks with a smacking kiss on Jaxon's forehead before he sits down.

"Not feeling well," Jaxon answers, handing the salad bowl to Drew.

"That time of the month? She always gets like this." Rob looks at his husband for verification.

Drew and Samson groan at the female issue conversation. "Really, Pop? At the dinner table?"

"It's a fact of life, Sam. Pass the chicken?"

I hand Rob the platter of juicy chicken breasts, doing my best to keep my eyes from the stairs leading up to the girl I'm obsessed over. Girl problems are something I have no issue with. Mom always needed painkillers and the heating pad, so this is definitely something in my wheelhouse.

I rush through dinner, drawing glances from both Jaxon and Rob. The food is delicious, but my concentration is elsewhere.

I mention being tired from a full day at the shelter and in the shop, and Rob excuses me from the table without an issue.

Longingly, I eye Delilah's door before closing myself in my own empty bedroom. I hate that I have to wait what will end up being hours for everyone to be asleep. Drew may suspect that Delilah and I have been sneaking around, but I won't confirm his suspicions by blatantly going to her while the sun is still up.

I shoot off numerous texts, but they go unread. She's more than likely asleep, resting like her dads said she was.

Head hung low, Drew walks into the room, phone in hand.

"What's wrong?" I sit up from my nap on my bottom bunk.

He shakes his head, clearing his throat but doesn't speak. He strips out of his jeans and t-shirt and crawls up into his bed.

I wait him out, but the time ticks slowly. My mind races with things that can cause his normally carefree personality to act like he's just watched his puppy get run over on the highway.

"I fucked up," he finally admits.

"You're fifteen. How bad can it be?"

"I sent a message to Aunt Kathy."

"Your dad's sister on the East Coast?" My brows draw together. He never has wanted anything to do with them.

"Yeah." His voice is shaky, and I can tell he's on the verge of tears.

I want to get out of bed and reach for him, but he's just as stubborn as I am. Doing that will make him lockdown, and we'll never get to the source of his pain.

"I just wanted to let her know about Mom. I know they hate her—"

"They never hated her," I cajole. "They were angry about Carl and how she allowed him to treat her."

He clears his throat again, but this time I can tell he's crying.

"Just get it out," I urge.

"She wants me to move in with her and Uncle Pete."

I shake my head. "No way," I hiss. "You don't have to go if you don't want to."

"They're my family." I despise the resigned tone of his voice.

"I'm your family," I spit.

"I'm a minor. I don't want to go. I love it here."

The girl I'm falling in love with is here.

"But they're blood, and Jaxon and Rob aren't related to me."

"Did they threaten you?"

"No," he defends. "I want to be near my family. You have yours now, and I w-want that, too."

Deep breath in, slow breath out.

"I don't want to keep you from your family," I admit. "I'll just have to come with you."

"You will?" I hear the relief in his voice.

"I go where you go."

Can a heart actually break, tear apart and die inside of your chest? With a rough palm, I rub my hand over the aching part in my soul. It does nothing to alleviate the burn that's starting to build.

"Your dad is here."

"My brother will be there. You're my responsibility no matter the sacrifice for me."

The quiet crying begins anew. Squeezing my eyes shut, I let him cry for both of us.

My fists clench at hearing his anguish, but at the same time I'm pissed that the second my life begins to look up, it's turning completely upside down again.

"When will they be here?"

There has to be time. Time for Delilah and I to plan; time for me to assure her that things will be okay between us.

"School starts next week in Fall River."

No.

"They'll be here tomorrow."

Shattered. Broken. Left for purgatory.

It's not enough time to assure her that things will work out.

Long distance relationships aren't that bad my mind says in an attempt to convince me. We can make it work. She'll wait for me if I ask.

How the fuck can I ask her that? How can I demand she put her life on hold for me?

The answer is simple.

I can't.

Chapter 22
Delilah

Five seconds is all I give the heat of his body to soak into mine.

"You shouldn't be in here," I warn.

"Jaxon said you weren't feeling well."

"I'm fine," I lie. Well, I'm not sick in the traditional sense.

"I wanted to hold you," he confesses with a desperation that sends chills over my skin. "Make you feel better."

"I'm fine," I repeat. Maybe saying it over and over will convince my own mind.

"So you said," he mutters with a quick kiss on my shoulder before he pulls at my shoulder until I'm flat on my back.

"You shouldn't be in here."

"You said that, too."

His lips hover over mine, an endless pause before he presses his mouth to mine. It's then that I feel the tremble in his body. Anger? Need? I'm not experienced enough to differentiate.

My groan of resistance transforms into a moan of arousal as his lips continue their coaxing and his hard length presses against my hip. My neck flexes, reaching for him when he pulls back.

"You're the best thing that's ever happened to me," he whispers before taking my mouth again.

Soft pecks turn into aggressive licks of his tongue. Floating above it all, I somehow feel overwhelmed with sensation and completely separate from it at the same time.

He ignores the tremor in my hands as they find the over-heated skin of his chest. Fingers flexing against his pecs, I dig in to keep my hands from roaming lower, which my brain is telling me is the right thing to do. Never in this position before in my life, and instinct is trying to drive me to the next step.

Will my heart survive taking what we have one step further, only to slam on the brakes the second that it's done?

I fear that it won't, but living my life without sharing this with him seems like an even more unmanageable burden.

"Touch me," I beg.

"Delilah," he pants pulling his mouth from the delicate skin on my neck. "That's too much."

"It's not," I promise.

"I can't," he hisses and backs off of the bed.

For a long moment, I stare up at him, his chest heaving as if he is running from demons I can't see.

I slink out of bed. One thing he may never learn about me is that rejection hurts more than a physical blow.

Growing bold even though I know it's a risk, I reach for him, my hand hovering over the elastic band of his sweats.

With eyes clenched as tight as his hands, he turns his head up to the ceiling, as if he's warring with his restraint.

With the slightest movement, the palm of my hand brushes against his erection. It increases in size as if it senses me and is seeking out my embrace.

"Law," I whisper against the column of his neck. "Touch me."

His eyes find mine, his throat working on a thick swallow.

Resolve and something sinister fills his icy-blue eyes. I don't even try to fight the heat it causes low in my belly. No matter the will he was trying to keep alive, the resistance he was holding on to, my need, my own form of manipulation has worked.

"You need me, Princess?"

"Touch me," I repeat for the third time, embarrassment marking my cheeks at my inability to tell him everything I want from him.

"Turn around," he commands.

The soft fabric of my pajama shorts abrades my skin as I shift on my feet. It's too heavy, too thick, and restrictive to what my body is demanding.

I reach for the waist of my shorts as his feverish skin presses to my back.

"Stop," he pants in my ear.

My body obeys before my mind has the chance to catch up.

"Where do you want to be touched?" I hate the calmness in his hands as they both grip my waist.

"Everywhere," I moan with a quick shift on my feet.

"Here?" he asks as one rough thumb sweeps over the tightened bud on my left breast. "Or here?"

My knees nearly give out when his right hand finds my center with a skilled precision I choose not to consider in fear it would ruin this moment.

"Oh God," I breathe. "Yes."

"Filthy slut."

I stiffen in his arms, but it only lasts a second as both hands toy with areas only I've ever touched before.

I'm dizzy from lack of oxygen by the time his right hand runs up my hip and then lowers inside of my shorts and panties this time.

"So wet for me, dirty girl."

Dirty girl is better than slut, I guess.

Before the unease can settle, his fingers spread me, thumb searching for the spot that has never needed something as much as it does right now.

He presses harder against me, hissing in my ear at the friction against his own body. I squirm, unsure of what to do, but blissfully aware of the contact on my clit.

"I bet it'll only take one finger to get this perfect little pussy off."

"Oh God." I quiver, shake, and become putty in his hands.

The slow, teasing circles of his thumb is the best torture, the thing my body recognizes as essential for survival.

"Jesus," he mutters against my hand. "Come for me."

"For you," I pant as my body shudders in a release that nearly destroys me.

He pulls his hand away long before the tiny quivering comes to a full stop.

"Turn around." I obey. "Knees."

With the hand that was on my breast, he pushes his sweats down. His other hand, glistening with my arousal strokes the length of his erection.

"Lick it clean."

I want to refuse, insist that he not speak to me the way he is, but my mouth waters at the prospect of tasting him, of tasting me.

He takes a step forward, resting the blunt head of his penis against my lips. I swipe at the pre-cum on the tip with my tongue, my senses flaming to life at our combined tastes.

I lick again, hungry for more. My hands find his powerful thighs as his free hand fists my hair. The small bite of pain, the same as the night we first kissed in here, stokes the fire that was already burning from my orgasm.

"Open wide," he commands, his voice growing unsteady. "Take it all."

He presses in, and my throat constricts immediately at the foreign intrusion. Gagging, I pull my head back. Surprisingly, he allows me to take a deep breath before he pushes in slower.

I look up, hoping to find pleasure in his eyes, but they stare back at me, empty and shuttered. He's not even here right now. He's lost in his thoughts, somewhere other than in this monumental moment with me. The tingle of awareness that I'd pushed down earlier at his horrible words begins to travel to my brain, pushing away the desire to please him.

"I told you you'd have those pretty pink lips wrapped around my cock."

I rip away, the haze of need doused as if I'd been thrown into the Antarctic.

"What is wrong with you?" I sputter wiping the back of my hand over my mouth.

"Don't stop now, Princess. We were just getting started."

"Was this your plan all along? Get me to fall for you just so you can get me on my knees."

Doubt tugs at the corner of his eyes before he shelters it and sneers at me.

"I can fuck your mouth while you lie on the bed if it's easier."

I shake my head, the slickness between my legs growing cold and becoming too much to ignore. I feel dirty and wrong and used. None of the things I'd anticipated feeling after getting to know him these last couple of weeks.

"You need to leave." The resilience I feel in my bones doesn't translate as strength in my voice.

With arms wrapped around my waist, I step back until my thighs hit the mattress. My body is near convulsing as I watch him swallow. His fingers twitch as if they're going to reach out for me, but I stiffen, and he backs down. I'm confused and my heart, which I'd planned on breaking myself soon, has now been ripped out by a guy that only paid attention to me to manipulate me into this exact situation.

He turns to leave, and I expect him to open and slam the door behind him. When he turns and the light of the moon catches on a single tear on his cheek, I've never felt more confusion before in my life.

"Have a nice life," he says with a trembling voice. "Hating me has always been what's best for you."

My door closes with a soft click, the tiny noise echoing in my skull.

The shaking continues even as I bury myself under the covers on my bed. The house alarm goes off, ringing loudly for all to hear, and then the front door slams.

Chapter 23
Lawson

The alarm blaring at my back has nothing on the sirens ringing in my head. The warmth of the New Mexico night only serves to irritate my already over-heated skin.

Fighting the insistent demands to go back to her, to apologize and find some way to make us work with me all the way across the country causes a stutter in my steps. I fight the urge, knowing that walking away right now is best for both of us.

The shop, the mechanics of machines with their structured uses, pulls me away from the house. I need the consistency, the perfect way they fit together, and if done right, work in sync with each other. Motorcycles and cars make sense. Loving a girl I could never ask to sacrifice a damn thing for my unworthy ass is a complication I can't focus on right now.

Laughter meets my ears, but my feet keep on moving. Being under the scrutiny of the Cerberus MC guys is the last thing I want, but the draw to get my hands dirty, to work on something I can fix is stronger.

Scooter, Rocker, and Kid all sit around a small table, beers and cards in their hands as they joke about their stupid perfect lives.

"Hey, Lawson," Rocker says angling his beer at me in salute.

A nod is all I'm able to manage as Kid looks at me, reading me like a book.

"Guys." The rough voice at my back causes the same tension in my muscles as it did the first time I showed up on the clubhouse steps.

They look behind me and move to leave the garage without one word of rebuttal. Kid slaps my shoulder, but I stand my ground, not shying away from the sympathy in his eyes.

I know how they see me. I'm just some fucked up kid with a chip on my shoulder, getting pissed off over the simplest things. I don't acknowledge the fact that my heart is being torn in two to the point that breathing is difficult.

"Sorry about the alarm," I mutter as I pull out some tools and sit on the ground beside an old project bike Shadow and I have been working on.

"No big deal," Jaxon says as he pulls up a chair and sits down beside me. "Want to tell me why you stormed out of the house?"

I treated your perfect daughter like shit while she had my cock in her mouth.

I resist the urge to draw my hand to my nose before losing her delicate scent to oil and dirt on the bike.

"Drew contacted his family."

He remains silent, and I'd give anything to be in his head right now. Does he know what's coming? Is he glad we'll be out of his hair tomorrow?

As much as I want to hate him, I let hope flicker that he'll be upset to watch me leave.

"They're coming tomorrow to get him."

He clears his throat.

"I'm going with him."

He shuffles his feet.

"How do you feel about that?"

I sigh feeling as if I need a couch to stretch out on while he plays one of the many therapists probation tried to get me to connect with.

"I can't let him go on his own," I reason.

"Are they bad people? I can put an end to it."

I shake my head. "That's his family. They're good people. His dad was a piece of shit, but luckily he was the black sheep of the family."

"But you don't want to go?"

I shake my head. "I'd gotten it in my head that I was going to be here for a while."

"You can stay as long as you like, but I understand needing to make sure your brother is okay." He shifts again, the chair legs scraping across the concrete floor. "He's been your responsibility for a long time."

"You don't give up on family." I stare down at my hands agitated from the night's events but relieved to be getting all this shit off of my chest.

"And that's why I'll never give up on you." His words hit home.

Looking up into eyes that are the perfect reflection of mine if only with a little more creasing at the edges, I see the truth in his words.

"Delilah hates me," I confess without going into any detail.

"Delilah isn't the type of girl that hates anyone."

I shake my head trying to erase the pain I saw in her eyes when I walked away from her.

"She may be angry," he continues. "She may think she hates you now, but she'll be fine."

The sad downward turn of his lips are reflective of him knowing more information than what I've spilled tonight, but I don't elaborate.

"Where is Drew's family from?"

"Massachusetts."

His lip twitches, eyes growing brighter as if I've said something that pleases him.

He stands and claps me on the shoulder. "I get a feeling that things are going to work out just fine."

I clear my throat as he walks toward the door.

"T-thanks," I stammer, the words unfamiliar in my mouth. "Thanks for everything you've done for me."

He turns, a full smile on his tattooed face. "You're more than welcome, son."

He leaves, the sound of his boots on gravel a comforting sound I know I'll miss.

"Well?" he says returning and startling me to the point I drop the wrench I was holding.

"What?"

"Come to the house with me. I have some things to show you."

***

"Hey."

I come awake in the desk chair with a rough shove to my shoulder.

"What's up?" I ask Drew as he looks down at me. "Are they here already?"

He shakes his head. "Not yet. Jaxon and Rob wanted us to have breakfast with them before we leave."

I rub tired eyes, only having gotten a couple of hours of sleep last night.

"I'm up," I tell him and stand from the chair. "You head down, and I'll be there in a few minutes."

"I went ahead and packed for you." He points to the duffel bag that is bulging compared to when I first brought it up to this room.

"Thanks, man. Give me a few minutes."

All I can think about is getting to Delilah. I have to apologize. I have to make her understand that last night wasn't even close to a true reflection of my feelings.

I wait, antsy and trembling, for Drew to make his way downstairs before heading to Delilah's room. If I know her like I think I do, she'll be holed up in her room, avoiding the sight of me.

My gentle knock goes unanswered, but there's no way I'm leaving today without her understanding what she means to me.

I push open her door, surprised I don't have to pick the lock like I did last night to get to her. The room is empty, bed made and no sounds coming from the bathroom. The dock where she charges her cell is empty, but I check the bathroom anyway.

My shoulders sag as I close her door behind me, hating that I'm going to have to sit across from her glaring eyes at breakfast without explaining.

Only, when I make my way into the dining room, she's not there either. A quick look into the kitchen remains unfruitful as well.

I look at Jaxon, at the head of the table as he passes a tray of bacon and sausage to Drew.

"Delilah went in early to the animal shelter," he explains.

A knot forms in my gut, but the satisfied look on Samson's face has me taking my seat rather than insisting on keys to a car to go to her. I want to blame him, blame anyone for this change of events.

Jaxon doesn't mention the lengthy conversation we had after returning to the house last night, so neither do I. The dining room fills with laughter and talk of Drew's plans when we get to Massachusetts. Drew has always been one to roll with the punches, and I hope he remains happy and unaffected by the bad shit we've dealt with in our lives. I've protected him from almost everything in my power that could harm him, and I'll continue to do it even though I'm shattered myself.

It's not long after breakfast that the doorbell echoes through the house. A quiet, sad calm washes over the household as Jaxon opens the front door. Drew's Aunt Kathy searches the room, her eyes landing on me first with a quiet nod before coming to life at the sight of Drew on the couch.

He shoots up, and they embrace. It's not until that very moment that I realize just how much Drew has needed more than just me. Tears are on his face as Kathy pulls back to cup his cheeks in her hands. The pain at losing our mother is clear in his wet eyes as he nods softly at something she whispers to him.

"Don't forget what we talked about last night." Jaxon is only a few inches from me, talking low enough that only I can hear him.

"I won't." I turn to face him, both loving and hating the anguish in his eyes.

"I'm always here. Anything you need, even if it's just to talk."

"Del—"

"She'll be fine," he assures me. "Become the type of man she could never hate."

I don't even stiffen when his tattooed arms draw me in for a hug. The embrace lasts longer than one I've ever had, and I let his pride in me seep into my bones. I'm going to need every ounce of strength I can muster to walk away from her and leave the ball in her court.

Chapter 24
Delilah

"Where's Lawson?"

I tense at Dana's question as I get the last two dogs back in their kennels from our walk.

"Probably working in the shop."

I have no idea where he is. A million miles away would be best.

"Something on your mind?"

I've always spoken to Dana, told her about the things bothering me. I've used her more than once as a shoulder to cry on when something upset me at school. I've confided in her my frustration of not having a mother. I love my dads, but there are just some things, as men, they'll never understand.

As her question sinks in, I know this isn't a door I'm opening between us. Lawson said he still plans to work here, but that may be off the table now since his true colors shined through bright and blinding last night.

"Nope." I lock the kennel and begin to coil the leashes as I make my way to the supply closet. "Anything else you need before I leave?"

When I face her, she tilts her head to the side. She's not an idiot, so I know she can tell something is bothering me. What she isn't is a nag, so she won't hound me to tell her what's bothering me.

"Not a thing," she says with a quick smile. "You've put in ten hours today."

I nod and walk past her.

"See you on Monday."

"Drive safe," she says to my back as I make my way out to the parking lot.

The smell of Lawson's lingering cologne assaults me when I climb in the car, so I crank the AC to full blast and roll down the windows. All the way home, I pray that the car is aired out enough that I never have to smell him near me again. It also reminds me to wash my sheets. I fell prey to the beautiful scent last night as I cried into my pillow, but today is a new day.

He only acted that way as a defense mechanism. He's done it almost every day since he showed up.

To get the voices trying to convince me to forgive him out of my head, I crank the radio up and tap my fingers on the steering wheel. I ignore the fact that people are staring at me at the red light. I can't be the first person to ride around with the windows down and radio blaring as a distraction.

I turn the music off as I pull through the front gate in front of the clubhouse, parking in the main lot rather than driving around to the back.

If I need to leave quickly, it's faster to go from here than navigating the narrow driveway on the back of the house.

No talking or laughing is coming from the shop. Not one person is in sight when I make my way around the clubhouse and toward my front door.

"Hey."

Ivy. As much as I love her, being alone is the only thing on my mind right now.

"Hey," I say turning toward her front porch where she sits with a book in her lap.

"Only a week before school starts. Are you ready?" Her eyes are wide and bright even though there's a light sheen of sweat on her forehead. The fan above the porch swing is working overtime to no avail.

"As ready as I'll ever be." I sit beside her, realizing this conversation will postpone the inevitable argument with Lawson once I get to my house.

"The birthday party was pretty epic. I'm sure your popularity will be at an all-time high."

I raise an eyebrow at her. "You sound more like Gigi than the girl I know."

She shrugs. "It's just our senior year, you know? I love my life and my small group of friends, but at the same time I'm a little jealous of the attention Gigi gets from all the guys."

"You want the attention Gigi gets from *Griffin*, you mean."

"Exactly like you beam anytime Lawson looks at you."

"Nope," I say without delay. "There's nothing between Lawson and me. I doubt we'll ever speak again."

"What happened?" she asks on a whisper.

I look away, begging the tears burning the backs of my eyes to stay put.

"His true colors coming to light is what happened." I sniffle, the action pissing me off because I swore to myself after last night I'd never shed another tear at thoughts of him.

"As in?"

I ignore her question for as long as I can, but she's relentless.

"I'm your best friend, D. You can tell me anything."

So I do. I lay out the last couple of weeks right at her feet. By the time I'm finished, and the sun is setting, shooting pinks and oranges across the sky, Ivy hates Lawson O'Neil as much as I do.

The air is thick, filled with unease, as I open my door and close it behind me. The familiar sound of Drew and Samson playing video games is oddly absent.

"Hey, sweetheart," Pop says walking out of the kitchen drying his hands on a dish towel.

"Where is everyone?"

His face softens as his eyes fill with a sadness that's peculiar on his generally happy face.

"Sam, Gigi, Sophia, and Jasmine are down at the pool." The hesitation in his voice is clear as day.

"And Drew?"

He shakes his head and clears his throat.

"Drew's family from the east coast showed up to get him today."

Confused, I just stare at him.

"Lawson went with them."

The second it seeps in that he's gone, all of the anger I'd had for him disappears.

"W-where?"

"Massachusetts."

"That's all the way on the other side of the country." I shake my head. "They didn't have a family. Darby died, and Drew's father's in prison."

"It's his dad's sister that showed up."

I swallow past the dryness in my throat and pull my eyes from his.

"Okay." What else could I possibly say?

"I know you'll miss them, but you'll still be able to see them."

I shake my head again, the almost violent action causing my temples to throb. "No, this is for the best."

He reaches for me, but I back away.

"I'm filthy. I'm going to go grab a quick shower before dinner."

Without another word, I hit the stairs, making sure to keep my eyes focused on my door rather than looking into their empty room as I walk past.

I strip my bed, strip out of my clothes, and climb into the shower long before the water warms. I blame the frigid water rolling down my spine as the cause of my shivering. I convince myself that I don't need him, that I have my whole life ahead of me and he'll do nothing but drag me down.

What I don't realize while I tremble in that shower is that I'll spend two years building up walls against my feelings for Lawson, only for him to come crashing back into my life as if he never even left.

Chapter 25
Delilah
2 YEARS LATER

"Are you going to call him?" Ivy looks hopeful sitting across from me at the restaurant.

I shrug. "Of course not."

"Really?" She looks confused, but she should know how I am by now. "He was crazy hot. Popular. Muscles for days."

"They all are." I wink at her, and she only sinks lower in her seat.

"Don't do that," she mutters.

Refusing to look at her, knowing what's coming, I give all my attention to the straw between my fingers. Stirring my already flat soda is better than facing the best friend that knows me too well.

"You can act flippant right now all you want. You can put on this carefree brave face for everyone else, but keep in mind I hear you crying through the walls when they drop you off."

"It's my life," I argue. "I can do what and who I want."

"Until it involves someone else who loves you." She pauses, letting that sink in. "Until you get pregnant or end up with an STD."

I glare at her. "I'm on birth control, and I use protection every time."

"And you go to parties without a friend."

"You won't go with me." She hasn't changed much since high school, opting to stay closer to home than get involved in any outrageous campus activities.

"You risk the chance of getting drugged," she says without acknowledging my statement. "Getting raped."

"You sound like Dad." I hang my head even lower. I can't hide my true feelings, not even the hatred I have for who I've become.

"He sounds like a very intelligent man."

I chuckle. Leave it to her to throw out some hard truths and still make me laugh. I didn't start Brown University last year as a freshman with the intention of hooking up with guys that lead to nothing but one-night stands. I've had a few encounters but nothing like some of the girls around campus. What I'd wanted was to be different, to be free from the stereotype that I left behind in New Mexico. It took me the better part of a year to build up the courage to accept an invite to a college party, and after a few drinks, nearly everything sounds like a good idea.

"No more random guys," I vow.

"No more risky behaviors," she counters.

"One hundred percent studious and no life," I mutter. "Got it."

"Poor D. has to actually go to class so she doesn't lose her scholarship."

I grin at her. "You know as well as I do that my grades are great and my scholarship is in no danger."

She shakes her head. "What I know is that you started all of this wild behavior in May and it's only gotten worse as summer progressed. There's no telling what the semester will look like in two weeks if you don't shut it down now."

"True." I smile. "So stop the partying in two weeks when school starts?"

Her head twists back and forth in disbelief. Her finger stabs the table to emphasize her point. "I think you need to practice. Starting now."

"Buzz-kill."

"You have to be responsible." She pushes the ticket across the table. "Now's as good a time to start as any."

"Only because you paid yesterday," I concede as she excuses herself to the restroom.

The waitress takes the ticket along with my card on her next pass by the table. I spend the time looking around the restaurant. Dark, mysterious eyes across the room catch my attention. As if trained around good looking guys, my mouth tilts up in a seductive grin, and he looks away.

Total turn off.

Men who know what they want, who are insistent in their attraction to me is what gets my blood running. Shyness and men that need to be chased don't appeal to me in the slightest. After the waitress returns my card, I make a second sweep around the room. He makes eye contact again, only to duck away.

Nope done.

"Leave that poor boy alone," Ivy says walking back up to the table.

"He's not my type anyway," I tell her and stand from the booth.

I follow her through the front door toward my car.

"Wanna go do some shopping?"

"Not particularly," she murmurs.

"It's Saturday, two weeks before we start our sophomore year at college. Surely there's something you need," I urge.

"I need shampoo and a few more notebooks." She shrugs. Ivy is the easiest chick to please. Her obsession with spirals, pens, and stationery should be sad, but somehow it works for her.

"I'm not spending my Saturday at Wal-Mart," I insist.

I grin, and she grins back.

"Target," we say at the same time.

"Starbucks first," I say as I climb behind the wheel.

"You just drank an entire carafe inside," she reminds me. "You're going to end up with holes in your stomach lining."

"Judgmental much?" I say with a grin. "I didn't get home until early this morning. I need more caffeine."

I smile and focus on starting the car. It's the best I can do to try to get the hazy memories of last night's party out of my head.

Turning the key, absolutely nothing happens. The radio nor the AC kicks on, and there's no clicking.

"I told you," Ivy says looking out the window.

"Yeah, yeah," I mutter. "I'll call Dad."

I pull out my phone and unlock the screen.

"Call a tow truck. Jaxon is in New Mexico. There's not much he can do for us in Rhode Island."

"Hush," I hiss playfully as the phone begins to ring in my ear.

"Sweetheart," Dad answers in lieu of a hello.

"Hey, Dad. I have a problem."

"Don't tell me you spent all the money I sent last week."

I shake my head. "No. I've barely touched it. My car won't start."

"Did you check the battery? Is it out of gas?"

"It has gas, but check the battery? Seriously? I don't know crap about cars."

"I told you to trade it in last year."

I sigh. "'I told you so' doesn't exactly get me out of this parking lot."

He laughs. "Fair enough. I'll call a towing company, but you seriously need to get a new car."

"Tell her I'll send her some links later," Pop chimes in from the background. "There are a few dealerships in town that are running some great end of summer deals."

I narrow my eyes. "Don't you need to know where I am?"

I hear both of them laugh. "Sweetheart," Dad says. "I always know where you are."

"Creeper." I look over at Ivy who isn't surprised that my dads know our location even from thousands of miles away. "I bet you have a satellite on me."

"That's ridiculous. The White House turned down that request, but I do track your phone." He hangs up, and my mouth just drops open.

"Dad does the same with me," Ivy mutters. "Gigi got a new phone when she left last year. So he has no idea where she is. Drives him nuts."

I cringe at the idea that something could happen to me and they couldn't find me. Having grown up with the stories of horrors going on around the world, there's no way I'll insist on them pulling their "surveillance." Safety first, as I always heard growing up.

"Control freaks," I whisper but loud enough for Ivy to hear me. I push open my door to let some cooler air in. "I hope it doesn't take forever."

"I don't think they're control freaks."

I snort. "I wouldn't be surprised if they had microchips planted in Sam and me when we were adopted."

"Oh." Her eyes scrunch together. "I thought you knew about the chips."

I grin when she runs her hand behind her left ear, implying hers is planted there.

"I hope it's something simple. I'd rather not spend my day looking for a place to rent a car."

"You should just junk it and get something else."

I run my hand over the recently cracking dash. "I've had this car since I turned sixteen."

"And it was ten years old then. It's time for something newer."

Sighing, I look around the parking lot. I've heard it all before from everyone in my family. Many were surprised the old clunker actually made it across the country last summer.

"That was fast," Ivy says angling her head so she can see out of the side mirror better.

The side of a massive towing truck blocks my car at the rear bumper.

"What does that say?" I squint, but the reflection off the shiny metal door makes it impossible to read.

"Camel Towing?"

I laugh. "Yeah. Dad would definitely send something like that my way."

The height of the truck combined with my low to the ground car makes me unable to see the driver through his window. I don't have to wait long, as his door swings open.

"Nice," I say with genuine appreciation when the driver opens the door and his muscular legs and firm, jean-covered ass steps down from the truck.

I'm nearly drooling as I watch him face the truck again and reach in to grab a yellow reflective vest. The sliver of revealed skin on his back makes my mouth water.

"I think the 'no boys' rule is going to have to wait until Monday. This guy is just too sexy to pass up."

I step out of my car and turn in his direction. Seductive smile playing on my lips, I give it all I've got.

Shielding my eyes from the sun in an attempt to actually see his face I say, "You're my hero for coming to my rescue."

I hear him chuckle, throaty and low, and echoing low in my belly. "So does that make me your prince, Princess?"

Chapter 26
Lawson

There is not enough saliva in my mouth to keep my lips wet at the sight of Delilah Donovan. Two years have transformed the quiet, demure angel of my dreams into a sex kitten with a low riding top and lace shorts that make my mind wander immediately to lingerie that would look best on my bedroom floor.

"Oh shit," Ivy mutters as she climbs out of the passenger seat and notices me, but I can't even manage a glance in her direction.

The long tan legs that I remember vividly from her time around the pool seem to have lengthened. She's gorgeous, my memories not serving her justice at all.

"What the fuck are you doing here?" she spits, and the only thing I can do is grin.

She ignores the wind whipping her blonde hair around her face and glares at me. If I didn't know any better, I'd believe she truly hates me.

"If you ladies wait, I can pull the wrecker around the front and get the car loaded up."

She shakes her head and with stubborn defiance crosses her arms over her chest.

"I want someone different."

"I am someone different." Her eyes narrow at my declaration.

"Another wrecking service," she specifies, ignoring the implication of my words.

"Not gonna happen, Princess. Now go stand over on the sidewalk and let me work."

Ivy, having come around the trunk of the car to join her friend, tugs on her arm. She's reluctant at first, but eventually lets her friend guide her out of the way.

I make quick work of the disabled vehicle, and before long, I'm standing in front of her once again. This moment, being a long time coming, is one I savor. Ivy has a weird, yet happy, look on her face. Delilah? Well, if looks could kill, I'd be a pile of ash on the ground with the fiery daggers she's shooting my way.

"Your chariot awaits, Princess." I sweep my arm toward the open driver's door on the wrecker.

Ivy moves first, climbing in and scooting across the bench seat so she's against the passenger door. It puts Delilah where she belongs, right next to me where our thighs will be touching the entire way back to the shop. Man, am I thankful it's a twenty-five-minute drive.

"Not gonna happen, Lawson." She takes a step back rather than one closer to the truck. "I'll call an Uber."

"You're beautiful," I whisper and reach out to push some of her wild hair behind her ear. It only serves to anger her more.

When she slaps my hand away before I can make contact, I know it was the wrong move.

"Don't touch me, and keep your meaningless comments to yourself."

I shrug, the smile never leaving my face. She's going to be a tough one to get on my side. "Just telling the truth."

She takes another step back. "I experienced your true character two years ago. I want nothing to do with you."

For a split second, my mind races, wondering if this approach is the best way to go about trying to win her back.

"Oh, Princess, don't be like that."

"Don't 'Princess' me."

"Your dad told me to make sure you get home safely. I promised him I would. I don't break my promises. So." I scrub my hand over the light stubble on my chin. "You can get in the truck on your own, or I can carry you there."

Her eyes dart from me to the open door of the cab and back to me. It's as if she's evaluating if I'm serious and can't make up her mind.

"Personally, I hope you refuse. I've thought about getting my hands back on you for the last two years."

She huffs. "And my mouth around your cock, right?"

I stiffen as my past and bad decisions are tossed back in my face.

"We can talk about that right now if you like. I can explain my fucked up reasoning, the reasoning of a boy."

"You always said you were a man," she mocks in a lower voice.

"I said a lot of things while trying to protect myself." I take a step toward her, arms out, my intention to lift her over my shoulder clear. "I'm an open book now. You can ask anything you like, and I'll tell you anything you want to know, but I'd rather have that conversation in private and not on the damn sidewalk. Now make up your mind, Delilah."

She glares at me, tension in her cheeks and stubbornness in her jaw.

"Walk on your own or be carried?"

"Asshole," she mutters as she walks past me and climbs inside.

My hands clench as the need to help her up with a gentle push on her ass hits me in the chest. I think my greasy handprints on her amazing ass would be the best thing ever, but I have a feeling she wouldn't be receptive.

"No fucking way," she hisses and tries to climb back out.

Her body meets my chest as I climb in behind her and give her no room to escape.

"What's wrong? The seat's clean. You won't get anything on your clothes."

"Let me down. I'm not straddling your damn gear shift."

I press against her, a challenge. She can either sit down, or she can continue to grind against me. I'm fine either way.

"I think I like this even more," I whisper in her ear, my voice going hoarse when the scent of her lavender skin hits my nose.

She elbows me in the gut but sits down. At first, she tries to position both of her legs to Ivy's side of the seat, but then she splits them apart when she realizes it won't work. I notice Ivy trying to take up more room than necessary for her slight frame. I wink at her when my spitfire isn't looking. It's great to have someone on my side, because I know I have a very long damn road ahead of me, and I'll take all the help I can get.

I settle into my seat and shut the door. The intensity of her scent grows in the enclosed space. I do my best not to look like an idiot when I draw her into my lungs.

"Seatbelt, baby."

She bites her lip so hard I wait for the blood to run from her mouth, but she just looks ahead and uses her fingers to find the belt and click it in place. Safety first has always been her family's motto, and right now it works for me. No matter how upset she is with the pet names, she wouldn't purposely put herself in danger just to spite me.

The truck, idling the entire time I loaded her car up, responds immediately when I put it into first and pull away from the parking lot. Not pressing my luck, I keep my hand fisted around the top knob of the shifter. What I don't do is pull my hand away when I'm at cruising speed with no need to shift anytime soon. The heat of her thigh against my forearm is enough to make me thicken in my pants.

I sense some form of nonverbal communication going on between the girls and watch them out of the corner of my eye.

"So," Ivy begins, and Delilah freezes beside me. "You live out here?"

"More like lying in wait like some weirdo fucking stalker," Delilah mutters.

I ignore her. If she only knew that I've purposely stayed away from her until a situation presented itself maybe her opinions would be different. I've known she's been close for the last year, but I didn't press my luck by going to her.

"I've been in Providence since shortly after I left New Mexico," I inform her.

"And Drew?" Delilah shoulders Ivy for continuing to talk.

"He's not far. Starting his senior year in Fall River." I keep my eyes on the road but can feel my beauty relax a little next to me. She may act angry that I showed up out of the blue today, but I know she has no ill will toward my brother, and she's curious about him. "His Aunt Kathy is an amazing woman. He's adjusted well. Makes good grades. Stays out of trouble, mostly."

"You're not here because of me?" Delilah asks softly, confused as if she really had it in her mind that I'm stalking her. The sadness in her voice hurts me, but it also makes my heart smile because no matter how much she wants to pretend she hates me, I know she doesn't.

"I'm here for you as much as I am for Drew. Never doubt that."

"Whatever," she mumbles.

When I look past her at Ivy, she's the one to wink at me this time. I pull my lip between my teeth to keep from smiling as I drive up to the front of the shop.

"You work here?" Ivy asks as she leans forward to get a better look at the building through the windshield.

"Yep," I answer. "Almost as long as I've been on the East Coast."

I put the truck in park and open my door. "Need help getting down, Prin—"

I frown when I see that she's already climbing down behind Ivy.

I have a long ass way to go, but luckily she's going to be worth every ounce of pushback she gives me.

Chapter 27
Delilah

"I won't ever forget which side you chose," I warn Ivy.

She grins at me as I jump down from the cab of the wrecker. Getting away from the warmth of his thigh and the amazing scent of his spicy cologne is all I could concentrate on since leaving the parking lot.

"I don't know what you're talking about." She feigns interest in her surroundings.

"Like hell you don't," I hiss at her back as she walks around the back of the wrecker.

"If you ladies hold tight and let me get this off the flatbed, I'll take you home."

Even in a bright yellow vest, grease stains on his jeans, and a smudge on his left cheek, he's still the hottest guy I've ever seen. Acknowledging that, even in my head, pisses me off. The least he could've done is to turn gray or grow warts on his face. The thought of him having salt and pepper locks makes me tingle, and my anger grows.

I've learned a lot in the two years since he treated me like shit and disappeared into thin air. Well, it wasn't exactly thin air, but I avoided any talk of him in the house and made no effort to reach out to him. He made his feelings more than clear that night in my bedroom.

"It would've taken less time for you to drop us off before we drove all the way across town."

I cross my arms over my chest again, an action I've done more than once since he showed up. His eyes dart to the swell of my breasts as the action pushes them a little higher in my tank top. His eyes piercing into me does more to my libido than the boy from the restaurant could ever hope.

"Yet you didn't say anything when I drove right past your street on the way here," he challenges.

Busted.

He winks as Ivy laughs behind me.

We stand off to the side as an older man comes out of the huge roll-up door on the front of the shop. He stops short and just watches us. I stare, unabashedly at Lawson, as he strips out of the vest and begins to work on getting my car off of the wrecker. I know my mouth is hanging open by the time he's done. I'm also well aware of the show he's putting on. It's not very hot out here so when he lifts the bottom of his shirt to wipe at his face, I know it's not because he's sweating and overexerted.

I sneer even though my face is as deep as my irritation goes. Ivy laughs again when a grunt slips out at the sight of the dark trail of hair snaking from his belly button and disappearing into his low-slung jeans.

"Jesus," I say before I can stop myself.

"Do you need a minute alone," Ivy jokes with a quick shoulder bump.

I shake my head. "A minute wouldn't even do him justice. A month would probably barely scratch the surface."

"He's always been very handsome."

"I hate him."

I stand straighter, my back stiffening in defiance, but I never pull my eyes from him. My brain warns that I may have limited time with him, and is insisting I get my fill while I can. It makes no sense. I've spent two years doing my best to not think of him. Two years of wasting time with other men who just don't seem to measure up. Two years of silently comparing him to everyone I encounter only to find them lacking. The problem is, he's an asshole, a jerk who treated me like a whore when he had me believing there was something building between us.

"You're still mad?"

I'm not surprised by Ivy's reaction. I haven't spoken out loud to anyone about Lawson O'Neil since I explained what had happened between us on her front porch before I even knew he was gone.

"He treated me like shit," I tell her, angling my head to see him when he steps around the wrecker and I lose track of him.

"People change," she says.

"Not really," I argue. "But that doesn't mean I can't have some fun once or twice."

She grabs my upper arm, turning me and forcing me to look in her eyes.

"What exactly do you have planned?"

I shrug, but even the thought of what I could do to Lawson O'Neil heats my blood. "Fuck him and forget him of course."

"Delilah," she chides. "I don't think that's a good idea."

"It's the best one I can come up with."

"You need to reconsider that plan," she urges. "You'll only get—"

She stops abruptly when Lawson, smile on his handsome face, comes walking back up.

"Ready to go?" He points to a silver truck parked directly in front of the building. "Four doors so you don't have to straddle my stick."

The innuendo is plain as day, the words frighteningly similar to something he would've said two years ago. My faith in my 'love him and leave him' plan begins to slip. I know exactly what Ivy is getting at. She's well aware that there's no way I can play with his fire and not get burned. I reason with the voice in my head telling me to run far and fast. I figure if I can be the one to turn the tables on him this time, I can walk away with my pride intact.

I walk away from him and toward the truck without a word.

"Icy, Princess," he mutters walking close enough to my back that I feel the heat coming off of his skin. "Good thing I like it."

I shake my head, but a grin he can't see lights up my face.

"You don't stand a chance. Might as well get over it and move on."

"Nice truck," Ivy praises as she climbs into the back passenger side.

"Selling drugs?" I ask and immediately hate the inference to some of the things he admitted to being forced to do when he was younger to help support his family.

"Nope," he answers, schooling his face back to the gorgeous smile that's been there since he got out of the wrecker in the parking lot. "I just work a lot."

"An honest living?" I continue despite the bile rising in my throat at the mean words. "What a change of pace."

Ivy hisses in the background, and I cringe, ashamed, as my behavior reminds me of Gigi.

"Sorry," I mutter, turning my eyes to look at him as he drives down the road.

"Lots of things have changed," he says softly but refuses to look at me.

Ivy reaches between my seat and the window, pinching my arm in chastisement. Jerking my arm out of her reach, I don't bother to say anything to her. I deserve worse for what I just said.

"Turn right up here," Ivy instructs.

"I know where your apartment is," he tells her with a quick wink in the rearview mirror.

"You've been this close to me for two years, and I'm just now running into you?"

Now he looks at me. The red light we're waiting at giving him the opportunity.

"If you wanted to see me sooner, you could've asked your dad where I was," he challenges.

"I didn't care to know where you were." Even as I say the words, I know, deep down, that it's a lie.

"And that's exactly why we haven't seen each other before today."

"I'm glad you're close," my traitorous best friend adds from the backseat. "I feel safer knowing family is nearby."

"We're not family," Lawson and I say at the same time.

At least we can agree on something.

"Not yet," he says with so much conviction, I almost believe him.

"What do you do at the shop?" Ivy just won't give it a rest.

Tension still thick in the cab of the truck, Lawson grins at her over his shoulder.

"Mostly motorcycles, but we get the occasional car. I'm apprenticing with Joel, the old man you saw back at the shop."

"And when you're fully trained?" Ivy speaks for me. I both love her and hate her for it. I'm hungry for the knowledge, but we all know I'll never ask the questions myself. Vocal curiosity about what his life has been like the last two years gives him power I'm not willing to relinquish.

"Joel is retiring. The shop will be mine by the time I turn twenty-five."

Unwanted pride swells in my chest.

"That's amazing," Ivy says, once again speaking my words out loud.

"Jaxon has helped me a ton. I couldn't have done anything without him and Rob."

Dad and Pop never mentioned anything of the sort. Why would they? Dad tried to talk to me about Lawson and Drew when I got home two years ago, but I shut him down and asked him to never mention them again. He respected my wishes, but it doesn't surprise me that they would've stayed involved in Lawson's life. Moving across the country doesn't mean giving up on your son. I respect them immensely for any help they may have provided.

"You planning to keep everything the same when Joel retires?"

"Ivy," I chide. "What is this twenty questions?"

"I don't mind," Lawson says with a quick chuckle. "I plan to re-image. Joel isn't exactly happy with his life work changing, but I have to do something to bring the business into this century."

They continue on, talking and asking each other questions all the way to the apartment. He's spoken more, revealed more in the twenty minutes it takes to get home than he did in the weeks that he was in New Mexico.

"Oh look, there's Cindy." Ivy pushes open her door the second the truck is in park. "Thanks for the ride, Lawson. Hope to see you again soon."

I scowl at her back as she darts across the parking lot to talk to her friend, effectively leaving me alone in the truck surrounded by Lawson's cologne and soft leather.

"I've missed you," he confesses, turning slightly, so his upper body is angled in my direction. "I can't take back how I treated you, but I want you to know that I'm sor—"

I'm out of the truck and walking toward my apartment before he can even finish his apology. I don't regret leaving him sitting in his truck, but him driving off without coming and trying to talk to me stings more than it should've.

Chapter 28
Lawson

Watching her walk away was harder than I could've ever imagined, but she's not ready to hear what I have to say. Hell, I've been practicing it all in my head since I moved here. Leave it to the gorgeous Delilah Donovan to throw a wrench into my perfectly constructed plans with her snarky attitude.

I imagined her running into my arms the second she saw me, telling me how much she missed me, and how she's happy we can finally be together. I knew it would never happen, but daydreams and fantasies aren't ever rational.

At the first red light I catch, I use the truck's Bluetooth to call Jaxon.

"Hey, son," he answers after the second ring.

"Dad," I return.

"How's our girl?"

I love that he extends the possession to include us both, but even more, I love that he no longer sighs happily when I call him Dad rather than Jaxon. I can still remember the day it changed. He and Rob came to my house after getting Delilah settled into her freshman dorm. It wasn't the first time they'd flown across the country to visit, but something shifted. He gave me partial responsibility for his daughter, grateful I was here in case she needed me, so I gave him something in return.

"She's safe. Just dropped her off at her apartment."

"That's great. Did she give you any trouble?" Laughter is barely masked in his tone, but I'm still flying high from seeing her after so long, I don't complain about him sending me into the lion's den today. Rather, I'm indebted to him once again for the opportunity.

"She hasn't changed a bit."

"Are you purposely lying to yourself, or just saying shit so I feel better about my daughter on the other side of the country?"

"I'm not sure. Do you want to fill me in on what you're talking about? Would make it easier for me to make informed observations."

She's a spitfire, just like always, but she acted that way when we were alone back in New Mexico. She behaved differently in front of Jaxon and Rob.

A sad chuckle echoes in my ears. "I'm not spilling any secrets, but just let me say, I'm glad I was able to send you her way. Maybe things will calm down now."

I wait for him to elaborate, but he never does, so I change the subject. "I'll make sure she gets a rental car first thing in the morning. I think she tolerated me as long as she could today."

"Use the credit card I gave you for emergencies," he instructs.

"Find her a new car," Rob says in the background.

"I'll take care of it."
"Use the card, Law."
"I will."
"Liar. You never do."

"A rental car isn't an emergency," I mutter, having pulled up in front of the mechanic shop. Three cars I don't recognize are now parked there. Joel is speaking with one man about a mid-sized SUV. The driver of a black BMW is nowhere to be seen, but a woman stands, leaning against the driver's door of her red Camaro. I already know she's trouble by the smirk she gives me as I pull my truck in and put it in park.

"Dad, I have to go. Got three customers waiting at the shop."
"Sure thing. Let me know how tomorrow goes."
"Will do."
"Love you, son."
"Have a good day."

I hang up. I may call him Dad, but the 'I love yous' haven't happened yet. I have no time to feel like an asshole this time as I climb out of my truck. My focus is on the driver I can see when a paunchy bald man walks out of the front office. I frown in his direction, irritated that no matter how many times I've told Joel we need to keep that door locked when we're not in there, he still just leaves it open for everyone. He can't get it through his head that we aren't living in the damn fifties anymore, and the trust you had in people back then can't be given to assholes of this day and age.

"About fucking time someone else showed up," he hisses as he closes the distance between us.

I just stare at him.

"There's some sort of rattling noise," he says pointing to his car.

"Give me just a minute," I tell the woman standing outside of her car.

"I'll wait all day for you," she purrs.

I chuckle. She has to be in her late fifties, but it's clear she's taken very good care of herself.

"Quit fucking flirting," the bald guy hisses when I finally make it over to him. "I've been waiting twenty minutes, and that geezer over there doesn't seem to be in any hurry."

"We don't do imports." I cross my arms over my chest, legs spread shoulder-width apart.

"Bullshit," he sneers. "You got a fucking Toyota up on the rack."

I don't bother looking over my shoulder. I'm well aware that Delilah's car is in the first bay of the shop.

"Family car," I appease. "My insurance wouldn't cover me if I fuck up your pretty little car. It's newer and should still be under warranty, take it back to the dealership."

He's cursing me and muttering about it getting repoed since he hasn't made the last three months payments, but I ignore him. If I had to guess, I'd bet he got fired from his job because of that nasty ass attitude he's sporting. Tires squeal when he pulls out, but I just continue my trek across the lot to the last waiting customer. I swear I'm going to lose my shit if she asks for blinker fluid, which, oddly enough, we get on average twice a week. Always from women dressed to the nines with a coo in their voices like either Joel or I would be interested.

"How can I help you?" I ask, keeping a respectful distance between us.

"I need a full body inspection." I cock an eyebrow at her. "I mean the emissions thing or whatever."

"I hate to turn you away, but we ran out of stickers two days ago."

We do more inspections than anything else. Mostly on cars that pass with flying colors, by owners who wear tons of makeup and jewelry. It's serious craziness, especially for a shop that specializes in motorcycles and ATVs.

"Surely you can help me out."

I grin when her pink lip juts out in a pout.

"I can't do anything for you without a sticker, ma'am."

A devious smirk lights her face. "Oh, I'm sure there's plenty you can do for me."

Ignoring her, I point down the street. "I'm pretty sure Mack's just down the block still has some."

"But," she begins, but I turn away from her.

"Have a great day," I say over my shoulder and walk toward Joel and the customer he's been chatting with.

When I round the corner, I take in the scene. The man stands, not stiff, but also not relaxed in this environment. His MC cut stands out like a waving flag.

"Hey, Law," Joel says when I walk up. "This is Eric Quintal. President of the Ravens Ruin MC."

I offer my hand while he eyes me up and down, until his scarred-knuckled hand clasps mine.

"The old man here tells me you're the best in town at keeping bikes running." I nod because it's the truth. "How are you with modifications?"

"Get better with each one I do."

I take in the grime on his cut, 'Lynch' in bold print just above his 'President' patch, the old scar running down his left bicep. I'd wager that he didn't earn the damage to his body doing recon and rescue like Cerberus.

I'm not sure I want business from this man, so I don't elaborate.

"He's great at paint, exhaust mods, bodywork. You name it, this kid can do it."

I can hear the pride in his voice, but now is not the time for it. His emphatic trust in all people isn't helping in this situation.

"I'm more interested in the body mods," Lynch says with narrowed eyes.

"We're booked up," I lie.

Thankfully Joel keeps his mouth shut. We never turn business away without scheduling them on the books to ensure a greater chance of them returning.

"Check back in a couple weeks, and we may be able to get something lined up."

"I'll be back." Simple words that still feel like a threat.

I don't turn to face Joel until he's on his bike and halfway down the block. Three other bikes pull out further down the block. Assuming they're the vice president, sergeant at arms, and possibly the road captain, they get into formation and drive away.

"How long has he been harassing you?" I ask Joel once the sounds fade out in the distance.

"Since about ten minutes after you left." I follow him to the stool on the far wall of the building, surprised he's been able to stand as long as he has.

Apprenticing is what I called it when speaking with Delilah and Ivy earlier, but it's more like point and yell. He sits on the stool and tells me shit like he's right beside me. His knowledge is unparalleled, and his instruction is the same if he's sitting beside me or fifteen feet across the room.

I wait for him to get settled in before speaking. "Any clue what he wanted?"

"Of course, child. I'm not an idiot."

"So you're well aware it's probably illegal?"

He shakes his head as if I'm an idiot, but I can see the smile playing on his wrinkled lips.

"If you consider built-in hidden compartments for their wallets and jewelry store purchases illegal."

He eyes me, toying with me, waiting for me to respond.

"Jewelry, right."

He's chuckling as I walk away. I close the door between the garage and the office and settle down in the chair. My phone is out a second later. What does any young man do when faced with potential danger? I call my dad.

Chapter 29
Delilah

A headache, more from the banging on the door than the over imbibed wine from last night, taps away in my skull.

"Ivy," I yell from in front of my bathroom mirror. "Can you get the door?"

She doesn't respond, and the banging continues.

"Dammit," I mutter and toss my eyeliner on the vanity.

Passing by Ivy's room, I notice that she's gone, bed made just like she does every morning.

"I don't eat cookies," I mumble loud enough for the visitor to hear as I turn the deadbolt on the door. "And I already found Jesus."

"Tell me, Princess. Just how many times do you cry 'Oh, God!' each week?"

Lawson.

"More times than I can count," I lie. "Depends on how good he is with his mouth."

I watch his throat fight down an angry swallow. Not the response he thought he'd get apparently.

"Don't give me that kicked puppy look." I turn away from him, leaving him standing in the doorway and walk to the kitchen.

The front door clicks closed, but I know he isn't gone. He has a force that surrounds him. It literally affects the hair on my arms whether I can see him or not.

"I'm sure you have tons of stories to tell, a line of women fighting over the opportunity to choke on your cock," I continue.

"Not even touching that one." He pulls a chair out from the table and sits down, uninvited yet undeterred by my glare.

I rise up on my toes to get a cup out of the very top cabinet even though there are clean mugs in the dishwasher. I love torturing him, and I know how well it's working when I look over my shoulder and find his eyes on the backs of my legs. The short skirt wasn't something I did on purpose for him, but the everyday wardrobe choice is helping me right now.

"Like what you see?" I taunt as I make a cup of coffee, rudely not offering any to him.

"More than I could ever describe," he whispers.

Keeping my back to him does nothing to abate the shiver running over my body.

"Why are you here?"

I lean my hip against the counter, refusing to join him at the tiny table. There are only two chairs, and he's larger than life, so there's no way I could sit without part of my body brushing against part of his. My fingers already tremble against my warm coffee cup. I'm certain if we just barely brush against each other, I'll pounce on him.

"I'm here for you." In my mind, it sounds like a seductive whisper, but from the look on his face, he said it like any normal person would.

"How very Denny and Izzie of you."

"Huh?"

Seriously? Can you trust a man who doesn't watch Grey's Anatomy?

"The rental car?" he says with a tilt of his head like it's supposed to remind me of something.

"Okay?" I give him the same head tilt. "I'm getting one later."

"Right after you finish that coffee. I don't allow liquids in my truck. Don't want anything spilled on my seats."

"One, I'm not going any damn where with you, and two, I'm not a child. I can drink in a vehicle without spilling shit."

"I would tell you to hurry up; that I don't have all damn day, but it would be a lie. I cleared my schedule for you." His grin is almost contagious, but I catch myself before my lips part to mirror his.

"Nope." I drink the last sip of my coffee and rinse the cup before placing it on the counter.

"Your dad told me to make sure you got one so let's go." He sweeps his arm out toward the door.

I stay exactly where I've been standing and give him a pointed look.

"You keep mentioning him. How often do you talk to him?"

"If you want my life story, Princess, you're going to have to get into my truck."

I need a rental car, and I also need answers, but I don't know if I need them enough to be alone with him. I remind myself that I'm alone with him right now, in the apartment, where there are beds and a very comfortable couch.

"I'll grab my purse," I say and run out of the room.

He waits, somehow a little too close yet still too far away while I use my key to lock the apartment door, and his hand finds the small of my back as we descend the stairs. Once we're buckled in, he cranks the truck and puts it in gear.

"Every day," he says out of nowhere.

"Huh?"

His smile is blinding. "You asked how often I speak to Jaxon. We talk every day."

"No way," I hiss. "I don't even talk to him every day."

"And he misses you when you go days without checking in."

Well, if that isn't a kick in the gut.

"I'm trying to be independent," I mutter, already guilty over my sporadic contact with my dads before he even mentioned it.

"I get it."

"He doesn't talk to me about you." The meanness I hate so much rears its ugly head once again.

"You told him long ago that you didn't want to know anything about me."

I stiffen. "You talk about me? Did you tell him why I didn't want to hear about you?"

He laughs at my ridiculous question. Of course he didn't. He wouldn't live to tell the tale if he did.

"We talk about you all the time."

I let that sink in and stare out the window. We drive, five minutes longer than it would take to get to the rental place.

"Where are we going?"

"Figured we could find someplace quiet to talk." He looks over at me, and I instantly want to shut him down. If not for the sincerity and pleading in his eyes I would've. For some reason, today, being this close to him for the first time in years, I just don't have the strength to push him away.

We ride in silence for another fifteen minutes, until he turns off of the highway, pulling into the State Park. Slowly, he drives along until he finds a deserted parking area near the water. He surprises me when he parks with the nose of his truck against the trees and the tailgate facing the water that's on the other side of the lot. I anticipate him climbing out so we can sit and watch over the water, but he puts it in park and makes no move to get out.

"Tell me about your relationship with my dad," I plead.

"Tell me about school," he counters.

The fire in his eyes makes me think he's asking more about the nightlife and parties than the core classes I took last year and have already registered for this year. I realize now why he parked the way he did. This way there's nothing to look at but trees, so he's forcing my hand. There are, however, worse things to look at than his sexy lips and clear blue eyes.

"Don't," he murmurs.

"Don't what?"

"Lick your lips and stare at my mouth."

The corners of my mouth twitch before turning up with a wide smile.

"Tell me about my dad," I insist.

"Tell me about the boys you've met at college," he counters.

"Men," I correct. "And I thought you said you haven't been stalking me."

"So there have been others?" I stare, stunned at how quick he is to ask about my romantic life. "Are you seeing anyone?"

"That's none of your business."

"It's my business now," he says with quiet authority.

The domination in his voice is exactly what was missing in the darting gaze of the boy from yesterday.

"You want details?" I ask, unclicking my seatbelt and shifting my weight. I bite my lip as he stares, fingers tightening on the steering wheel. "You want the truth?"

"Always the truth," he says, voice cracking at the end.

"You want to know that your voice does more to my body than their mouths, their fingers, their," I lean over the console close to his ear, "cocks?"

"Stop," he commands, loud enough that I back away into my seat.

I told myself that my choices were just that, mine. I reminded myself each time I cried after a boy dropped me off at the end of the night that I was getting exactly what I'd wanted. I wasn't being used; I was the one doing the using. No regrets, I'd told myself each and every time.

I lived by that rule over the last three months. I was having fun, partying, and living life to the fullest.

Right now? This very second? I hate the woman I've become. I despise each of the three guys I used. More so, I hate the look of disappointment in Lawson's eyes as he realizes I gave something away that should've belonged to him. I hate him even more, blame him, for who I've become.

"What?" I ask defensively, another mask to my pain. "No dirty talk from you? No declarations of how much better you'd be?"

"I'm not that angry kid that moved away from New Mexico, Delilah." The intensity of his stare holds my eyes. "Now, I'm simply a man who knows what he wants."

"What do you want?"

I swear if he says anything about my mouth on his cock, the police will never find his body.

"You," he answers. One simple, three-letter word. How in the hell is it enough to tilt my world off of its axis?

Chapter 30
Lawson

Her lips are on mine before I can consider that honesty is the best aphrodisiac for women.

My first thought is to push her away, but at the end of the day I'm not a saint, so I kiss her back. I let the warmth of her tongue sweep over mine, and I offer her mine in exchange. In amazing contradiction, a sheen of sweat and goosebumps trail down my spine and branch out all over my body.

My cock, pressing against the denim of my jeans, having been hard since she agreed to talk, throbs in need of attention. The sound of coins clanging echoes around the cab of the truck as she flips up the console and tugs me closer to her.

We're in dangerous territory. I'd wanted to be alone with her. Wanted the chance to talk without interruption, but the way her lips are gliding over mine will only lead to one thing, and talking isn't it.

She's not quite straddling me, but her chest is pressed against mine, and the contact is beyond amazing. "Delilah."

I pull my head back but don't loosen my arms. They managed to find their way around her back, one hand resting dangerously low near her ass.

"Missed you, too," she whispers.

For the first time since I saw her yesterday, I see sincerity in her eyes. It's brief, only lasting a couple of seconds, but my heart soars at the possibility of what it could mean.

"Princess."

Her mouth hits mine again, and rather than push her away, my fingers dig in harder and pull her closer.

The heat between her thighs burns my cock as she shifts her weight to straddle me.

"Fuck," I groan.

Her hips rotate as she grinds down on me. Jesus, the tell-tale tingle is already present in my underused balls.

"Slow down," I urge.

With a mischievous grin, she swivels her hips in the slowest, most delicious circle. I grip her hips, but I'm no fool. My hands may be on her body, but I haven't made any real effort to make her stop. I'm powerless against her, against the situation I've envisioned while I stroked myself off in the shower, her name on my lips for the last two years.

If I concentrate hard enough, I can still feel the warmth of her pussy as it constricts around my finger. Can still feel the swipe of her tongue over the tip of my cock.

I squeeze my eyes shut, doing my best to stave off the orgasm that's churning with hurricane strength force in my nuts.

When I open them, Delilah has her shirt pulled up and both cups of her bra tugged down. Her perfectly round, pink-tipped breasts are mere inches from my mouth. Saliva pools as if I'm a hungry dog tempted with a T-bone steak.

Tilting my head back, I look in her eyes. Having dreamed of this moment, I don't want to give in, but I only have so much strength.

Lips parted, her breath ghosts out in uneven pants. She leans in, placing the puckered tip of her breast on my bottom lip, in similar fashion to the way I rested my cock on hers back in New Mexico. I want to shake my head to clear out thoughts of how epically I fucked that up, but doing so would break the contact with her perfect skin. That sacrifice isn't one I'm strong enough to make.

I don't waste time. I don't give her breast a gentle swipe of my tongue. I wrap my lips around it and suck like I'll never be offered it again. She whimpers, squirming once again as I draw her puckered flesh deeper. When her fingers get lost in my hair, I'm lost in her. I disappear into her scent, into the glorious taste of her warm skin. I'm entranced by the irregular breaths leaving her lungs. I'm adrift in the sound of her erratic heartbeat, or is it mine that's reverberating around us?

The pressure surrounding my cock is relieved. So much so, that I have to look down to see if I've just busted a nut in my jeans. It nearly comes to fruition when I look down and see her small hands gloriously wrapped around my cock.

"Oh fuck," I hiss as her black skirt clears her thighs and her bright pink panties are revealed.

"Feel good?" she asks, swiping the tip of my cock at the wet line on the pink fabric.

"Too good," I hiss.

"What about this?"

My mouth, once flooded, now runs dry as I watch her pull her panties to the side and use my cock to stroke that perfect bundle of nerves. I've felt that sensitive flesh on the tips of my fingers, but fuck me sideways if it does any justice to what she's doing right now.

I'm concentrating so hard on the sight of her skin against mine, that I don't even notice that she's produced a condom until she caps the end of my dick with it.

"Delilah," I groan but don't make a move to stop her.

"Lawson," she mimics.

"I can't tell you no."

My mind is screaming for me to put an end to this, but my grip holds tight to her hips, even helping her as she situates me at her entrance.

"Then don't," she pants against my lips as she slides down my cock.

We moan in unison when she seats herself fully and begins to rise.

"Help me," she begs.

Holding her against my chest with one hand, I use my other to push my jeans down to the floorboard. I gain the leverage I need with my thighs no longer being restricted and press into her as she sinks down.

I hold her up, easing into her and retreating in the most delicious way. I opt for slow, hoping to have the lasting power to take her over the edge with me, but she wants nothing to do with slow. I want romance, to make love to her. The look in her eyes tells me she needs to be fucked. She needs to be taken in the filthiest way possible. Being in the truck and not a bed covered in rose petals dictates that she gets what she's searching for.

We move in sync with each other, her forcing herself down as I pound up. The brutality of it is also beautiful in its own right.

"Fuck me like a filthy slut," she hisses when I pull her down, thrusting deeper. "I'm your dirty girl."

God help me, I wish I could stop the train that's barreling down my spine ninety to nothing as she throws the words that ruined us years ago in my face. I squeeze my eyes shut, a feeble attempt to gain some control, but lose the battle. Her words, even as bitter as they sound, send me straight over the edge and fuck if that first pulse of my cock isn't the heaven I've always imagined it would be.

"Fuck, fuck," I hiss. "Too soon."

Somehow still cognizant, I lick my thumb and swipe it repeatedly over her clit as I fuck her through my orgasm.

"Yes," she moans before she clenches around me.

The rhythmic clenching of her core around me is enough to keep me thick inside of her. When I can focus on something other than her flushed cheeks, I notice the condensation from our breaths covering the windows. If people weren't able to determine what we've been up to by the rocking of the truck, the windows would be a dead giveaway.

"I've never," she says, the look on her face almost worshipping. Shaking her head, she just stares down at me. "It's never been like that before."

I smile up at her, reaching up to brush my lips against hers. "You deserve more than this fucking truck."

"I figured it would've lasted longer with your sexual prowess and all." I'm unable to tell if she's joking or not.

"I haven't come with a girl present since before my mother passed away," I confess.

An emotion I can't distinguish marks her face as her brows draw together. The brief tremble in her lower lip makes my heart clench. It's gone as quickly as it showed up.

She looks down as she slides off my still semi-engorged cock.

"Looks like I still managed to get your seat wet, even without bringing a cup of coffee in here."

I don't bother to look down. I can feel the evidence of her orgasm pooling below me on the seat. My truck is going to smell like her for a long time to come, and I'd be lying if I said I wasn't looking forward to climbing inside and letting the scent settle in my lungs every day.

"Let me help you," I say and grip her hips before she can move away fully. Leaning over, I flip open the glove compartment and pull out a few napkins stashed there from random fast food places.

When she trembles against my hand at the contact, I swear I'm ready to take her again. My eyes meet hers, and I immediately know whatever moment we just shared has come to an abrupt end.

"Thanks." Her tone is flat as she repositions her panties and once again conceals her perfect little pussy. Next, she's back on her side of the truck and covering her breasts. I mourn the loss as I tug the condom free and wrap the napkin I used on her around it.

"Well, that was awesome." I look around my truck for some place to stash the evidence as she uses the visor mirror to put more lip gloss on.

"It was okay," she says absently, smacking her lips and refusing to look my way.

Anger at her unwillingness to acknowledge how great we were together when only moments ago she was quivering around me during her release pisses me off. I jam the trash in the cup holder in the driver's door and turn to glare at her.

"Excuse me?"

I clench the steering wheel as I fight the urge to grab her chin and force her to look at me.

"I mean," she begins, still looking down at her clothes. "Most guys don't fuck me in a truck. I at least get a bed."

My eyes nearly bulge out of my head at her words.

"You jumped me. You took my cock out. You rolled that rubber down my dick and sat on it like it was yours." I put the truck in reverse and back out without even checking my surroundings. When I pull out far enough, grateful to not have run over some kid or hit a guy unloading on the boat ramp, I put it in drive and peel out heading toward the main road. "Don't regret your actions now, Princess."

Chapter 31
Delilah

The echo of him inside of me is almost unbearable as we bump along the road, heading back out to the highway and eventually back into town to get my rental car. Clenching my thighs together does nothing but make me yearn for more.

I've been lying to myself. I can tell myself repeatedly that I was using the guys I slept with, but after what Lawson and I just did, there's no denying that those men were using me.

I didn't mean for my confession to slip past my lips, but I was delirious with pleasure, my orgasm the first by another's touch since the last one he gave me in my childhood bedroom.

If I were using them like I've proclaimed more times than I can count, they would've made me come, would've been invested in my gratification. Having been focused solely on their own release, makes the truth sit heavy in my stomach, souring the coffee there from this morning.

I find the courage to look over at him. He doesn't acknowledge me, but I know he's aware of my gaze because his hands tighten on the steering wheel.

How do I tell him the truth? How do I explain to him that his confession rocked me to my core?

"I haven't come with a girl present since before my mother passed away."

I can't presume he was waiting for me, but while he was living a life of self-imposed celibacy, I was getting drunk and letting vodka make major decisions for me. Blame wasn't one hundred percent on the alcohol. I made my choices, and I'll live with the fallout.

"Are we just going to ride in silence with you over there bristling like a wet cat?"

He stretches his neck, first to the right, then to the left before he speaks. The tension doesn't ease up in the truck as he figures out what he's going to say. My eyes narrow, hating that he just doesn't speak his truth without worrying how I'll respond. It feels calculating and manipulative and pisses me off.

"Talk to me," I demand. "Tell me what you're thinking."

He shakes his head. "It's not that simple. My feelings are... confusing."

"Confusing? Just use your words, Lawson. It's not that difficult."

He chuckles, his hands easing up slightly on the steering wheel. "We're going to my house."

My eyes widen. "No, we're going to go get a rental car."

"You implied that I took advantage of you, or treated you less than you deserve because we fucked in the truck. I'm going to take you home, lay you out on my bed and make it better than anything you've ever had before. Make you forget every other encounter you've had before me."

I wince at his words, wishing that he would be able to make me forget. Praying the amnesia took the guilt and self-recrimination right along with it.

"No."

He looks over at me. "What do you mean, no?"

"Take me to get a rental," I insist. "I have no desire to go back to your house."

It wasn't part of the plan, and resisting him after today is only going to be a million times harder.

"I waited two years for you."

I do my best to ignore the pain and pleading in his voice. Walls up and defenses on high alert is the only way I know how to maintain imaginary control over this situation.

"Well," I look out the window, hating myself. "I didn't wait for you."

And, God how I wish I had.

"I have a past, too," he says with more understanding in his voice than I deserve.

"It was a one-time thing." My body trembles in disapproval at my words.

"So you're just going to fuck me then walk away?"

I don't respond immediately, and my anger grows as I think about how offended he sounds.

Lowering my voice to sound more masculine I say, "I told you you'd suck my cock."

He nods. As he swallows, I watch his Adam's apple work under the pressure.

"So it comes back to that?"

"The last two years, all of my decisions have centered around the moment you made me feel like a whore," I confess.

"I was hurting." He holds his hand up when I try to respond. My jaw snaps shut, and I wait for him to continue. "Drew had just told me about his Aunt. I knew he was leaving, and I knew that meant I was going to leave with him."

I huff. "So you just figured you'd get me on my knees before you took off?"

The truck jerks and rocks back as he puts it into park. Looking around, I realize we've made it to the car rental place. I'd been so lost in my own head, I hadn't even noticed we'd traveled so far.

"You begged me to touch you," he hisses as he shifts his weight to look at me.

I pull my eyes from his, the scrutiny of his gaze more than I can handle. "So I was a whore then, too."

"You're not a whore!" He rages. "I've never seen you that way. Not once since I met you have I let that thought cross my mind."

"You manipulated me. You told me exactly what I needed to hear to get me to sink to my knees in that bedroom."

"I figured you hating me would've been easier on you."

"Hate." I bite my lip to keep the sob from slipping out. "More like hating that I loved you."

"Delilah." He reaches for me, but I pull my hand away before he can make contact.

"Don't worry, Lawson. I crushed that shit a long time ago."

"I couldn't ask you to put your life on hold for me," he barters a few years too late.

Tears spill down my cheeks. "I would've," I whisper.

"What?"

I look at him, not hiding my pain. I need him to see it, to feel it. "I would've waited for you."

"I'm here now." His eyes plead with mine, but there's no use.

"It's not even an option now. Too much time, too many bad decisions."

I push open the door to the truck and climb down. When I reach back in to grab my purse, he once again reaches for me.

"Talk to me."

"There's nothing to talk about. Let me know when my car is fixed."

I make it to the front door of the rental office before I feel his heat at my back. I'm torn between wanting him there and wanting him to leave me the hell alone.

"I'm perfectly capable of taking care of this myself," I mutter as he reaches past me to open the door.

I walk through, and he follows behind me.

No one is at the front counter, so I tap the top of the small bell and wait. His warm breath is in my ear, and there isn't a sliver of possibility that I can hide the tremble that takes over my body.

"I get that you're hurt. I've felt the pain from that night just as much as you have. We've both made bad decisions, the wrong choices, but if you think you making some declaration and getting all growly and mad will make me walk away from you again, you'd be wrong."

I try to turn, but he clasps my hips, pressing against my back until my front is flush against the tall counter.

"Listen," I say softly as if I'm a negotiator talking him down off the ledge of a building. "We had sex. It was decent."

He's the one growling now.

"But it will never happen again," I continue. "I've always wondered what it would be like with you. That opportunity presented itself today, and I jumped at the chance."

"I'm going to be making love to you for the rest of my life." There's so much surety in his voice, I almost believe him. "There's no getting rid of me this time, Princess. You're stuck with me."

Before I can respond, a tall man with a wiry beard comes to the counter.

"How can I help you?"

"Lawson O'Neil," he says reaching over my shoulder to hand the guy a credit card. "We're here to pick up a car."

I glare at the red and black logo on the front of his card. The familiarity of the three-headed Cerberus dog on the front makes my heart skip a beat.

Lawson, feeling the tension in my shoulders moves to my side and looks down at me.

"That card," I begin but don't say another word.

He smiles and shrugs. "It has a great interest rate."

The man at the counter takes the card and sweeps his eyes over me. "And will you, your girlfriend, or both of you be driving the car?"

"Not his girlfriend," I spit at the same time Lawson says, "Only my girlfriend."

The guy, Jerry if you believe his name tag, smiles at me and my explanation.

"Do you have a death wish?" Lawson watches Jerry, his tone no different than if he was asking the guy for a pen.

Jerry shakes his head, asks for my driver's license and gets to work. I should be angry or mad, but the possessiveness, even when I'm confused, turns me on like nothing else.

Chapter 32
Lawson

My cards have been played, my hand dealt sooner than I'd wanted, but letting her drive away in that rental car without her knowing my intentions wasn't a possibility.

My cock throbs as I inhale and pull her scent into my lungs. It's the best kind of torture and nearly has me turning right instead of left. Heading to the shop rather than her apartment is an exercise in restraint that's ten times harder now that I've had her.

Trying to ignore the insistence in my nuts, I do what I always do when I'm driving.

Dad answers on the second ring, his voice echoing around the cab of the truck through the hands-free.

"I forgot to tell you about my visitor when we spoke last night," I say after we both deliver our hellos. "Are you familiar with the Ravens Ruin MC?"

"The name's familiar, but I haven't had any dealings with them personally. I can have Blade look into them." I hear him mention the name to Rob. "Did they threaten you? Who did they send?"

"I had the pleasure of meeting Eric "Lynch" Quintal, the president. He didn't threaten me, didn't even tell me what he specifically wanted other than body mods for bikes."

"Body mods can mean a lot of things, son."

"I know. I told him I was booked out and to get with me in a couple of weeks."

"That was smart." I smile at the nonchalant praise. "He didn't give you any grief?"

"No, which surprises me. Joel told me after he left that he'd mentioned compartments for their wallets and jewelry."

My dad's laugh rings in my ears. "So they're either running guns or drugs."

"That's my guess. Rhode Island has concealed carry, so there's no reason for them to need to hide a weapon inside their bike."

The weight of the pistol in my boot increases at my statement.

"I'll have Blade look into them. Hopefully they're just fishing to see if they get any bites around town, but let me know immediately if you see any of them hovering around."

"I will," I agree.

"And how's Delilah?"

More gorgeous every day. The best thing that's ever slid down my cock.

That's the last thing I can tell him, but the reminder doesn't keep the low groan from escaping my lips.

"Something you want to tell me?"

I clear my throat.

"Man to man?" I ask testing the waters.

"That's always a good policy."

No guts; no glory, right?

"I'm going to marry that girl someday."

I'm met with silence, which I guess is better than him threatening to kill me from over two thousand miles away.

"Dad?"

"She's not very fond of you," he finally says amusement tinting his voice.

"I won't give up." I put my truck in park outside of the shop and run my hands over my hair. "She's the one who made me want to be a better man."

"She's an amazing woman."

"I don't know where my life would've ended up had I not met her. Had I not met you and Rob."

It's his turn to clear his throat, but he doesn't speak. I'm met with dead air so long I have to check the dash to make sure the call is still connected.

"Good luck, son."

His voice, sounding much like his blessing, eventually sounds through the speakers.

I turn my gaze to look at her car, still in the first bay on the rack. "Thanks. I'm going to need it."

"Before you go," he begins. "Rob had Blade run an initial check on the Ravens Ruin MC. They're not anyone you want sniffing around you. Feds are all over their asses."

"Got it," I say thankful he transitions so easily from my declaration and future plans.

"Take this seriously, son. These fuckers are sick, deadly, and nothing but trouble. Lynch got his name because his alleged calling card is hanging people from fucking trees in their family's yards. You don't need that kind of heat."

"Jesus," I mutter.

"Call immediately if you see anything suspicious. You're not going to like this, but I need you to distance yourself from her. I don't need them connecting the two of you. If you even get a Spidey tingle that something is off, you get her to the safe house."

"Yes, sir."

"Keep her away from the shop until I get the all clear." I hear him speak away from the phone, more than likely to Rob. "And, as much as I love him, don't tell Joel a damn thing. He runs his mouth too much. That poor bastard is living in the fifties. You and I both know times are much different now."

I let the heavy silence and weight of his words wash over me. Stay away from her. Don't tell the only person I've longed to see over the last two years a damn thing about what's going on. My life just went to shit over a visit from some psycho, asshole biker.

"Did you hear what I said?" His voice isn't exactly frustrated, but there's a hint of uncertainty in his voice that wasn't there ten minutes ago.

"Yes, sir." I swallow around the thick lump that's formed in my throat. "If I'm being honest, it scares the shit out of me."

Just the command to stay away from her for now, right after getting her back in my life, is like a sledgehammer blow to my chest.

"You're a man. You can handle yourself. I have no doubt. But you would be a fool to not have a little fear in the back of your skull."

"Delilah," I whisper.

"She's safest where she's at right now, Lawson. It's not for forever. A couple weeks tops." His tone is sure and full of faith I don't think should be placed on my shoulders. "Besides we'll have something in place soon."

Weeks? Damnit. I press the heel of my hand into my chest as the restriction grows tighter.

"Care to expand?" We're talking about the safety of my girl. She may be reluctant to that idea, but it doesn't make it any less true.

"I'll let you know more when I know more."

"Okay." I can't hide the defeat in my voice.

"Keep your head down, work, and I'll call you when I know something."

"Got it." Overwhelmed with the news I just got, coupled with the fantastic sex, and weighed down with the oath I made to Delilah earlier, I end the call without even telling him goodbye.

I'm diligent in my duties the rest of the day, but I keep one eye on the door and my ears open for the rumble of motorcycles. My pulse quickened no less than three times. Twice when customers drove up on Harleys for scheduled work, and once when a lone rider cruised in front of the shop. He wasn't wearing a cut, and I know for a fact that an MC member, especially one in a one-percenter club wouldn't be caught dead on a bike without letting everyone know where his loyalties lie.

As much as it pained me, I went home after shutting down the shop and making sure the doors were secure.

"This shit has got to stop," I mumble looking at the mess on the living room floor.

I reach down and pick up the pile of fuzz at my feet, then take a few feet and scoop up the carcass of the monkey that was in pristine condition when I left the house.

"What did he ever do to you?"

I hold the destruction in my hands. Per his usual, Raider has his forehead against the wall, the only sound he makes coming from the occasional thwap of his tail on the hardwood floor.

"You won't chew on a rawhide or a tennis ball, but you maim every stuffed toy I bring in the house."

I grin when he looks away from me, eyes down, thoroughly chastised. I drop the wreckage in the trash and walk over to him. His tail thumps harder on the floor.

"Did your mom drop you on your head when you were a pup?"

More tail thumping, only this time he actually puts some energy into it.

"I thought service animals were supposed to be regal and well behaved."

His jowls flutter, popping against his teeth as if he knows I should know better than to expect more from him.

"Come here," I call and slap my leg. He turns, jovial, all signs of remorse gone from his smiling face as he bounds the couple of feet across the room and nearly knocks me on my ass.

He licks my face, and I rub him all over as he squirms under my hands. When I snap my fingers twice, he's all business again.

"Good thing," I say reaching into the bottom drawer of the cabinet I have the living room TV on and pull out another monkey, "that I have a spare."

His eyes dart from me to the monkey and back again. He's begging, but after I've given him a command, he won't break until I relieve him. Smiling, I pat my leg and toss him the monkey whose fate is sealed the second he catches it in midair and trots off with it between his teeth.

I click the TV on, turning to some random channel I can't concentrate on. I need to shower. I'm filthy as hell, a deep, hard scrubbing the only thing that will get my hands clean, but fuck if I want to clean Delilah's scent off of my body. Hell, I stood over the toilet at the shop earlier to take a piss and nearly sprayed the damn wall. When the delicate scent of her pussy made it to my nose, the good Lord couldn't have even stopped the erection.

Jaxon Donovan better get his shit together and quick because staying away from Delilah is going to be next to impossible, and waiting isn't my strongest trait.

Chapter 33
Delilah

"Why are you frowning this time?"

I pull my eyes from my phone and look up at Ivy. The scowl on her face rivals the one that has marked mine for the last week.

"There's a party near campus," I mutter and slap my phone on the coffee table.

Tucking my legs up and resting my head on my knees, I watch her as she stuffs her purse full of lord knows what.

"And you didn't get invited?"

I huff. "I'm always invited. It looks like it's going to be a blast and yet I'll be here, seeing as I promised to stop partying."

"Such a travesty," she mocks. "Now tell me the truth."

My head lifts from my knees, and I look out the window.

"No clue what you're talking about."

"Don't give me that crap." Sitting down on my left she forces herself into my line of sight. "You've been grumpy for days."

"I haven't," I argue.

Her eyebrow cocks up, and she gives me the look, the one that says she knows I'm full of shit and I just need to spill it.

"I'm pretty sure it has everything to do with Lawson. You told me he took you to get the rental, but something else happened didn't it?"

"I'm going to be making love to you for the rest of my life," says the man who then never calls or stops by.

I close my eyes, but the heat of her gaze burns hot on my face. She's relentless, and I know she won't give up.

I squeeze them tighter, the sting of the tears I allowed on the drive back from the rental place renewed with thoughts of him.

"We had," I begin, but stop short. "We fucked in his truck."

"He had sex with you in a truck?" I can hear the disdain in her voice, and for some reason, it rubs me the wrong way.

"I fucked *him* in his truck." I don't question the defense of his honor. I can hate him all day long. I can regret the things we did, a week ago as well as back home, but I won't put the blame on him for something of my own doing. I won't let anyone else do that either.

I hear her sigh. Opening my eyes, I find sadness in hers.

"Well, you said you were going to." A comforting hand reaches out and rests on my shoulder. "So it was awful? You built him up all this time, and then he sucked at the banging?"

"*Banging?*" I chuff a laugh. "I wish he sucked at it."

A wide grin spreads across her face. "You liked it too much, and now you're having trouble with the one and done."

Not a question. She reads me like a book.

"Not like I have much of a choice. He hasn't called or come by all week. Seems he doesn't have a problem with one and done."

"He will. I'm certain of that. He's not like the shitheads you meet at those stupid parties. The way he looked at you." She looks away, a dreamy light shining in her eyes. "I'd give anything for someone to look at me like that."

"You mean Griffin."

She snaps her head back in my direction. "What?"

"You want *Griffin* to look at you that way."

Her lips tilt up in the corners, but she catches herself before it turns into a full smile.

"I'm no longer waiting for him," she says with confidence.

It's my turn to reach out to her. "If you love him, you need to wait. He's worth waiting for, Ivy. Believe me, you don't want to live with the regret if you get a chance with him."

I should know, my own regret nearly levels me every day.

"He's supposed to be home for Thanksgiving," she adds changing the subject.

I may have silently pined after Lawson for two years, but Ivy has been infatuated with Griffin since she realized boys existed. He was the first boy she ever saw, and she's been watching him ever since.

"I say corner him and kiss him senseless."

"I wish," she mutters.

Before I can offer any more sound advice, my cell phone rings.

Although the number is unfamiliar, I can see that it's local. I shrug at Ivy and answer.

"Hello?"

"Ms. Donovan?"

"Speaking. How can I help you?" I eye Ivy as she gets off of the couch, grabs her gym bag and waves her goodbye.

"This is Joel from Camel Towing. Your car is ready to be picked up."

I let out a relieved sigh. "Awesome. Give me about an hour? I have to drop the rental off."

"Sure thing," he replies. "We're open until six."

***

"Ready my ass," I hiss as I climb out of the Uber and see my car still up on that damn rack inside of the shop.

On a mission to rip Lawson's ass, I stomp across the parking lot to the big garage door, stopping short when the man of the damn hour appears wiping his greasy hands on a shop towel.

He looks over my head, darting his eyes back and forth.

"What the hell are you doing here, Delilah?"

I take a step back, caught off guard by his irritation.

"Joel called and said my car was ready," I explain when all I want to do is find the heaviest thing in my reach and knock him upside the head with it. Violent idealizations are new to me, and the realization only makes me madder.

"Obviously he's mistaken," he says looking over his shoulder, first at my car and then at Joel.

The wide grin on the old man's face doesn't match what I would expect from someone sorry for making a mistake.

"What did you do?" Lawson asks his business partner.

"Wrong car," Joel murmurs and disappears back inside, but pops his head back out. "You've been bristly for a damn week. I was getting tired of it."

"This isn't your business," Lawson hisses.

Joel, I'm sure used to his attitude, just waves a shop towel at him and disappears again. I bite the inside of my cheek to keep from smiling. Just the thought of Lawson being as miserable as I have over the last week brings a certain joy.

"Ma'am," he says as he sweeps his arm toward the front door of the shop. His official tone enrages me.

Fuck me in the truck then pretend I'm some random customer? Not today, Satan. Not today.

"If you'll follow me, I'll be able to provide more info on your vehicle."

I follow him, only because I'm losing my shit, and crying this close to the street isn't something I'll ever do. I want to turn and walk away, but my rental car has been safely returned, and it would take ten to fifteen minutes for another Uber to show up.

He closes the blinds on the door the second I step inside. Next thing I know, I'm plastered against the wall, and his body is hovering over mine.

"The fuck are you doing?" I push at his chest, but I'm not strong enough to create even an inch of distance between us.

"Why are you fighting me?" The low purr of his voice combined with the desire visible in his eyes is more than I can handle.

"Get off," I spit.

I straighten my clothes when he backs away a few inches.

"Why?" he asks again.

"Seriously? You treated me like shit two years ago, you talk to me that way outside?" I point behind me for emphasis. "Then you want to jump on me the first fucking second no one is around?"

"You don't understand," he mutters, his large hand running over his face.

"I sure as hell don't. I also don't trust you. It's like you're two different damn people and I never know which asshole is going to come out and play when I'm around."

"I've got a lot of shit going on right now," he says taking another step back. "It's not safe for you to be here right now."

My blood runs cold. "Afraid your girlfriend will find out we fucked last week?"

I slide past him and sit down in the old chair in front of the desk. After pulling my phone out of my pocket, I use the app to schedule another driver to pick me up.

I realize too late that sitting in the chair only gives him more power over me.

With hands resting on the armrests, he leans in close enough that each of his exhales are breathed into my own lungs. "My girlfriend was there when we fucked, and she's sitting right here looking amazing, gorgeous, and totally fuckable."

I tilt my head to the side, the only way to get a couple of inches between our mouths. "You need your head checked."

"We've been apart for too long, and you're crazy if you think I'm walking away from you again."

"Two years," I lament more to myself than him before turning my eyes up to meet his. "Things would've been different if you'd only waited eighteen months."

He looks confused.

"I could've given you all of me then."

Why am I even vocalizing this to him?

"You gave me all of you last week," he counters.

The tears that only seem to make an appearance when he's around pool on my bottom lashes. He kisses each one, the moisture glistening on his lips when he pulls away.

"Quit fighting this," he begs.

"I'm not that same girl from New Mexico."

"You're better," he whispers.

I shake my head. "I hate that you waited. I hate that we've been so close for so long and you came to work every day and couldn't be bothered to reach out to me."

He backs away, his full face coming into view. "I was working on myself, becoming a man you could be proud of."

"I was proud of the man you were then." I frown. "Well, I thought I was, but your actions proved who you really were."

"I can apologize for that night a hundred times a day for the rest of our lives if you need me to, but eventually you need to forgive me so we can move past it."

"I don't know if I can."

A loud bang snaps both of our heads in the direction of the shop.

"Shit," Joel grumbles.

When Lawson looks back at me, all of the care and comfort that I love so much is there, but there's a tinge of agitation in his eyes that's making his brow furrow.

"Let me take you home," he offers.

"No need," I say and stand from the chair. "I called an Uber."

"Princess," he chides. "Just go get in the damn truck."

I smile as he escorts me with a hand to my back, but regain a look of impassivity before he can see it. I hate the alarm bells and constant arguments going on between my head and my heart.

Chapter 34
Lawson

My lips part, a puff of air leaving my lungs when I watch Delilah climb in my truck and breathe deep. I know she does not smell what I longed for every day when I got inside. To my despair, the scent of our love-making didn't last as long as I'd hoped.

"You like the smell in here?" She nods, pink creeping up her neck to her cheeks at being called out. "The leather of the seats?"

It's all I can smell now.

She shakes her head. "Your cologne. You've always smelled so good."

"I can say the same thing about you." I crank the truck and pull out of the parking lot, praying I hit every single red light between here and her apartment. "It smelled like both of us until Tuesday. Made me hard as steel every time I got inside."

Her teeth scrape over her bottom lip as chill bumps race up her arms and disappear under the short sleeves of her t-shirt.

"I was sore for two days," she confesses as her head tilts a few inches to the right. My mouth waters with the need to lick the delicate column of her throat.

She's right about not being the same girl from years ago. That young, innocent girl wouldn't have had a clue on seduction. The minx sitting in my truck right now doesn't have an ounce of cluelessness in her body. The realization of her words hits me in the gut and steals my breath.

"Things would've been different if you'd only waited eighteen months."

I look away from her, hating the patience I somehow managed even knowing she was only a few miles away.

"I could've given you all of me then."

White-knuckling the steering wheel and trying to focus on anything but her is an exercise in futility. Her movement catches my eye as we slow at a red light.

"Jesus," I mutter when her finger traces over her collarbone.

The tip of her pink tongue is trapped between her teeth, and her eyes never waver from mine.

"Want to go back to the park?" Raspy words filled with promise.

"I'm not making love to you in this truck again." If I don't get her home and put more than three feet of distance between us, my cock is going to revolt.

"Okay." A provocative word only because it releases on a breathy moan. "You can just fuck me then."

My eyes narrow, but they stay on the traffic in front of me. She's purposefully trying to piss me off by separating the act from the emotion it includes.

I'm fuming by the time we pull up to the parking lot of her apartment complex.

"What are you doing?" she asks, eyes darting from me to the front of the building.

"Walking you up." I close my door and walk around to get hers.

Regardless of her words and attempt at enticement in the truck, she's a lady and waits for me to open her door for her. She's also agitated that I didn't just drop her off and refuses to take my hand so I can help her down.

I steady her when she bounces out of the seat and wobbles from the impact.

"You know what they say about men who drive big trucks." She shoves off my aid and tries to walk past me.

Closing her door with more restraint than I actually feel, I urge her back against the door, crowding her and forcing her chest against mine. "I think you know I'm not compensating for shit, Princess."

"Meh," she mumbles.

I chuckle at her feigned apathy. "Sore for two days. You said so yourself."

I want to nip at her throat as it swallows roughly, but I keep my eyes on hers, my face mere inches away. She's not unaffected, but for some reason, she's fighting me every step of the way. If she wants proof that I'm not the same man, that I'm not walking away from her, I have no problem proving it to her in any way she needs.

"I was sore because you didn't bother to make me wet w-when..." She swallows again and the pink I love so very much creeps back into her embarrassed cheeks. "When we fucked."

I press against her harder, the thickness of my cock pushing against her stomach. I've never hated clothes as much as I do right now.

"One," I say nipping at her throat and smiling when she gasps, and her body shudders. "We made love. No matter where, no matter how hard I pound into that sweet pussy of yours, it's still making love. I don't care if I have you bent over my motorcycle on a deserted gravel road in broad daylight with you begging me to slip inside of your ass, it's still making love."

Her lips part, breath quickening.

"Two." I lick at her lips, but pull back as she opens her mouth further. Her small hands cling to my shirt as I lean in close to her ear. "You were wet at just the thought of me slipping inside of you. You creamed so much on my cock, your pussy juice coated my balls."

My pulse is pounding in my ears. My mouth dry from taking ragged breaths, and I'm seconds away from embarrassing myself by coming in my jeans.

"Gross," she hisses and pushes against my chest.

I take the reprieve she offers and move back a few steps.

"Seems you haven't changed a bit." She turns to walk in the direction of her apartment, but I don't miss the wobble in her first couple of steps. She's just as affected as I am.

I adjust myself in my jeans and follow behind her.

"I'm capable of getting myself inside," she mumbles as she begins to climb the stairs.

"I wouldn't turn down the opportunity to follow your gorgeous ass, ever."

She huffs as she presses her key into the lock on her door. The second it opens a terrified scream echoes around us. On instinct, I press Delilah's back against the outside wall and reach into my boot.

"Stay here, baby."

She nods, tears already welling in her gorgeous blue eyes.

"Ivy," she whimpers.

"Oh, God," Ivy screeches again.

I follow her voice down the small, narrow hall. I'm man enough to admit that I'm scared, my nerves causing a slight tremble in my hands.

Peeking around the corner to the small bathroom, I do my best to evaluate what's going on in the split second I give myself to look.

What the?

I lower my gun and take a step into the bathroom.

"Are you fucking kidding me?"

Ivy turns and screams again, this time pointing her can of hairspray and toilet brush at me, her new perpetrator.

Her eyes widen and sweep over me before going back to the spider clinging to the wall of the shower.

"Ivy," I nod and turn away.

She hisses, the hairspray and toilet brush clattering to the floor as she realizes that her robe was open. I can admit that Ivy has a great body, but I'm also so fucking thankful she still has on a bra and panties because this situation is already going to be awkward as fuck.

"Delilah," I call and watch as her tear-stained face comes into view around the door frame. I hold out my hand. "It's fine, baby. Come here."

She walks toward me, but her steps falter when she sees the pistol down by my side. Clearing my throat, I bend and place the weapon back into the holster in my boot.

Ivy slides past me, the width of the door barely enough to keep us from touching, but she manages.

"Spider," she tells her friend with a shiver that tells of a room full of black widows, not one little guy probably more terrified of her.

"Wuss," Delilah mutters walking past her into the room.

She picks the daddy long legs spider up and carries it out the front door.

"You should've killed it!" Ivy shouts as Delilah walks back in and closes the front door.

"Get in the shower," Delilah says and plops down on the couch.

I join her in the living room just as she's wiping the tears from her eyes.

She laughs when I reach for her but pulls her head away before I can make contact.

"I think that's enough excitement for one day," she says with a laugh.

"Scared me, too," I confess and sit down beside her.

"Why do you have a gun?"

She was apprehensive when she noticed the gun in my hand. I imagine being around her dad, and the other Cerberus guys have given her a ton of respect for weapons, but the way she eyed me is confusing.

"I have a permit."

"You have a criminal record," she counters as if I'm lying to her.

"Not anymore." More confusion draws in her brow. "It was expunged."

"Dad," she mutters.

"He's been very helpful in many ways."

We sit in silence. I want to talk to her about what was said outside. I want to assure her that she doesn't have to fight me at every turn, but she stares off, looking at nothing, and not saying a word.

For the first five minutes, I watch her, reorienting myself with every dip and delicate curve of her face. After that, I take in her apartment, waiting for her to speak. She doesn't tell me to leave, so I see that as progress and mentally put a tick in the win column for myself.

"Well, that was exciting," Ivy says breaking into the quietness of the room.

Ivy smiles at me when I look up at her. Her hair is still wet, but thankfully she's now fully dressed.

"I hope you're hungry, Lawson. I ordered pizza for lunch."

"He's not staying," Delilah huffs.

"I'm starved," I tell her friend and sink deeper on the sofa.

Chapter 35
Delilah

"Really?" I frown as I walk up to the couch and notice the new seating arrangement. "I leave to get napkins, and you pull this shit."

Ivy chuckles as Lawson spreads his legs further apart, taking up the center of the sofa. He was down on one end, Ivy was in the middle, and I was on her right, but thirty seconds later and they've both moved.

"You're as transparent as air," I mutter to Ivy.

"You can sit on my lap," Lawson whispers when I give in and claim the end of the couch.

My heart thumps behind my rib cage at his offer, one I'd love to take him up on, but keeping my distance is more important.

"Don't you have work?" I hand each one of them a napkin and pick my paper plate up off of the coffee table.

"Joel can handle things for the afternoon." He looks at me with seductive promise in his eyes. "I'm yours for the rest of the day."

I roll my eyes but grin behind my slice of pizza as I raise it to my mouth.

"If you had a little better work ethic, my car would be done already."

"I'm not wasting time or money fixing that heap of junk, Delilah." My eyes widen.

"What the hell have you been doing for the last week and a half?"

He shrugs as if it's no big deal that I've been in a rental car. I shouldn't complain because the car I've had is ten times better than the Corolla, but it's the principle.

"Fixing bikes. Working on cars that are worth fixing."

"Unbelievable," I hiss.

"Who's up for a movie?" Ivy interrupts, feeling the tension that's growing by the second in the room.

"I've got nowhere to be." The smug smile on Lawson's face makes me want to slap him and kiss him at the same time.

After wiping his mouth with his napkin, he stands and takes both of our plates to the trash and even slides the uneaten pizza into the fridge before excusing himself to the bathroom.

"You need to quit whatever it is you think you're doing," I tell Ivy with a pointed look. "It's not helping."

She just smiles at me. "I'm a virgin, but the sexual tension bouncing between you two is making me tingly."

"Stop," I hiss when I hear the toilet flush. "Sex isn't everything."

"Sex *wasn't* everything," she corrects. "That man loves you, and you'd be a fool to let him go."

She snaps her head back in the direction of the TV and scans through the channels as Lawson opens the bathroom door and sits even closer to me on the sofa.

"Game of Thrones marathon?" Ivy asks, already knowing how hot I get for Jon Snow. I refuse to acknowledge his dark hair and blue eyes because it means confessing my attraction to him over the years has more to do with him resembling Lawson than Kit Harrington.

"Love this show," Lawson says scooting even closer to me.

His warmth, his scent wash over me. God, this man will be my undoing.

"Come here, baby." His breath heats my neck, and my body responds with goosebumps. "I'll keep you warm."

Like the bipolar sadist I am, I allow him to wrap his arms around my back as I snuggle into his chest. I sigh my contentment, and it seems to calm him.

But true to Lawson form he ruins the moment of surrender with his damn mouth. "Try not to think about my cock while we watch Khal Drogo take command of his queen."

I try to pull away, slapping him the only thing I can concentrate on.

"Wrong," I whisper when I realize exactly which scene we're watching. "Daenerys owns his cock."

Lawson shifts uncomfortably as we both watch the scene playing out on the TV screen in front of us. It looks very similar to the way I straddled him in the truck and rode him until we both came.

He groans and shifts again when my fingers curl against his thigh.

"You own my cock," he pants, uncaring that my best friend is a few feet away.

I dart my eyes in her direction, but by the way she's nibbling on her thumb, I don't think she heard him.

"Hush," I tell him.

His chest rumbles against the side of my face, but he doesn't argue. Before long even the battles playing out on the TV can't keep me awake. The hand roaming from the top of my head and down my back in slow, rhythmic strokes is my downfall.

It isn't until I feel my body being lifted from the couch that I realize I fell asleep.

I cling to his shirt when he pulls away after placing me on the bed and covering me up. I'm begging without words as I look into his eyes. Normally, I would feel too prideful, but in the quiet of the room, with nothing but care and concern in his eyes, I feel a sense of freedom I've never felt before.

"Princess," he whispers against my cheek.

He could crawl in behind me, spread my legs, and sink deep inside and I wouldn't object. By the tension pulling at the corners of his eyes, I know he's well aware of that fact.

His hand cups my cheek just before his lips sweep over mine.

"I don't hate you," I tell him. "But my heart can't trust you yet."

He smiles against my lips, a reaction I wasn't expecting. I wait, looking into the blue depths of his soul, once again preparing myself for some remark that's only going to serve to burn another bridge so precariously built between us.

"That's the most honest thing you've said since we reconnected." He kisses me again. Soft, sweet, with love, not the fiery passion that seems to overflow between us. "Take all the time you need, baby. I'm not going anywhere."

***

I smile into my pillow, the scent of his skin all over mine from our snuggling on the couch. What I don't have is the warmth of his skin against my back any longer.

Maybe his promise of not going anywhere was meant in a not-quite-so literal sense, but that doesn't ease my anger very much.

I stagger to the coffee pot, only to find Ivy already at the small kitchen table.

"Sleep well?"

The playfulness of her voice tells me she suspects more happened last night with Lawson than actually occurred.

"Yes," I answer honestly. I didn't realize until he climbed behind me, insisting on staying on top of the covers even after I'd tried to persuade him differently, just how exhausted I've been. I haven't slept well since he showed up in the parking lot when my car broke down, but last night was different. I'm wide awake, though annoyed he's not here, and ready to take on the day.

"What's that?" I snap out of it and look over at her.

"What's what?"

I smile behind my coffee cup.

"That silly grin on your face." She smiles too. "Did you catch feelings for Lawson?"

"Catch feelings?" I mull over her words while my mind races for an excuse. "I didn't catch anything."

"True," she says with a quick tilt of her head. "I guess since they were always there, you can't really catch them again."

"That's not what's happening."

"Tell that to Lawson. He's head over heels for you." She points to a set of keys on the counter. "He left his truck. Said he had to get to work."

"He needs to stop doing shit like that." I hate the words the second they're out of my mouth. It's clear I'm not one hundred percent over my anger. I lock down the vulnerability I showed last night in the soft light of the moon.

"Don't do this to yourself." I turn my back to her, adding unnecessary sugar to my already sweet coffee. "You going to punish him for words he said so long ago?"

"He spoke to me like I was some filthy whore," I rebut.

"He said some pretty dirty things to you on the couch last night while watching TV."

"Exactly. See he'll never change."

She shakes her head in disbelief. "Did you squeeze your thighs together like you did last night when he said that stuff to you two years ago?"

I hiss, jolted by her words enough that I spill my coffee down the front of my shirt. I stare in disbelief, and if I'm being honest a little proud of Ivy as she leaves me reeling in the kitchen.

I've thought, probably more often than I should've, about that night in my room with Lawson. My mind was overwhelmed then, wondering if Samson was going to tell Dad and Pop about things he'd only suspected. I worried over whether they would kick him and Drew out. I know deep in my heart that had Lawson not done something to push me away that I would've done the exact same thing to him.

I can be indignant all damn day, but the outcome would've been the same, only he would hate me instead of me pretending to hate him.

Pretending.

It's the first time I've allowed myself to admit the truth.

I've never hated Lawson. If anything, seeing him again, feeling his lips on mine, takes me right back to where we were when I was just an immature, inexperienced girl who wanted nothing more than the love of a boy she shouldn't have wanted in the first place.

"Fuck," I grumble as I place my half-consumed coffee in the sink and make my way to the bathroom.

I turn the radio up almost loud enough to drown out the thoughts and images of Lawson that bombard me as I strip out of my clothes.

While I scrub his scent from my body and wash my hair, I steel my spine once more. Even with my feelings, there are a million reasons why Lawson and I shouldn't be together. The only problem is as I rinse the suds from my hair, I can't think of a single one.

Chapter 36
Lawson

"You sound frustrated."

I huff into my phone, ready to knock the head off of the Uber driver if he so much as looks over his shoulder while I'm in the back seat of his car thinking of ways to kill my dad.

"Explain it to me one more time," I hiss into the phone.

"Blade sent a few guys to Purgatory Chasm. Ravens Ruin has found a shop in Worcester that will do their bidding."

"And Cerberus is just going to let that happen?"

"Calm down, Rambo." His chuckle is like nails on a chalkboard right now. "They're under surveillance, and you don't need to worry about it. You didn't want the club."

"And you won't talk about it. I wasn't spending four years in the Corps to join." We've been through this a hundred times. The time in the service is a requirement for official acceptance in Cerberus MC, one I wasn't willing to commit to.

"I *can't* talk about it," he clarifies. "Why the attitude?"

I take deep breaths before I continue. "You said you found out two days ago."

"Correct." His voice lowers, calming and sedate. "Why are you upset?"

"Are you sure she's safe?"

"She was never in danger, Law. We were just keeping it that way."

"I spent a week away from her." I scrub my hand over my face doing my best to keep from telling the driver to take me back to her.

"I haven't seen her since May," Jaxon informs me. "So I know what it's like to miss her."

"Exactly," I agree too soon.

"You didn't miss her last night." There's mirth in his voice, but only having known him for two years, I still worry about when the conversation will change from support and morph into disgust.

"I swear nothing happened."

He laughs. The chuckles from farther away tell me I'm on speaker phone and Rob is nearby.

"You're both grown," he clarifies.

"I don't feel very grown with you tracking our phones," I murmur.

"When you have children, you'll understand."

I nod even though he can't see me. The thought of having kids doesn't scare me one damn bit because I know Delilah will be an incredible mother.

"In years," Dad says in a long breath. "When you have children years down the road. *Years*, right Law?"

I laugh.

"Law." Rob's voice this time. "His head's about to explode."

"Years," I concede as a smile spreads on my face. "We'll still be having children years from now."

I hear him yelling when I hang up on them. That's what he gets for not telling me forty-eight hours ago that Ravens Ruin MC wasn't a threat to her. I may have spent time with her yesterday, but we could've already had another day of connection under our belts. I need every second to build what Delilah is trying to reject.

***

"Put your shirt on."

I smile as the voice of my angel echoes through the shop. I was hoping she would stop by today, but as time dragged on, I let doubt creep in.

I turn in her direction, using the shop towel to swipe at the sweat running down my abs.

"You seem to be enjoying the view."

Her lips smack together as if she's getting ready to say something, but no sound comes out. Her eyes don't pull from my stomach either. If it's a weapon in my arsenal, I'll use it. Leaning back against the truck I was just bent over, I kick my legs out, crossed at the ankles. The position allows me to contract my stomach for optimal viewing.

"You look…"

"You're pretty fucking spectacular yourself." She's wearing the same lacy shorts she had on the day her car broke down, but her top is different. This one slides off of her shoulder, revealing a thin strap and hinting at the lace covering her perfect breasts.

Her eyes snap to mine. "Grungy and dirty. That's what I was going to say."

I hold my tongue as I watch her fight the urge to take another look.

"Where's my car?"

"Round back. Waiting for a tow to the junkyard."

I expect a fight, an argument at a minimum, so when her breath shudders, it catches me by surprise.

"Was it really that bad?"

"Sorry, Princess."

"I've had that car since I learned to drive."

I never thought I'd see her so emotional over a damn car, especially since I know she knows how much I care about her and she's all too eager to push me away.

"You've only been driving what three? Four years tops? You'll get another one."

"Is it that easy for you to just replace things that were once important to you when you get tired of them? When they're no longer pristine and perfect?"

I recoil at her words. "It's just an old car, Delilah."

She turns her back to me and mutters. I stop cold.

"What did you just say?"

She shakes her head and walks out of the front of the garage.

"What did you say?" I repeat.

She spins, wiping at fresh tears on her cheeks. "I said I loved that car."

I shake my head. "It sounded a lot like 'I fell in love in that car.'"

She shrugs, and I clench my fists so tight my knuckles pop. "His name was Danny. We spent a couple weeks together in the summer."

I growl at her but keep my distance. It's the only thing keeping me from shaking some damn sense into her.

A mischievous glint hits her blue eyes, the corner of her mouth twitching. I can already tell, true to Delilah form that she's going to mask her emotions with some damn joke as a distraction. "We laughed and sang together. Frolicked in the surf of the ocean."

I tilt my head, confused as fuck. "What?"

She nods towards the shop. "He loved cars, too. Seems I have a type."

Frolicked in the surf? Loved cars?

"Wait." I take a step toward her. "Did you just describe fucking *Grease* to me?"

She rolls her teeth to stop her laugh, but it's not enough as it bubbles up her throat. God, I love her smile.

"You realize every one of those songs is filled with tons of sexual innuendo. If you pay attention, you'd realize they have filthier mouths than I could ever dream of."

Her eyes dart to my mouth and down my glistening chest.

My phone buzzes in my pocket, and I make sure my stomach flexes in all the right places when I reach to get it. I look down at the text and frown.

"What's wrong?" I love the concern in her voice.

"An emergency," I lie. Well, not a total lie, but my neighbor may try to kill me in my sleep if I don't get home quickly. I pull my t-shirt over my head and sweep my hand toward my truck. She offers me the keys. "Your pussy wagon, my lady."

She snorts but walks in that direction. "Travolta drove a Ford."

"I'll trade the Chevy in tomorrow, baby. Hurry. I have to get home."

She hustles inside, still letting me open and close her door for her.

"You going to tell me what's going on?" she asks as we make our way around the block toward my house.

I smile at her but shake my head. "You'll see."

We drive, with the radio playing softly. She hums along to the lyrics of a song I've never heard before but has somehow managed to become my favorite.

"Why did you leave so early this morning?" I grin even wider at the insecurity in her voice which makes me an asshole.

"Miss me, Princess?"

"No," she insists, but I see the smile on her face before she turns it from view.

"I had to make sure Joel didn't burn my shop down yesterday. Had a few things to check off my list before the weekend, and then I planned to come right back to you."

"I don't want you—" She stops right before shutting me down once again. "Is this your house?"

I frown because I know she's just putting off the inevitable.

"It is." I turn the truck off and point. "And that is my very pissed off neighbor."

I open her door for her, and it surprises me when she places her hand in mine to climb down and doesn't pull it free when we start to walk across the yard.

I whistle and wait for the clinking of Raider's dog tags. The sound never comes, but a bark can be heard from inside the house.

"Mrs. Houston?"

She hitches her thumb over her shoulder. "I'm calling the Home Owner's Association if that satanic dog isn't locked up immediately."

Delilah stiffens beside me.

I smile when the dark headed woman appears behind Mrs. Houston.

"Hey, Lawson," Cynthia says as she wraps her arms around her grandmother's shoulders. "Raider's been agitated more than usual. I normally wouldn't bother you while you're at work."

"I'll take care of him. Thanks for letting me know."

I tug on Delilah's hand as I pull her toward my house and Cynthia turns her grandmother around and guides her back to her house.

"She's pretty," Delilah says with a huff as I unlock my front door. Jealousy coming from Delilah Donovan has to be the best thing to happen since Harley came out with its Softail. "And she has your cell phone number. That's lovely."

I remain quiet as she enters my home for the very first time, but I can tell she's working herself from mild envy of Cynthia to full-blown agitation.

"Does she come to visit when the old lady goes to sleep?"

I grab her by her shoulders and spin her around. "She has my number because sometimes her grandmother can't hear when the phone rings and she gets worried about her. She's never been inside of my home. Hell, I don't know that she's even stepped foot on my grass. And yes, Delilah, Cynthia is very pretty. A trait I'm absolutely certain her husband loves about her."

A banging noise bounces off of the walls down the hallway. I give her a quick kiss on her stunned lips and head to my dog.

I whistle and the banging stops.

When I open the door to the nearly empty guest bedroom, Raider doesn't even bother to act ashamed of the mess he's created. He lunges for me.

"You," I tell him scratching at his face as he licks my neck. "Are defective. I'm going to take you back if you keep this shit up. How does such a smart dog close himself inside of a bedroom?"

He yips, keeping to his inside voice and licks me more.

"You would never take a dog back to an animal shelter." Delilah sounds thoroughly offended behind me.

Standing on his back legs, Raider is almost as tall as I am which makes it very easy for him to peer over my shoulder. I've never seen his tail wag so hard in the time we've been together.

"Shelter?" I laugh. "A shelter animal would be smarter than this dummy."

Raider withdraws his legs and makes it to Delilah in less than a handful of steps. She's knocked on her gorgeous ass before she can prepare herself for the dog's attention

I snap my fingers, and he backs away immediately, a low whimper his only sign of discomfort.

"That's impressive," She says wiping dog spit from her face. Her smile is the biggest I've seen since before I left New Mexico.

"He's not a shelter dog?" Sad eyes look up at me. "Please tell me you didn't get him from a breeder. Tons of places breed animals in horrid conditions. Unless you visit there yourself, you never know how they're treated."

"He's a therapy dog," I confess waiting for the shame to hit me in the chest, but it never comes.

She grins back at Raider and pats her lap. The longing look he gives me over his shoulder is almost enough to make me let him go, but he knocked her down and could've hurt her. I don't care how excited he is that another human being is in my home, that's entirely unacceptable.

"He seems fine," she says but frowns when the dog stays. "Does he have a brain condition?"

She pats her lap again and the dog whimpers.

"Raider." His ears perk up, tail giving the slightest twitch. "Be gentle."

He eases toward her, almost crawling on his stomach until his head is on her lap, tongue lapping at her hand for attention.

I sit beside them on the floor in the hall.

"He's *my* therapy dog," I clarify. "I was struggling about a year after I got here. Drew was living his life, doing better than anyone expected. He was busy with his friends, and even though I was working crazy hours at the shop, I was lonely. Da-Jaxon suggested a counselor, but I shut that shit down the second the word was out of his mouth."

I expect her to laugh with me, but her face softens when she looks into my eyes.

"A week later he and Rob showed up with this asshole." I rub the scruff on the back of Raider's neck. "They told me he was super smart, knew every trick in the book, but as you can tell from his behavior just a minute ago they were fooled."

Indignant eyes look from me and back to Raider. "How would you act if your person left you locked in a bedroom with no way to use the restroom, eat, or drink?"

I reach for her arm and guide her to the kitchen and point to his food and water bowl, both nearly full. She looks dumbfounded as I guide her to the back of the house and show her the dog door that gives Raider access to the backyard. "Do you really think I'm the kind of guy who locks his dog in a damn room?"

Her head angles in the direction of a soft click. "What was that?"

"Perfect timing," I mutter and tug her arm once again until we're standing in the hallway.

The door to the spare bedroom rattles and Raider whimpers from the other side.

"He shuts the door," I tell her as I push it back open.

"You need to put a stopper under it," she suggests.

"I've done that. He pulls it out and chews it up." I stare down at the deviant who looks up at me as if he understands exactly what I'm saying. "I don't know what else to do."

"Put a dog door in," she says and walks back toward the living room. She looks back over her shoulder. "Aren't you glad you have me?"

I close the distance between us, wrapping my arms around her stomach and pulling her against me.

"So glad I have you," I whisper in her ear before nipping at the spot on her shoulder that drives me wild. "How have I survived without you?"

A low moan escapes her lips as her arm reaches over her head and her fingers run through my hair.

"If it's for my safety, then I think it's best if you just move in tonight."

Chapter 37
Delilah

I stiffen in his arms.

"Stop," I demand as my fingers leave the silk of his jet black hair and claw at the forearms trapping me. "Why do you say shit like that?"

"Like what?"

He doesn't release me but rather turns me in his arms so I'm facing him.

I lower my voice to sound manlier. "Move in. I'll be making love to you for the rest of my life. Take your time, Princess. I'm not going anywhere." I swallow around the lump forming in my throat. "Is this all a damn joke to you?"

"I mean every word I've said to you." His brows draw together, and I resist the urge to run my thumb over the crinkles.

"You can't ask me to move in fifteen minutes after I step inside of your house for the first time."

"I just did." His eyebrow raises in challenge.

"You claim you'll be making love to me forever, but you denied me last night."

"Princess." He cups my cheek and brushes his lips over mine. They part of their own volition as my breathing grows shallow. "You were exhausted. So bone weary, you were asleep seconds after you suggested..."

I love the rush of heat that turns his cheeks pink as he clears his throat.

"After you mentioned us making love."

I shake my head, a smile marking my face as my frustration slowly begins to fade away. "That's not even close to what I said." He grins back at me, hips grinding against mine. "Do you not like it when I talk dirty to you? You can dish it out but can't take it?"

He leans in, mouth less than an inch from mine before he begins again. "You were asleep seconds after you suggested you hug my cock with your tight. Little. Cunt."

My insides quiver. I knew I'd propositioned him and that he turned me down, but I didn't know exactly what I'd said. I just knew it didn't sound anything like 'make love.'

"You said you weren't going anywhere, yet I woke up alone this morning." My voice cracks and he holds me tighter.

"If I woke you to tell you goodbye, and you looked up at me exactly like you're looking at me right now, I never would've gotten out of your bed."

His lips devour mine in a heated kiss that sets every inch of my skin on fire. I'm panting yet reaching for him again when he pulls away.

"And if my tight. Little. Cunt," I punctuate each word just as he had with a smack of my lips against his, "wanted to give you a hug right now?"

"That word on your lips makes me as hard now as it did last night." His tongue snakes across my lips tracing the upper curve.

"I'm a dirty girl."

"*My* dirty girl."

My heart pounds in my ears as his fingers curl against my ass.

"Can I hug you?" I beg as his tongue teases the dips and curves of my neck. "With my pussy."

"Filthy mouth," he praises against my skin.

I stiffen and push his head back until his eyes meet mine. "Make one suggestion about my lips wrapping around your cock, and you'll never see me again."

"Delilah."

"No," I tell him taking a step back but not fully escaping his arms. "Hard limit."

He nods, understanding why I can't bear to hear that coming from his mouth again. Greasy hands run over the top of his head, and he looks harder, noticing the smear of dirt on his forearm.

"Shit," he grumbles. "I bet I ruined your clothes."

He spins me, eyes lowering to my ass.

"Jesus, D. Those shorts will have to be trashed." His eyes look up into mine as I peer over my shoulder at him. He's more upset about stains on my clothes than I am. "I'm so sorry."

"They're just clothes."

"Let me get you something to change into, and I'll grab a quick shower."

"Okay," I agree quickly.

His eyes search mine. "You'll be here when I get out?"

I smile at his insecurity, and the longer I look, the easier it is to tell just how genuine this man is.

"I don't plan to walk home, and I don't want to be arrested for taking your truck."

He laughs as he clasps my hand and pulls me toward his bedroom at the back of the house. Raider, the most amazing dog in the world, tracks us with his eyes and lumbers behind us once we've cleared the threshold to his room and he loses sight of us.

Having forgotten about the possibility of his mouth comment just as fast as I'd imagined it, I shake my head when he offers me a shirt to change into.

"Don't need it."

I watch his mouth go slack as I tug the loose shirt and camisole over my head in one movement. My lacy shorts hit the ground next, revealing that I didn't bother with panties before leaving the house today.

I stand in front of him completely naked for the first time ever.

"Ten minutes," he mumbles. "I'd say seven, but I want to make sure I'm clean."

"Ten minutes," I repeat as he backs out of the room and smacks his head on the open door.

I can't help the laugh that escapes when he turns and sprints down the hall. His boots tumble to the floor in the hallway, and a sock flies past his bedroom door, a pair of jeans comes a split second later.

"Ten minutes is going to seem like forever," I tell Raider as I climb under Lawson's comforter and get lost in his scent.

I'm tracing the stitching on the side of the pillow when I feel his mouth trail kisses along my spine.

"Sorry I took so long," he whispers against the curve of my ass. "I didn't want to embarrass myself again."

I turn over to face him, not realizing until it was too late that my new position put his mouth hovering right over the apex of my thighs.

"You pre-gamed in the shower?"

He nods, the stubble on his chin scraping in the most delicious way on my inner thigh.

"You said I came too fast in the truck." His tongue parts my most sensitive flesh, but his eyes never leave mine. "I didn't want to disappoint you again."

I shake my head, the overwhelming sensation coming from his mouth's contact with my body making the movements jerky and violent.

"I came, too. You didn't disappoint me."

"I don't want to rush tonight." Another swipe of his addictive tongue. "I want to savor you."

My back arches, the glorious licks of his tongue too much and not enough all at the same time.

His eyes close on a soft blink as he teases my entrance. His warm breath, although hot on release doesn't compare to the burn, the need in my clit. My flesh cools with the gusts then heats again on his inhale.

"You're torturing me," I hiss and grab his hair. My hips grind against his mouth.

My legs are spread even further as he devours me. My vision narrows as all the sensation in my body shrinks down to the tiniest pinpoint before exploding over every nerve in my body. I whimper, begging him to stop all the while pushing harder against his face.

"Fuck you're beautiful when you come."

A weak smile is all I'm able to offer him as he kisses up my body. He didn't bother to dress when he finished his shower, and I'm grateful he doesn't have to waste a second taking off clothes.

His fingers trace the lips of my pussy before diving in an inch and dragging back out.

"Just fuck me already."

He shakes his head, but a lascivious smile spreads across his beautiful face. "I have to make sure you're wet."

"I'm so fucking wet," I pant and wiggle my hips.

"I thought you were last time, too, but when you feel me for the next two days, I want it to be from overuse not because I dry fucked you."

I groan and cover my eyes with my forearm. Why I teased him about that is beyond me.

I hiss, my neck lifting off of the bed when his fingers are replaced with his thick cock.

"Damnit." His breath ghosts over my lips. "I don't think pre-gaming is going to even matter."

I start to laugh, but it comes out as a moan when he circles his hips and pulls my thigh higher on his. The soft thatch of dark hair at the base of his cock works wonders on my bare, waxed skin. The contact is absolute as he mumbles and pleads with his cock not to fuck this up.

"Hey," I manage between pleasure filled sighs as I look into his eyes. His hips slow, but that is the last thing I need. "Make love with your mouth, but fuck me hard with your cock."

He swallows my cries as his hips piston me through another earth-shattering orgasm, and he's still thrusting after he crashes over the edge himself.

"Jesus," he pants as he pulls his cock free and sits back on his heels.

I mewl like a kitten when his finger sweeps across the overly sensitive bundle of nerves.

"I never thought your pussy could look more amazing, but my cum dripping out of it tops all I've ever seen."

"What?" I look down, and sure enough, there's a puddle between my legs. "You didn't use a condom? Why didn't you use one?"

I'm frantic, pushing at him with my feet so I can climb out of his bed.

"Why are you freaking out? I'm clean, D. I swear it. I'd never put you at risk."

He clasps my shoulder before I can get away.

"And if I get pregnant?" I ask turning on him like a rabid dog.

His eyes waver between mine and my stomach, with a longing look in his eyes that heats my blood and somehow makes it run cold at the same time.

"My baby growing in your stomach would be the best thing that could happen to me." I glare at him.

"You can't be serious. So that's your plan? Get me knocked up so I can't walk away from you?"

"I felt your IUD jab the head of my cock on the first thrust, Delilah."

"So what," I say shrugging off his arms. "You think that gives you the right to creampie me?"

His eyes light up, and a chuckle falls from his lips.

"And now you laugh at me. Perfect," I mutter and reach for my clothes on the floor.

"Don't," he says with humor still in his voice. His arms wrap around me from behind. "I'm not laughing at you, but the words *creampie* coming from your pouty lips is funny."

"Let me go." I twist and try to escape him even knowing I won't be released from his strong arms until he wants me to leave them.

"Where do you think you're going?"

"We fucked," I say stating the obvious. "It's time for me to leave."

"Stop," he says turning me to face him. There's more anger in that one word than I've ever heard from his mouth before. "Quit running from me."

"You got what you wanted." I lower my eyes. "Just let me leave."

"Got what I wanted?" He catches my left hand and holds it against his chest. "I won't get what I *want* until there's a ring on your finger and our vows have been spoken before our friends and family."

"It was just sex," I insist even though I know the words are a lie.

"It's not just sex with you, and you know it."

I shake my head, rejecting his words before they can sink into my heart and make me want things I don't deserve.

"If you keep running from me, I'll never be able to prove to you how much I care."

When he pulls me against his chest this time, I don't push him away. I let myself give in to the fantasy.

"Stay with me," he pleads as he inches us closer to the bed.

I don't say yes, but I don't stop him from lowering his mouth to mine and spreading me out on his tangled sheets.

Chapter 38
Lawson

As if I can sense the empty bed in my sleep, I wake with a sheen of cold sweat covering my body.

"This is not happening," I mutter as I climb out and pull on a pair of jeans.

The house is empty, my truck keys left abandoned on the counter in the kitchen, right where I dropped them off last night.

We'd made love a second time before falling asleep tangled in each other's arms. I'd cleaned her after releasing on her flat stomach, not willing to take the chance of another outburst.

"Where did she go?" I ask Raider as if he'll be able to tell me. His head cocks to the side, and I know he's calling me an idiot. "How did she get home?"

The clock on the oven says it's after three in the morning.

"Fuck it," I hiss and head to the bathroom.

Less than ten minutes later, I've dressed, brushed my teeth, and I'm out the door, refusing to let another sunrise happen without getting it through her thick skull that we're going to happen whether she likes it or not.

I bang on her door and pray someone doesn't call the cops.

"Really?" Ivy says when she pulls the door open. "Get your shit together. It's starting to interfere with my life now."

I follow her, going down a door farther when she goes back into her room. I'm in the room and on top of Delilah before she even knows I'm there.

"What are you doing?" She presses ineffectual hands against my chest, so I seize the opportunity to pin them over her head.

Dammit, she smells like sin and everything I need.

"I was a complete asshole to you two years ago. From the day I showed up, I told you all the dirty things I wanted to do to you."

I run my nose up her neck and let her sensual moan wash over me.

I squeeze her wrists harder, and she squirms under me.

"Do I need to treat you like shit again to get you to see me?"

She shakes her head but her lips part on a soft pant.

"I hate being this way to you."

"Liar," she challenges. "You're hard."

I press into her harder, hating the covers and clothes separating us.

"It's biology. I can't help it. You breathe near me, and I get hard. You look at me, and I'm hard. I think about your lips, and I'm hard."

"So fuck me then."

"No."

"You know you want me." Her hips rotate against mine, grinding the zipper of my jeans against my cock.

"Always," I swear. "Every minute of the day I want to be inside of your body."

"You can have me," she offers.

"I won't deny I want to be here." I punctuate my words by pressing my straining dick against the center of her thighs. "But I want to be here more."

I press my mouth over her heart, my lips warming against her heated skin.

"That's not part of the deal," she whispers and turns her head as her eyes close.

I rest more of my weight on her. "That's what you're not getting, Delilah. You can fight this between us as much as you want and it will only serve to make me fight more."

"Don't." The plea from her lips is sad and full of despair as if she can't accept the things I'm saying to her.

"I'm going to fight for you," I promise. "For your time, your heart, and most importantly, your love."

"Loving you has never been the problem."

My heart soars...

"Trusting you not to walk away when things get hard is what I can't allow."

...And crashes to the earth, shattering into a hundred pieces.

"I'll do anything for a chance to prove that we belong together." I softly kiss her lips. "Tell me what you need, baby, and it's yours."

"I need time."

I shake my head. "You'll only use it to push me away."

"You're smothering me."

I lean back some, taking most of my weight back and putting it on my knees.

"Not in the literal sense." She reaches for me when I release her hands and pull away. "I love the press of your body against mine."

"That's contradictory, Princess. I don't know if I'm coming or going with you."

"You could be coming soon." She swivels her hips again, and I back away entirely and sit on the edge of the bed.

My head hits my hands as I press my elbows into my thighs.

"You make me wonder if you're only using me for sex."

The tinkle of her laugh meets my ears and makes my throat burn. Now I know how she felt when I laughed at her earlier in my room.

"That's funny to you?" I ask and angle my head so I can look in her eyes.

"You're an amazing lay. The best I've ever had."

The words sting like a thousand pinpricks on my skin, but I don't know if it's her callous delivery or the knowledge that she's been with other men.

"You've probably ruined me for other men."

"Enough," I roar and pin her back down to the mattress. "You won't have to worry about comparing me to other men, Princess. My cock is the last one that will ever have the pleasure of bringing you to orgasm."

"Your cock is the only one that's managed it to begin with."

"You gave yourself to men who didn't deserve you, baby. Now I'm tasked with making up for my mistake for the rest of your life." I lean in close, our mouths a mere inch apart. "Challenge accepted."

"*My* mistake," she says, her voice breaking on the last word.

"I own it a million times over, baby. I should've shown up and banged on your dorm room door the minute you arrived. Fuck that," I correct. "I never should've left New Mexico without telling you how I feel."

"How do you feel?" There's a softness in her eyes I haven't seen since I kissed her the very first time.

"I love you with every molecule of my soul." She gasps. "Don't act surprised. I've told you as often as I can."

"You never used those words." Her eyes squeeze shut.

"Don't block me out when I've laid my heart in your hands. If you can't see yourself feeling the same way, I have the patience of a saint. I'll spend every second of my life making you realize that you're safe." I press my lips to her forehead. "Your *heart* is safe with me."

I back away from her.

"Where are you going?" she asks when I climb off the bed.

"Home," I answer, still unable to face her.

I don't know what I was expecting from her when I finally had the courage to say those words to her, but the sting of her not saying them back burns more than I'd like to admit.

"Stay," she pleads, but I shake my head.

"I can't."

"You can."

"If I climb under those covers and feel the warmth of your body, I'll end up sinking inside of you."

"Sounds like an incredible plan to me." The playfulness after such a serious conversation gives me hope and makes my already hard dick twitch in my jeans.

"That's not what either of us needs." I lean in and kiss her one more time, lingering on her lips for a long moment before standing up again.

"Who's walking away now?" She asks my back as I reach for the doorknob. I know she's teasing but now is not the time.

"This isn't a game, Delilah."

"I never said it was." The hint of anger in her voice comes from nowhere.

"Then quit playing. Your words have consequences."

Her bottom lip quivers in the darkness. "I asked you to stay, and you say you have to go. I can't beg you, Lawson. I don't have it in me."

My shoulders slump forward at the thought of causing her pain, but I need to back away, go home, and lick my wounds. Only then can I regroup and figure out how I need to approach this situation.

She turns over, giving me her back before she speaks again. "I just wanted you to hold me."

"Damn it," I grumble and kick off my boots. My jeans and t-shirt hit the floor next.

She moves forward, giving me more room behind her when I pull the covers back.

"You left my bed," I remind her as my arms wrap around her. "We were lying just like this when I fell asleep. Tell me why you left."

"I don't feel like I deserve you."

I hold her tighter. "You deserve the world, baby, and I plan to give it to you."

Chapter 39
Delilah

"Do you think he even noticed?"

I smile at the guy from my Ethics in Psychology class as he follows me out of the building.

"I don't know how he couldn't. He wasn't wearing any underwear," I tell him with a quick laugh.

"Exactly! If my fly was down while going commando, I know I'd feel the cold air on my dick."

"What would you feel on your dick?"

I stop cold at Lawson's words, but my heart warms at the sight of him standing in front of us, hard scowl and everything.

The guy I was walking with, whose name I don't even know, takes a step back.

"What about your dick?" Lawson asks again with more fire in his voice than the first time.

"Stop," I tell him with a gentle hand on his chest and a quick kiss on his lips.

"Not my dick, dude." He holds his hands up in mock surrender, but Lawson's face still doesn't settle.

"Umm..." I look at the guy from class.

"John," he says eventually.

"John and I were discussing whether our professor knew his fly was down."

"He was commando. I was telling Delilah that he had to have felt the cold air on his dick." He clears his throat. "His dick, nothing about my dick."

"Which class?" Lawson asks without pulling his glaring scrutiny from John.

"Ethics in Psychology," I answer when it seems John has suddenly become mute.

Only then does Lawson look over at me, his eyes softening immediately. "He was testing you. I wouldn't be surprised if he failed all of you for staring *unethically* at his junk all through class without telling him."

I grin at Lawson, knowing full well he's full of shit. I had the same professor last semester, and he's a hot mess on his best day.

"Fuck my life," John mutters. "I already failed that damn class last year. My parents will kill me if I don't pass it this time around."

Lawson's arm curls around my hip, and he turns me away. "Nice meeting you, Jim."

We walk away, John refusing to correct the man at my side.

"Stop," I tell him with a playful slap to his hard stomach. "You'll give that poor boy a heart attack."

"You need a bodyguard," he mutters as we near his truck.

"Where are we going? And you need to stop worrying about the boys in my class."

"Lunch," he tells me offering his hand so I can climb inside. "And that *boy* wanted to fuck you."

I wait to roll my eyes until he's behind the wheel of the truck. "He's awkward at best, besides you have nothing to worry about."

"Yeah?" He cranks the truck but doesn't make a move to put it in gear to leave the parking lot. "And why is that?"

"Lawson O'Neil, are you fishing for compliments?"

He shrugs. "I'll take what I can get."

"Waking up in your arms again this morning was amazing." I flip up the console separating us and crawl closer to him. "But my body misses you. It's hard being so close to you and not feeling you between my legs."

His hands clench the steering wheel until his knuckles turn white, but he doesn't touch me.

I lean in and swipe my nose up the stubble on his chin, relishing his sharp inhale.

"We've slept in the same bed the last three nights." I lick at his ear. "I miss you."

"I'm right here, Princess."

I cup him through the denim of his jeans.

"And ready for me," I whisper in his ear.

"I'm not fucking you in the truck again."

"Then make love to me on the hood," I tease.

He finally turns his face so I can kiss his lips. "You have the ability to test the virtue of a saint. I'd bet my life on it."

"Yet, you're the only one I want to sin with."

"No." He pulls my hand away from his cock, but the strain on his face tells me it pains him to do so. "You're on a new diet."

I raise an eyebrow at him.

"Cock light."

I chuckle at the ridiculousness, but it doesn't thwart my efforts like I'm sure he hoped it would. I turn his palm in mine and press it between my legs. I've never been so glad to be wearing a skirt than I am today.

"Cock light?" He nods and a grumble roars in his chest at finding me wet. "So just the tip then?"

"Sorry, Princess." He pulls his hand away, and I whimper at the loss.

"What's your end game?" I say giving up and flopping back in my seat.

"Your heart." Two simple words that leave me speechless as he puts the truck in drive and leaves my college in the distance.

"This is all your fault to begin with," I accuse with my arms crossed over my chest. "I wasn't even worried about sex until I straddled the damn gear shift in the wrecker."

"I could smell you then," he whispers. "I had a wet spot on my jeans from my cock leaking the rest of the afternoon."

"Gross." I cross my legs but resist the urge to roll the window down. "No, you couldn't."

"I swear it, baby." He licks the tip of his finger that he just had against my panties. "Smells even better now that you've gotten past the hating me stage."

"That's disgusting." Those are my words, but my body responds differently by softening, quickening, and begging for him to take me.

He inhales deep into his lungs when we pull up to a red light.

"Stop," I say with a laugh and slap his chest. "You're crazy."

He grabs my hand that I left lingering against the muscled wall of his chest and brings it to his lips. I pull it back when my phone chimes a text. I pull it out and frown at the screen.

"What's that look for?" It's the same question Ivy asked last week when a similar text came through.

"Party," I mumble. "I left all the groups on social media, and now people are texting me about them."

"I'm not going to stop you from having a good time."

I roll my eyes. "I've never had a good time at a single party I've gone to. Well, it no longer seemed fun the day after."

I look out the window and pray he asks me about them. I have a ton of things that need to be out in the open, for us to talk them through before I ever have a hope of getting past them.

"Really? I thought you couldn't go wrong at a college party, but hangovers suck."

"And vodka makes everything seem like a good idea."

He chuckles, not catching on to the serious tone of my voice.

"The three guys I slept with this summer, I met at college parties."

He stiffens, squeezing my hand a little too tight at my admission.

"Sorry," I mutter. "I shouldn't have brought it up. I know you don't want to hear about it, but I swear I didn't bring it up to make you mad."

I try to pull my hand back, but he maintains his grasp.

"I hate hearing about it, but I understand that you need to get it off of your chest." He kisses the soft skin on my wrist. "Put it out there, baby so we can work through it."

I wait until we're moving again, his focus on driving making it easier for the words to come.

"The first party I went to was after a long conversation with Samson. I was feeling brave and admitted my feelings for you. Put some of the blame on you hurting me right at his feet."

We stop at another red light, and I wait, keeping my eyes focused outside even though I can feel his eyes on the side of my face.

He inches forward, turning right which leads to a more rural area with fewer red lights. He's already caught on and wants me to keep talking.

When the open road stretches out in front of us, I continue.

"We'd had a similar fight the night you snuck in my room. I had every intention of pushing you away that night. He'd threatened to talk to Dad and tell him what was going on between us. He only had suspicions but he can read me like an open book, and I was scared for what that info in Dad's lap would mean for you and Drew."

I trace the window seam with my finger searching for the words.

"That night three months ago, he was an asshole all over again. He told me that I just needed to get over it, get over you. I went to that party and took every drink that was offered to me. When a guy I didn't even know suggested we go somewhere private, I thought it was the best idea in the world. I mean I went there on a mission, but that didn't mean I wanted to do all of that with an audience."

I swipe at the tears rolling down my cheeks and ignore Lawson's ragged breathing.

"When it was over, I felt vindicated. Free from whatever ties I had to you, but then I woke up the next day realizing what I'd done. I cried for a week. I cried until the next party. Then I did the same thing again, praying it would be different. Hoping that I'd feel something, anything with him, but I only felt empty and used."

I look over at Lawson as he pulls the truck over to the side of the road. The tears staining his cheeks makes the bile crawl up my throat, but I'm not done.

"I did it a third time." His eyes search mine, and I have no clue what he's looking for. At this point, I imagine he's going to call me a whore and kick me out of the truck. "The day before my car broke down I was with someone else."

Shame weighs heavy on my shoulders. "I don't even know their names. I was drunk every time. Not that I'm using that as an excuse, but I had to have the alcohol to go through with it."

"Baby."

I shake my head when he tugs my hand, an indication for me to get closer to him. "I cried each time. Even Ivy heard my sobs through the bedroom wall. I cried after we made love in this very truck."

Another squeeze of my hand.

"Not because I was ashamed of you, but because I ruined what could've been between us. I understand if you hate me, but please don't make me walk home from here."

He releases a pitiful laugh. "I could never hate you."

"You should've been my first," I tell him. "It was always meant to be you."

"And you should've been mine," he adds quietly. "But it didn't work out that way."

"You're being too nice."

"Do you hate me for the women that came before you?"

"I hate that there were others," I confess.

"But do you hate *me*?"

I look into his red-rimmed blue eyes and shake my head. "I never hated you."

"Then understand that I feel exactly the same way."

I finally allow him to pull me into his lap. His lips rest against my temple as he cradles me to his chest.

"Even now with all of this sitting heavy in the air around us, my body hums for you," I confess against his t-shirt.

"Is it only your body that wants me?"

I know exactly what he's asking, and I know that if he can forgive me for what I did while hurting, then it's damn time I forgive myself.

Chapter 40
Lawson

"Where are we going?" There's a smile, a lightness in her voice that hasn't been there in a long time.

"You'll see." I wink at her and take the next road to the left.

"You mentioned lunch back on campus. Are you planning some romantic picnic?"

I frown. "I wish I'd thought of that, Princess, but honestly I'd just planned to eat a meal with you while staring at your mouth."

"Oh." She doesn't sound disappointed, but there's an edge to the word that I don't like.

"The conversation got super serious really quick, and that wasn't planned either." I make another right and come up to the fast food place. "I don't have a picnic planned, but we can grab something quick and then go someplace where it's just you and me."

"That sounds perfect." She leans her head on my shoulder as we wait in line at the drive-thru. I'm thankful for the adjustable console in the truck. She'll never sit apart from me again.

The speaker crackles with a generic menu suggestion when we make it to the ordering sign. "No onions," she whispers.

No onions mean kissing, and I'm totally down for that. I place our order and wait to move up to the window.

"How was class today?"

"Are you asking about school or the boys in my classes?"

"Both," I say telling the truth.

"Was Jim one of the guys you umm... met at the parties?"

"His name is John," she corrects. I know that, but don't want to give her the satisfaction. "And no. I haven't seen any of them since their respective parties. There's a chance they aren't even college students."

She leans away long enough for me to pull cash out of my wallet, but then her tight little body is back against mine.

"Why are you asking?"

I shrug and hand the cashier the money.

"You planning on tracking them down and beating them up."

"Fuck, I wish," I mumble.

Her lips form a smile against my skin.

"Does it turn you on that I want to beat up the men that hurt you?"

"*I* hurt me," she corrects. "They were just the catalyst that allowed it."

I take my change and pull up to the second window.

"I love how possessive you are."

My heart clenches at the word *love* coming from her lips. She may not be saying it in the context I want, but I'll take what I can get.

"I love how you fight for me, knowing exactly what you want and not taking no for an answer." She nips at my neck and as sweet as her words are, it doesn't stop my cock from jerking in my jeans. "How you knew what I wanted, what I *needed*, even when I didn't."

"It's my job, Princess."

"I let less than a dozen words spoken in one sentence two years ago ruin me. I let them have power over me."

She pauses as our food is passed through the window. I hand her the bags so she can place them beside her on the seat and reach to place the drinks in the backseat console. I'll be damned if I'm separating us while this conversation is still going.

With my mind, I beg her to continue, but she remains silent as we head out of town. It isn't until the city scene transitions into empty fields that she begins again.

"I wasted two years of my life pretending to hate you. I let my anger fuel my bad decisions while I was self-destructing."

I pull over at a deserted rest stop, no longer able to concentrate on driving, and when I turn her face up to mine, I no longer see the pain that's been on her beautiful face all afternoon. I find acceptance and a small smile that tells me everything is going to be okay.

"I'm tired of wasting time."

"What are you saying, baby?"

Her eyes drag down to my lips before focusing back on mine.

"I'm not fighting you anymore. I'm not running from you. I'm not pulling away when all I want is to be near you."

I kiss her lips, soft and sweet, full of promises of forever rather than instant sexual gratification.

"That's the second best thing I've heard from your lips."

I kiss her again.

"And the best thing?"

Smiling I turn her chin and run my tongue down the soft slope of her neck, and nip at her earlobe before whispering, "That tiny whimper you make when I sink inside of you."

She makes that sound now, and my balls tighten as if programmed to respond. I groan and flex my hips up when her hand strokes down my length.

"You sure are a dirty talker." She squeezes with just the right amount of pressure. "Are you sure about my new diet?"

Her lips find mine, tongue seeking entry which I allow without hesitation.

"I think you can splurge." My hand wraps around the back of her head, and I angle her mouth to the perfect position. "A cheat meal so to speak."

She stiffens in my arms, and that's when I know that although she may want to forget about her anger and her pain from two years ago, it's still something she's going to have to work through.

"Seeing as I know how hungry your pussy is." She relaxes. "I might be persuaded to feed it my cock."

"Right here?" she pants, pulling back and reaching for the hem of her short skirt.

"No." Damn, that was difficult to say. I ease the rejection with a swipe of my finger over the wet lace between her thighs.

"You know I thought it was hot fuc... making love in this truck the first time." Her hips swivel against my fingers, and my resolve begins to slip. "Don't you want to smell my pussy in here for the next couple of days?"

"Jesus, Princess." I conjure the willpower that seems to be non-existent around her. "I won't be able to smell your pussy, taste your pussy, or thrust every inch of my cock inside of it if I'm sitting in jail pending addition to the sex offender list."

Her eyes narrow until I point down the road. The Rhode Island State Police car rolls by, the officer taking in the scene. Delilah shoves her skirt down and repositions herself in her seat as the patrol car turns into the rest area and parks behind us. I pull out my license, insurance, and gun permit placing them on the dash.

A couple of years ago, my first instinct when watching a cop walk up to the back of my truck would've been to run. Today? I simply roll the window down and place my hands on the steering wheel, smiling when he introduces himself.

"Hello, Officer." The purr of Delilah's voice pisses me off because it's not directed at me, but my cock doesn't mind and remains thick in my jeans.

Officer Hamill leans in further, looking around and I don't miss the deep inhale of his breath.

"You folks eating lunch?" His knowing smile tells me he can smell more than just the fast food.

"Yes, sir," I answer.

He takes the documents from the dash and tells me he'll be right back after making sure everything checks out.

"We weren't doing anything wrong," Delilah mutters as she looks over her shoulder at the officer as he slides back into his car.

"We were only minutes from getting arrested." My eyes trail up her golden thighs.

"He had no clue what was happening before he pulled up."

I shake my head. "See the way he leaned in." I check the rearview mirror and run my finger up her thigh, the fabric of her skirt lifting the higher I go. "He knew exactly what we were up to."

She slaps my hand away. "You're giving me a complex. I feel like I need to shower."

"You have the sweetest pussy in the world, Delilah and you smell positively intoxicating." I pin her with my eyes. "I wouldn't be surprised if he has to wait in his car for his erection to dissipate, or worse yet, trump up some fake charges and arrest me, so he can have a chance at you."

"I'm yours," she whispers.

"I know, baby, but you can't blame the man for being desperate."

She catches movement out of the corner of her eye and straightens again just before the officer reaches the window.

"Everything looks good, Mr. O'Neil." He hands me the documents back. "Have a nice day. Drive safe."

I chuckle when I hear him mutter 'lucky fucking bastard' as I situate my license back in my wallet.

"You're incorrigible," she mutters and puts her seatbelt back on. "Let's get out of here. I'm hungry."

The look in her eye tells me that our meal has been forgotten. I can't get out of that rest area and back to my house fast enough.

Chapter 41
Delilah

"Does he always do that?" I ask around a bite of burger.

"I told you he was useless," Lawson says with a chuckle, but he tosses Raider a French fry anyway.

"I love that you have a dog," I tell him after a quick sip of my drink.

Raider catches another fry with a quick snap of his jaw. "I always liked dogs, but I began to love them when I helped you at the animal shelter."

For the first time, I don't stiffen when he references our time then.

I pat Raider's head and give in when all he wants to do is lick my fingers. "I wanted a dog when I moved here, but I knew I didn't have enough time for one. It wouldn't be fair."

"You can visit him anytime," he tells me with a smile on his face. "If you moved in…"

"Too soon," I mutter, but there's no venom in my voice.

"Never," he whispers, which is just barely audible over the sound of him crushing the take-out trash in his big hands and walking to throw it away.

"What now?" I ask when he returns from the kitchen.

"Stay the night with me?"

I grin.

"Please? I sleep better with you in my arms."

I melt into a puddle on his damn couch.

"And you think you'll get any sleep if I stay?"

His teeth scrape over his bottom lip, and I long for that on my nipples, my clit.

"Eventually," he says as he prowls closer.

"I thought I was on a cock light diet."

His hand cups my cheek as he leans down and brushes his lips across mine. "I thought I mentioned a cheat day."

"So I go back on a diet tomorrow?"

He shakes his head. "Three nights is my limit."

Smiling against his lips, I twine my arms over his shoulders and around his neck. "We had sex here before you went all caveman and showed up at my apartment. So it's only been two nights."

"I'm a weak man."

My fingers flex on the corded muscle at his nape.

"You feel incredibly strong to me."

"You flatter me, baby." With this, he lifts me from the sofa. My legs, instinctively, wrap around his waist as he carries me down the hall.

"So strong." I nip at his chin and slide my hand down until I'm gripping his length. I moan at the brush of my own hand against my panties. "Every long, thick inch of you."

"I love it when you touch me," he hisses into my neck when I squeeze him harder. "Love it when I wake in the morning, and your scent is all over my skin."

"I love *you*," I confess.

"Baby." His voice cracks as he's unable to hide his emotion over my words.

I move my body with him as we strip each other naked before falling onto his bed. When he nibbles at my breast and presses inside of me, I finally feel complete. I'm whole after having been shattered and broken for such a long time

"Every day," he vows against my throat when he pushes to the hilt. "Every single day for the rest of my life, I need this with you."

I clench around him, my body agreeing before I can find the words. His back arches when my short nails scrape down his spine, and it drives him even deeper.

"You're close," he predicts with the truth. "You get hotter, tighter."

I moan my response.

"Fuck, baby. I'm going to come inside of you."

"Please," I beg.

The bite of his teeth on my neck beckons me to the edge, and I crash over not even a second later. The trembling of my body is matched by his as we both struggle for breath.

"Tell me again," he urges after pulling from me and holding me against his chest.

I trace the ridges of his stomach with the tip of my finger. His muscles are rock solid and standing out, the exertion of our love-making acting as an incredible ab workout.

"I love you."

He holds me even tighter, and as I fall asleep, sated and completely in love, I pray that he never lets me go.

***

"This is lovely," I say looking around at the small café. "Seems like we're the wrong clientele though."

"What do you mean?" Lawson asks as he blows over the top of his steaming hot coffee.

"We're the oldest ones here, and that's saying a lot since I'm only nineteen."

"Just a baby."

I give him my best, salacious grin and lean in closer. "You didn't treat me like a baby this morning."

He clears his throat. "Was I too rough?"

I lick my lips, drawing his attention to them. "I don't think that's a possibility, but I still feel you deep inside."

"Princess," he warns. "I don't care if I have to shove a dozen teenage boys out of the bathroom, I'll fuck you in there if you don't stop."

I slip off my flip-flop and run my toe up his leg until my foot is nestled against his hardening cock.

"Make love," I correct.

"No, baby." He leans closer, and I mirror his action. "I will stuff your panties in your mouth, hike that too short fucking skirt up, and bend you over the sink. I'll twist that blonde ponytail around my fist until your back bows to the perfect angle and pound into you until you beg me to stop."

"There's your problem," I coo while stroking his length with my foot under the table. "I'd never beg you to stop."

"Bathroom, now," he hisses, but before he can stand fully, a shadow looms over the table.

I look up into the familiar eyes of a boy I never thought I'd see again.

I nearly knock everything over on the table in my rush to get out of the booth and my arms around his neck.

"Drew!"

He squeezes me, holding me against his hard chest. I push back a few inches, my hands placed over muscles he didn't have a few years ago. His hands slide lower on my back to give me the room I need.

"Nice," I tell him. I'm beaming, probably looking like an idiot in this café full of adolescents, but I don't have a care in the world.

"I swear, little brother," Lawson sneers. "If your hands go any lower you won't be able to hold your lacrosse stick."

"He seems as sunshiny as ever," Drew mutters before giving me another quick hug. As his brother commands, his hands stay where they are.

"He's very possessive," I whisper as Drew reaches out and shakes his brother's hand. Lawson scoots over on his side of the booth, but Drew, being the shit stirrer that he is, sits beside me and wraps his arm around my shoulders. Unconcerned with the mirth and feigned anger on Lawson's face, I allow Drew to cradle me against his chest.

"Fuck you smell good."

Lawson chuckles at Drew's comment, and I kick him under the table. He winks at me, and I pull away from Drew immediately.

"What is that," Drew asks not giving up.

When his nose sweeps up my neck, inhaling like a maniac, even the smack on his chest doesn't stop Lawson from growling at his brother.

"Quit," I tell Drew and scoot a few more inches closer to the wall.

He looks down at me. "Fuck, I've missed you."

He shifts in his seat and swipes a lock of blonde hair behind my ear. A second later he's being hauled out of the booth and repositioned on the opposite side of the table.

"Get your own," Lawson says sitting down beside me and practically pulling me into his lap.

A wide grin spreads across Drew's face, one so similar to the first one Lawson gave me in the dark back home on his first night with us, my breath catches in my throat. Oh, this boy is going to be a lady killer.

"Believe me, big brother, I get plenty." He winks at me, and all I can do is shake my head and laugh at how even years later he's riling his brother up. "None as pretty as Delilah though."

"Stop," I tell him on a laugh. "Lawson is the most protective man I know."

"Not even blood will keep me from breaking your hand." Drew smiles even wider, his eyes never pulling from mine. "Or poking your eyes out if you keep staring at my girl like you want to eat her."

Lawson slaps the table, making the condiment basket jump an inch when Drew over-exaggerates licking his lips at the suggestion.

His eyes sober when they find his brother's, and his throat works on a hard swallow. He's not afraid of Lawson so I know that's not the cause of his change in emotion. They share a look, Lawson nodding at his brother as he holds me tighter.

"I'm so fucking happy for you."

Tears clog my throat at witnessing the relief in Drew's face at finally seeing his brother happy.

Chapter 42
Lawson

"Quit fidgeting," Ivy whisper-hisses to her best friend as we near the front of the clubhouse.

I tried to hold her hand in the back of the SUV after all of the hugs Dad and Rob showered us both with, but she jerks her hand away from mine.

Sitting between Ivy and myself, she doesn't have anywhere to go.

"Stop." Her eyes dart to the front of the vehicle before turning her fiery blue gaze back to me. "We haven't told them yet."

Rob twists the knob on the radio and turns the volume down. "What was that, sweetheart?"

I chuckle finding Dad's eyes in the rearview mirror.

"N-nothing, Pop."

Rob insists on taking our suitcases upstairs the second we make it through the front door, and my fingers itch to guide Delilah to the dining room with my hand on the small of her back. Knowing she'll freak out is the only reason why I don't.

The last three months have been the most blissful time of my life. Sure we fight and argue, but I can always pull her back before she storms off. We don't say things in anger or bring up our past. We left all of that on the floor of my bedroom the night she told me she loved me the first time.

"Smells great in here," I say to the room, but my words ghost over Delilah's back and I revel in the sight of goosebumps crawling up her back.

She steps away as if I swatted her on the ass.

"I've missed you," she tells Samson as she wraps her arms around his neck.

He gives me a quick nod before spinning her around. It's not the evil eye, so it seems like progress. When he releases her, he shakes my hand and pulls me into a back-slapping hug, I wonder what Dad used to bribe him with. Samson has never been my biggest fan, so the olive branch is a little weird.

"How was the trip?" he asks when we separate.

"Good," Delilah answers giving us a wide berth. I hate the distance between us right now, but I know how seriously freaked out she is about informing them of our relationship.

I spend the next couple of hours talking with the guys while Delilah, Rob, and Dad take turns baking, mixing, and preparing things for Thanksgiving dinner tomorrow.

I love spending time with them, but exhaustion hits me hard in the chest and my night isn't even close to being over. I tell everyone good night while Delilah is in the pantry searching for a lost can of sweet potatoes. She's made a plan, one we discussed ad nauseam about how we will go about the next four days.

One of us is to go upstairs while the other waits an acceptable amount of time, then the other can go up. At first, she insisted we just sleep separate, but after a three-hour session where I toyed with her but didn't let her come, she agreed to let me join her after she was sure everyone else was asleep. That's not happening either.

The wait is miserable, thirty minutes of lying in her bed waiting for her to join me.

"You can't be in here," she hisses but closes her door quietly. "Damnit."

She cusses when she damn near trips over my suitcase.

"Why did you bring your luggage in here?"

She's still standing in the middle of the room, petulant fists on her slim hips.

"I didn't bring them in here." Her arms fall. "Rob did."

She hisses, but remembers herself. After looking over her shoulder, she closes the distance between us.

"They know?"

"Do you think we could hide it from them if they didn't?"

"I'm an open book."

"You are, baby."

Her bright white teeth scrape over her bottom lip as she reaches for me, and the rule she'd made me swear to chooses this moment to infiltrate my brain.

"You can hold me at night, but we can't have sex."

"Keep looking at me like that, Princess and I'm going to break my promise."

"The last time we were in here together," she begins, and my blood runs cold.

I have no idea what being back here is making her feel, but I pray we've made enough progress that we can work through her feelings quickly.

I groan when her hand runs over my cock. He's been behaving but gets her message loud and clear as he thickens for her on contact.

"The last time we were together here, I started something I didn't finish."

I'm breathless by the time she drops to her knees and molten lava when she unzips my jeans and pulls my cock free.

It's my turn for my teeth to sink into my lower lip, and when I look down at her, I see a different expression on her face than I did back then. Tonight, the softness of her features are combined with more love than anyone has ever offered me.

"Baby, you don't have to." In fact, she never has before, and I'm not asshole enough to even raise the subject around her.

"I want to." I wobble as her tongue snakes out and swipes the dew from the tip.

"Fuck," I moan as she widens her jaw, cheeks hollowing as she sucks rhythmically on the tip.

She smiles, lips pulling away revealing the slight contrast of my deeper pink tinted cock on her perfectly pink tongue.

"Say it," she urges me.

"I love you." My hand trembles as it cups the delicate curve of her jaw.

"Not that."

"No." With resolute surety, I shake my head and try to take a step back. She clings to my thighs with both of her hands preventing my retreat.

"Say it," she repeats.

"Baby, I can't. I *won't*."

"Please?" Begging isn't something she often does, so I'm well aware of how serious this situation is. "Say it."

She must see the resolve to please her in my eyes because her mouth goes to work on my cock, sucking, stroking, and teasing her fingers over my tight sac.

"I told you, you'd have those pretty pink lips wrapped around my cock."

Brightness fills her eyes at the same moment I fill her mouth.

"Goddammit," I groan when she sucks me through my release. "Stop."

The sensation of her tongue licking the tip sends bolts of electricity up my spine.

She smacks her lips, grin never faltering as she stands. I accept her mouth against mine and hiss when her tongue, heady with the taste of me, slides against my own.

"I bet I can still make you come with one finger."

Her pants become my own as she pushes against my chest until I'm flat on my back on her childhood bed.

"Add in that talented tongue of yours, and you have a deal."

"Be quiet, baby," I warn when I grip her hips and position her over my face.

A minute is all it takes with my tongue, my finger, and the grinding of her hips. She, in fact, doesn't stay quiet as she comes down my throat with a roar.

"Do you think they heard us?" Even in the soft light of the moon, I can see the pink tint to her cheeks, there, I'm certain, from both her orgasm and the embarrassment of being heard by her family.

I chuckle as I slide off the bed and dig in my suitcase.

"Answer my question, and I'll answer yours."

She rolls over to her side, unconcerned about the exposure of her breasts and the shadow at the apex of her thighs that is hiding the luxury between her legs.

"And what is your question?"

I hit my knees on the edge of her bed. With the odds in my favor, the moon hits the diamond in the ring at just the right moment.

"Lawson?"

"Put me out of my misery and marry me?"

"But Dad—"

I press my fingers against her lips.

"Your Dad accepted my love for you long before you did, baby."

"You asked?" I can hear the wobble in her voice, but I know what she's going to say because there's only one viable answer to the question.

"Three months ago."

"Three?" I smile at the edge of shock in her voice.

"The night you told me you loved me."

"I love you so much."

"Baby, you still haven't answered my question."

A tear streaks down her face as she looks from the ring and back up to me. "Ask me again?"

I swallow, emotion clogging my throat in the best way. "Delilah Donovan, will you marry me?"

"Yes!"

Her arms wrap around my neck, the warmth of her happy tears on my chest. I slip the ring on her finger at the exact moment I slip my cock inside of her. Bliss.

Chapter 43
Delilah

"Jesus, everyone is here already." The sounds of multiple conversations wash over us as we enter the clubhouse from the back door.

"That's perfect." Lawson pecks me on the lips. "Stop shaking. Why are you nervous?"

He stops near the door to the laundry room and pulls me to his chest.

"Are you happy?" I nod against his soft t-shirt. "Then they'll be happy for you."

I take a deep breath, kiss his perfect lips, and let him lead me to the family room.

"She said yes!" he yells the second we cross over the threshold.

"Real fucking subtle," I mutter as applause and yells of joy fill my ears.

Dad and Pop are the first to reach me.

"I couldn't be happier for you," Dad says in my ear before releasing me to wrap his arms around Lawson.

"Sweetheart," Pop says before engulfing me in his big arms. I edge away from the tickle of his beard on my neck, laughing as he squeezes me again.

"Congrats, brother." I freeze at the sound of Samson's voice and nearly faint when I look over to see him hugging my fiancé.

Hell has officially frozen over.

"Thanks," Lawson says just as shocked as I am.

"I couldn't imagine a better man for my sister."

Lawson only nods, the same emotional look on his face when Drew gave his approval three months ago. I know if he talks right now, his voice will crack, so I do the only thing I can; I cry for him.

The endless line of congratulations and hugs seem to take forever but stops eventually. It isn't until I see Gigi across the room that I realize she's the only one who didn't walk up to us during the procession of well-wishers. She gives me a small smile, and there's more heartbreak in that one action than I've ever experienced for myself.

I go to walk in her direction, but Lawson pulls me against his chest.

"I told you everything would go just fine."

I'm lost when I look up into his eyes, forgetting all about the pain in Gigi's eyes.

"I've never been happier."

"Let's go have a seat until dinner," he suggests, but I pull away from the warmth of his chest.

"Can't." I step away from him. "I have to make the rolls."

I expect him to head over to the guys and talk about manly shit, but he follows me into the kitchen, helping me butter the tops before slipping them into the oven.

Wrapped around my back with his hands low on my belly, he kisses my neck. "I can't wait to put my baby here."

I smile but shake my head. "Not for some time. I want you all to myself for a while. Plus, I need to get through school."

A throat clears behind us, and Lawson turns both of us without releasing me. Dad is standing there, and I freeze. I know he knows we're together. I know he said he was happy for us, but it doesn't make facing him all wrapped up in Lawson any easier.

"Do I need to spray you two with the hose?" His voice is serious, but the smile on his face makes me think he's joking, mostly anyways.

"No," I say and try to pull away. Lawson only holds me tighter.

"What were you talking about?"

"Babies," Lawson answers immediately.

Dad's hand stills mere inches from the handle on the refrigerator. When he turns and shoots lasers at Lawson, I freeze.

"You promised me at least two years, Law." He holds up two fingers for emphasis. "Two."

"About that." My eyes widen when Lawson runs his hand low on my belly. "Will Pop still go by Pop when he's a granddad? What do you want them to call you?"

I swear my dad stops breathing.

"Them?" I've never heard my dad's voice squeak before.

"Quit." I step out of Lawson's arms and reach for my dad, laughing at how wide his eyes are as they focus on my stomach. "I'm not pregnant, Dad. He's messing with you."

Dad's eyes narrow as he looks at Lawson. "You're sleeping on the couch."

"The bunk bed would be more comfortable," Lawson counters.

"Like hell," Dad mutters. "You snuck in her room two years ago, and I know you'll do it again. The couch is all yours."

"Yes, sir."

Not the response I was expecting, but I also don't expect the wink Dad gives me before he walks out to repair his damaged nerves.

"That was fun," Lawson says with a wide smile on his face.

"You're awful," I tell him with a soft laugh and turn back to the oven to pull out the first batch of rolls.

***

"How are you liking that *cream pie*?"

I nearly choke on the bite in my mouth when Lawson whispers those dirty words in my ear.

When the wheezing stops, I turn and glare at him and shrug. "I've had better."

"It's a shame that so many people think Boston makes the best ones, but I know mine is better."

"I'd ask for proof, but that would be rather difficult from the couch."

He chuckles, but when he focuses on something across the room his brow furrows.

"What's going on with those two?"

I follow his line of sight and see Griffin talking to a very straight-backed Ivy.

"Don't you know," I tell him in a low whisper. "Ivy is so in love with that boy she doesn't see anyone else when he's around."

"Really?" He sounds surprised. "I thought he was into Gigi."

"And thus lies the problem," I mutter.

The mention of Gigi's name causes me to look around the room and search for her. She was abnormally quiet during dinner and excused herself before she'd eaten half the food on her plate. Something's going on, and everyone at the table could feel the tension between her and her parents.

When I find her, she's across the room and Diego is in her face. I can't hear what they're talking about, but if the tears on her cheeks are any indication she's not happy one bit.

"Gigi doesn't have a clue, and I'm pretty sure Griffin is clueless about Ivy," I respond to him without pulling my eyes from the parental confrontation.

"Shit. That's kind of sad."

"Incredibly," I agree.

"Ready for bed?" The suggestion in his tone has my thighs squeezing together.

"That's not even a possibility. It's barely seven. There's not one person in this house that would believe we're going back to the room to sleep."

Lawson, facing the challenge raises his arms over his head and yawns. In a voice loud enough for everyone near to hear, he says, "Man, that turkey is making me sleepy."

I swat at him even though he gets several agreements from the room.

"Worked like a charm," he says with a quick grin. "Let's go."

"Not so fast." I tilt my head in the direction of my Dad and Pop.

"Dammit," he mutters when Dad glares at him and shakes his head.

"You should've kept your damn mouth closed." I lean my head on his shoulder. Just the mention of being sleepy in relation to the big meal I just ate makes me truly sleepy. "Too bad because now I have to sleep alone."

"We'll get a hotel ro—"

"I forbid it!" Diego roars across the room.

"Yeah, well. I'm fucking grown so what you say doesn't even matter," Gigi hisses before turning and walking out the front door of the clubhouse.

I make to stand, but Lawson puts a hand on my shoulder. "Stay out of it, baby."

"She's upset."

"She'll be fine," he assures me.

Little does anyone in this room know we won't see her for a very long time, and when we do, we won't even recognize the woman she's become.

Hound
Cerberus MC Book 7
UnEdited Sneak Peak

Chapter 1
Hound

"Best job ever," I mutter to myself as the topless waitress bring me another glass of whiskey.

Leaning in close, she runs her hand down my arm. "I don't normally offer private lap dances, but for you, I'll make an exception."

I only acknowledge her with a quick wave of my hand and keep my focus on the stage. The best pair of tits and abs tighter than I've ever seen on a woman before, I'm mesmerized as the red-headed seductress as she twirls around the pole in the center of the stage.

I toss back half of the whiskey in my glass but never take my eyes from the woman I plan to have before the sun comes up.

The girl I came here to find is nowhere to be seen. I did my job for the night, looking for the whiney kid who's giving her dad fits by not staying under his command. I searched the front of the house as well as the back of the house where the girls getting ready before taking it all off on the center stage. The blonde girl with bright blue eyes that I tasked with finding and removing is nowhere in the building. Determining that she must be off tonight, I let loose. Having a few drinks and watching the topless entertainment is only a perk of the mission. Of course, it's not recognizance, infiltration, and extraction, but there are benefits to this type of works as well.

The girls flitting around with bare tits and asses exposed in glittery thongs are nice to look at, but they each pale in comparison to the siren on the stage.

Hips rolling and long red hair following her like a smoky shadow dancing at her command, she's got the attention of every single man in the room, and I'm not immune to her charm. Hell, if all of my money wasn't tied up in savings accounts I'd write her a check for the sum of all of them just for the taste of her skin and the tight embrace of her cunt.

My mouth grows dry as I breathe heavily, short panting breaths taken in an attempt to keep my cock from busting through the seam of my suddenly too tight jeans.

Strippers are nothing new. Seventeen years in the Marine Corps traveling the world has led to more adventures with loose women than I can count, but there's something about this beauty that has me chomping at the bit to get her beneath me. The great thing about underpaid whores is that for the right amount, they'll let you do just about anything to them. I imagine this one will be no different.

Paying for sex used to make my skin crawl, but bedding a professional woman who will have no expectations when the sun raises gained appeal as I got older. Leaving broken hearts in my wake never appealed to me, and lying to a woman just to fuck her, I've decided, is more fucked up than paying for a hole to fuck for the night.

She hits her stride, the deep bass of the song ricocheting off of the walls, and the hoots and hollers become almost unbearable. Enthralled by the sway of her hips, just like every other man in here, I don't notice when the song ends, and she bends to gather the bills tossed at her feet on the stage.

I move my eyes from the sway of her firm tits to look into her eyes. Soulless, dead almost. She's definitely not one of the ones who get off on dozens of men fawning over her naked body. I wish I could say I feel sorry for her, that seeing her misery so clear but ignored by every other guy in front of her will make me change my mind, but it doesn't. We all have demons we have to fight, and she's no different. Since I have my own shit to deal with and things to prepare for in the near future, I can't be bothered to concern myself with her issues. What I can do is make her come like a freight train and give her enough cash to make it easier to leave this life if it's what she chooses.

When her eyes lock with mine, a tingle of anticipation rushes down my spine and straight to my cock. The swipe of her tongue over her full lips as she takes me in is enough to make the tip of my cock thicken and weep for her. I wink, pretending to be as unaffected as I can and mouth 'soon' to her. She's flushed from the exertion of her dance, but it doesn't stop her cheeks from pinking even more. She gives me a slight nod, acknowledging that our plans for the evening include each other before she stands and exits the stage with enough sway to her hips to keep every man in the building pining for her.

The DJ announces that "Orphan Annie" will be back at the top of the hour, forcing me to look down at my watch. Contemplating if I should find and fuck her now or wait for another show on the stage, I think about her odd choice of stage name. The little, redheaded girl with no family, as the story goes is adopted by a mean woman who is never short of voicing her dislikes even after her husband, Daddy Warbucks comes into the picture.

I huff a small laugh, thinking about the storyline in today's age and why a woman no older than twenty-five would pick it. Was she abused? Did her Daddy Warbucks take advantage and that was the real reason for the discord with the wife? Is she into older men?

That thought makes me smile considering I'm probably ten years her senior. Attraction to older men would benefit me in the persuasion part of the night. I shake my head. Honestly, it wouldn't matter. The wad of cash in pocket ensures I'll be inside of her tonight.

I drain my whiskey and wait for her next performance. Once again as she makes her way on stage, I can't pull my eyes from the glistening skin of her body. The sweat dripping between her tits, rolling down the tight muscles of her stomach makes my mouth dry no matter how much whiskey I pour down my throat. Bad Girlfriend by Theory of a Deadman blares from the surround sound as she keeps perfect tempo to the beat.

Her eyes find mine, holding them captive. Her emerald eye bewitches me as I consider an attempt to access those savings accounts I thought about earlier in the night. Paid whore or not, I know one night with this temptress will never be enough.

She seems to be the headliner, the one woman who draws the men in, which means, from my past experience, her night is over. She's closing out the stage with one final dance as the waitress who's been serving me all night tells me it's last call.

I decline the offer for a final drink and head to the door before she walks off of the stage. I wait in the shadows near the rear exit listening to the men grumble as they're escorted out the front and wait for my redheaded beauty to make an appearance.

The wait is so long that I question the interaction between us, question the sincerity I saw in her wide green eyes. She's the perfect tease, making me think she wants me just as I'm sure she does with every man who walks through the dingy front doors of The Minge Palace.

I'm near giving up, realizing that Orphan Annie is more trouble than she's worth when the back door opens and a flash of red exits the building before laughing at something someone inside says before closing it again. I step out of the shadows when she's less than a handful of feet in front of me. I expect her to startle, to clutch at her chest in an attempt to ease her pounding heart, but she shocks me by staring directly at me as if I'm her puppet and waiting in the filthy alley is exactly what she expects. I clench my fists at the idea that she thinks she can have the upper hand.

"I've been waiting," I growl, loving the pink that returns to her cheeks.

"I searched for you out the front," she whispers closing the distance between the two of us and running her small hands over my heaving chest.

"I figure you'd want the cloak of darkness even though your screams of orgasm will echo down the alleyway."

"So confident in your ability to please."

Her hands leave my chest, trail down my chest, and run across my back as she circles me. I'm her prey tonight, and she's got even more confident in her power than she displayed on the stage earlier tonight. No matter how much I want to fight it, how much I want to prove to her that she'll be taking my cock as I see fit, I know without a doubt that Orphan Annie is going to use me and have me begging for more.

"Care to make a bet?" I offer as she stands in front of me once again.

Petite yet solid, she looks up at me as I imagine all of the ways I can easily take her.

"No," she pants, her pupils so big in the moonlight I question the small halo of blue circling them.

Didn't she have green eyes on the stage?

I don't give it a second thought when her tiny hand covers but a fraction of my cock over my jeans.

"You want to stand out here making bets?" She gives me a squeeze tight enough to make me groan. "Or do you want to fuck?"

"Brazen little thing aren't you?"

I drop my hands to my sides as she fumbles with my belt and the zipper on my jeans. The relief is immediate as she pulls the denim back and my cock springs free.

"Mmm." The tiny noise from her mouth not only makes me jump in her hands but forces me to wonder what that noise being made while she takes me to the back of her throat will feel like.

"Another time," I hiss.

"What?" she asks confused just as I lift her and turn her with her back against the cold brick wall.

"Enough talk." The insistent ache in my cock doesn't leave much room for anything else.

Urging her legs around my hips, I can see the pain the stretch is causing as she tries to get them all the way around me. She doesn't have a hope of doing it though. I'm twice her size and ready to handle her, to position her any way I see fit.

Her skirt rides high exposing the glistening slit of her pink cunt.

"Dirty whore," I hiss as my fingers move the wetness up to lubricate the friction of my fingers on her clit. "You came out here prepared to fuck me?"

Her eyes slam shut, a tiny whimper escaping her lips as she rolls her hips against my hand trying to find her pleasure. Without warning, I slip two thick fingers inside of her, watching her face for the response I know she'll give. Eyes dashing open, hers find mine.

"So fucking tight," I praise. "If two fingers are all you can take, there's no hope my cock will fit inside of you."

Lips parting, she tilts her head to the side. "Give me more," she begs.

I withdraw and delve back in with three fingers, working them in and out, preparing her as best I can.

"Please," she whimpers, near the edge, I refuse to let her fall over.

"I'm going to hurt you," I warn as I pull free from her tight pussy.

"Please," she repeats.

Against better judgment, I replace my fingers with the head of my cock and slam home.

She screams, half in pain, the other half in pleasure.

"Oh God."

"Fuck, Annie," I grunt as I pull back only to slam forward again.

"It's too much," she complains but relents when my finger begins to strum over the tight bundle of nerves at the apex of her thighs.

"That's it," I urge.

I'm certain her back is going to have abrasions from shoulders to tailbone, but the consideration isn't something I have to give as she clamps on my cock, the tightest thing I've felt since I fucked a virgin in high school. The quick thought of that night, so many years ago, makes me realize my mistake, the same one I made then. However fucked up and consequences be damned, I can't stop the ache of release already teasing my balls. My head flexes back, my orgasm becoming a living thing under my skin as I pulse inside of her. Bare. No condom.

When I'm done. I release my hold on her and stumble backward. I can't even look at her, so disappointed in myself for the whiskey I drank that allowed the haze of my senses to make such a monumental mistake. I fumble with my jeans. I get them up and zipped not even concerning myself with my belt.

"You said you'd make me come," she coos in front of me. "But you came too quickly for me to get mine. Want to go back to your place to finish what you started?"

"No," I hiss, keeping my eyes down as I shove my hand into my pocket and pull out a wad of cash.

She crosses her arms over her chest when I offer it to her.

"I'm not a whore," she growls, and it is then that I find her eyes.

"You just fucked me in a filthy alley after dancing for dozens of men on a stripper pole." I shove the money into her hands. "Believe me, Annie, you're as close to a whore as it comes."

"You mother fucker!"

"That," I say pointing at the cash she reluctantly holds in her hand. "Is for the abortion if my stupid ass put that shit into motion, or for your bus ticket out of this fucking town, because so help me God if I caught something antibiotics won't get rid of from that filthy snatch of yours I'll come back and kill you."

Her eyes narrow in challenge, and it gives me hope that VD isn't going to be in my future.

I don't give her a second glance as I make my way out of the alley and stumble back to my shitty hotel room. I try to push her from my mind as I fall on the bed and pass out.

When morning comes, and the incessant chirping of text messages on my phone is frequent enough to drive me mad, she's still on my mind. I almost feel guilty about the blood on my cock, knowing I was too rough with her. I check each one of my piercing, knowing that one of the barbells must have cut her, but they're all intact.

I don't however, feel the regret until I check my messages and see the first one from Blade which was sent a mere two hours after I left Annie in that disgusting alley without concern as to whether or not she'd make it home safely.

Blade: I told you to find Georgia Anderson. Not fuck her like a whore in the alley.

So much for my new life. That redheaded woman from last night just fucked me harder than I fucked her last night.

What do you think?
Join my group and let's talk about it!!
Marie James Stalkers

More From Marie James
Marie James Facebook: Marie James
Author Group: Author Marie James' Stalkers
Twitter: @AuthrMarieJame
Instagram: author_marie_james
Newsletter SignUp: HERE
Reader Email Share: HERE

Macon

Tossing a middle finger to Macon, Georgia as I made my way to Nashville was always the dream. Sing country music, go on tour, top the charts— with my popularity growing every day, I was on my way.

But then a gust of wind blew up your skirt, and those white cotton panties had me hooked. I didn't know your name, and you turned down every attempt I tried to throw your way. But I knew you were different, even though you told me I was the same.

"Friends" is what you offered, and I played by your rules, but, Adelaide Hatfield, you have to know, from that day, it was only you.

I just hope I can make you see how much you mean to me before we both drown in the sorrow of what heartbreak can truly be.

We Said Forever

Rock bottom.

They say the only way to go from there is up, but what is "up" when you're born into someone else's rock bottom?

At ten, football became my first love. It's what got me out of the house away from my self-destructive family. My love for football landed me at Las Vegas University with a full ride scholarship, and the orange on my jersey was my favorite color…until my eyes landed on the red dress Fallyn wore the night we met.

At twenty-one, I jumped off the cliff into the unknown the second Fallyn McIntyre danced in my arms at a party. I had the greatest girl in the world and the opportunity to play college ball every Saturday. My rock bottom was looking up, thanks to my two first loves.

Parties, sex, and football—life was perfect. But one drink too many, and my world came crashing down. When I chose pills over my second love, my head told me it was the best decision I ever made. The pills keep me warm and protect me from the distance Fallyn created. Percs don't judge me. They make me feel alive.

Threes.

They say the best things come in threes, but one leads to a stable future, one is my salvation, and the other drags me to hell—a hell I'd willingly burn in for eternity…if it weren't for my second love.

More Than a Memory

"You're gorgeous. Even better looking than the day I fell in love with you."

The words are a constant reminder of what true love is. Olivia Dawson's alarm goes off at the same time every day and she disappears into her room to hear Duncan's voice, see his face, miss him even more for being untouchable. Olivia loves with her entire heart, and her love for Duncan is unmatched, but there's something about her new roommate she just can't seem to ignore—no matter how hard she tries.

"I miss you so much."
"Can't be more than I miss you."

The words are a constant reminder of how unavailable Olivia is, and Bryson Daniels isn't one for competition off the baseball field, but since the moment he knocked on the door to his new apartment and his roommate "Ollie" wasn't who he expected, he can't help but consider bending a few of his rules—even if it means heeding to Olivia's.

"I love you, sweet cheeks. Chat with you later?"

Bryson hears the conversations through the paper thin walls, but there's a pain inside Olivia he can't seem to walk away from. He vows to be there for her when the voice on the other side of the computer inevitably breaks her heart, but will he ever be able to compete with someone who's more than a memory?

Hale Series
Coming to Hale
The only time she trusted someone with her heart, she was just a girl; he betrayed her and left her humiliated. Since then, Lorali Bennett has let that moment in time dictate her life.

Ian Hale, sexy as sin business mogul, has never had more than a passing interest in any particular woman, until a chance encounter with Lorali, leaves a lasting mark on him.

Their fast-paced romance is one for the record books, but what will happen when Ian's secrets come to light? Especially when those secrets will cost her everything she spent years trying to rebuild.

Begging for Hale
Alexa Warner, an easy going, free spirit, has never had a problem with jumping from one man to the next. She likes to party and have a good time; if the night ends in steamy sex that's a bonus. She's always sought pleasure first and never found a man that turned her down; until Garrett Hale. Never in her life was she forced to pursue a man, but his rejection doesn't sit well with her. Alexa aches for Garrett, his rejection festering in her gut. The yearning for him escalating until she is able to seduce him, taste him.

Garrett Hale, a private man with muted emotions, has no interest in serious relationships. Having his heart ripped out by his first love, he now leaves a trail of one night stands in his wake. Mutually satisfying sex without commitment is his newly adopted lifestyle. Alexa's constant temptation has his restraint wavering. The aftermath of giving into her would be messy; she is after all the best friend of his cousin's girlfriend, which guarantees future run-ins, not something that's supposed to happen with a one night stand.

Yet, the allure of having his mouth on her is almost more than he can bear. With hearts on the line, and ever increasing desire burning through them both, will one night be enough for either of them?

Hot as Hale
Innocent Joselyne Bennett loves her quiet life. As an elementary teacher, her days include teaching kids then going home to research fun science projects to add to her lesson plan. Her only excitement is living vicariously through her sister Lorali and friend Alexa Warner. Incredibly gorgeous police detective Kaleb Perez was going through the motions of life. His position on the force as a narcotics detective forced him to cross paths with Josie after a shooting involving her friend. On more than one occasion Kaleb discretely tried to catch Josie's eye. On every occasion, he was ignored but when her hand is

forced after a break-in at her apartment Josie and Kaleb are on a collision course with each other.

Formerly timid Josie is coaxed out of her shell by the sexy-as-sin Kaleb, who nurtures her inner sex-kitten in the most seductive ways, and replaces her inexperience with passionate need. The small group has overcome so much in such a short period of time, and just when they think they can settle back into their lives, they are forced back into the unknown.

Can Kaleb protect Josie from further tragedy? Can she let him go once the threat of danger is gone?

To Hale and Back

Just when things seem like they're getting back to normal and everyone is safe, drugs, money, and vengeance lead a rogue group into action, culminating in a series of events that leave one man dead and another in jail for a wide range of crimes, none of which he is guilty of.

This incredibly strong and close-knit group of six will be pushed to their limits when they are thrown into adversity. But can they come out unscathed? The situation turns dire when friendships and bonds are tested past the breaking point. Allegiances are questioned, and relationships may crumble.

Love Me Like That

Two strangers trapped together in a blizzard. One running from the past; one with no future. Two destinies collide.

London Sykes is on her own for the first time in her life after a sequence of betrayal and abuse. One man rescues her only to destroy her himself. An unfortunate accident lands her in a ditch only to be rescued by the most closed-off man she's ever met, albeit undeniably handsome.

Kadin Cole is at the cabin in the woods for the very first and the very last time. Since his grief doesn't allow for him to return home to a life he's no longer able to live alone, he's finally made what has been the hardest decision of his life. His plans change drastically when a beautiful woman in a little red car crashes into his life.

How can she trust another man? How could he ever love again? Will happenstance and ensuing sexual attraction be enough to heal two hearts enough that they can see in themselves what the other sees?

Teach Me Like That

Thirty-three, single, and loving life.

Construction worker by day and playboy by night. Kegan Cole has what many men can only dream about. A great job, incredible family, and more women fawning over him than he can count. What more could he ask for?

Lexi Carter spends her days teaching at a private school. Struggling to rebuild her life after tragedy nearly destroyed her, she doesn't have the time or energy to invest in any arrangement that could lead to heartbreak. That includes the enigmatic Kegan Cole whose arrogance and sex appeal arrive long before he enters a room.

It doesn't matter how witty, charming, and incredibly sexy he is. She plays games all day with her students and has no room in her life for games when it comes to men, and Kegan Cole has *'love them and leave them'* written all over his handsome bearded face.

When Lexi doesn't fall at his feet like every other woman before her, Kegan is forced off-script to pursue her because not convincing her to give in isn't an option.

How can a man who hates lies be compatible with a woman who has more secrets than she can count?

Can a man set in his playboy ways become the man Lexi needs? More importantly, does he even want to?

This is a full-length novel that has adult language and descriptive sex scenes. It is NOT a student/teacher book. Both main characters are consenting adults.

Cerberus MC
Kincaid Book 1

I am Emmalyn Mikaelson.
My husband, in a rage, hit me in front of the wrong person. Diego, or Kincaid to most, beat the hell out of him for it. I left with Diego anyway. Even though he could turn on me just like my husband did, I knew I had a better chance of survival with Diego. That was until I realized Kincaid could hurt me so much worse than my husband ever could. Physical pain pales in comparison to troubles of the heart.
I am Diego "Kincaid" Anderson.
She was a waitress at a bar in a bad situation. I brought her to my clubhouse because I knew her husband would kill her if I didn't. Now she has my protection and that of the Cerberus MC. I never expected her to become something more to me. I was in more trouble than I've ever been in before, and that's saying a lot considering I served eight years in the Marine Corps with Special Forces.

Kid: Cerberus MC Book 2

Khloe When Khloe Devaro's best friend and fiancé is lost to the war in Iraq, she's beyond distraught. Her intentions of joining him in the afterlife are thwarted by a Cerberus Motorcycle club member. Too young to do anything on her own, the only alternative she has now is to take Kid up on his offer to stay at the MC Clubhouse. As if that's not a disaster waiting to happen, but anything is better than returning to the foster home she's been forced to live in the last three years.
"Kid" Dustin "Kid" Andrews spent four years as a Marine; training, fighting, and learning how to survive the most horrendous of conditions. He never imagined that holding a BBQ fundraiser for a local fallen soldier would end up as the catalyst that turns his world upside down. Resisting his attraction for a girl he's not even certain is of legal age was easy, until he's forced to intervene when her intentions become clear. All his training is wasted as far as he's concerned, since none of that will help him when it comes to Khloe. Will the self-proclaimed man-whore sleep with a woman in every country he visits as planned, or will the beautiful, yet feisty girl living down the hall throw a wrench in his plan?

Shadow: Cerberus MC Book 3

Morrison "Shadow" Griggs, VP of the Cerberus MC, is a force to be reckoned with. Women fall at his feet, willing to do almost anything for a night with him.

Misty Bowen is the exception. She's young and impressionable, but with her religious upbringing, she's able to resist Shadow's advances... for a while at least.

Never one to look back on past conquests, Shadow is surprised that he's intrigued by Misty, which only grows more when she seems to be done with him without a word.

Being ghosted by a twenty-one-year-old is not the norm where he's concerned, and the rejection doesn't sit right with him.

Life goes on, however, until Misty shows up on the doorstep of the Cerberus MC clubhouse with a surprise that rocks his entire world off of its axis.

With only the clothes on her back and the consequences of her lies and deceit, Misty needs help now more than she ever has. Alone in the world and desperate for help, she turns to the one man she thought she'd never see again.

Shadow would never turn his back on a woman in need, but his inability to forgive has always been his main character flaw. Unintended circumstances have cast Misty into his life, but will he have the ability to keep his distance when her situation necessitates a closeness he's never dreamed of having with a woman?

Dominic: Cerberus MC Book 4

Dominic Anderson knows exactly what he wants in life: simplicity, safety, and solidarity with his brothers. He's vowed to spend each day living his life exactly how he chooses since the day his wife betrayed him and his four year military career turned into twenty.

Returning home after retirement from the Marines, he's traded the sand in the Middle East for that of the New Mexico desert, Humvees for a motorcycle, and the comradery of men in uniform for the occasional woman at his feet.

Life was perfect until Makayla "Poison" Evans, Renegade MC Princess, knocked on his door, bruises on her face, neck, and arms, and no money to pay the cab driver. Pink hair, perfect body, and a mouth that Dom yearned to teach a million lessons, Mak asks more from him than he's conceded to a woman in decades.

She needs his help, his protection, and against his better judgment, she expects him to keep her secrets. Only her secrets are deadly, dangerous, and have the potential to start a war between two MCs.

At what point does safeguarding a woman become a betrayal to the men Dominic calls his family? More importantly, can he get back the sanctity of his home once Makayla is no longer in the picture, or will he be forever tainted by her poison?

Snatch: Cerberus MC Book 5

I've been Jaxon Donovan since the day I was born, obviously. My road name, Snatch, came years later due to my ability to literally snatch up any woman I set my sights on. I've always been a connoisseur of the opposite sex. Tall, short, thin, thick and juicy, my tastes knew no limitations.

I didn't think there was a limitation to my sexuality, and I found out just how true that actually was the night my best friend took it upon himself to take me in his mouth. Sure, there'd been close calls before, the slip of a hand or misplaced lips. With our propensity to share women, it's bound to happen. That fateful night, I was met with pure intention and an experience I never want to forget.

How do you explain to your friends, your brother's in arms, that your extremely active sexuality has led you to your best friend's doorstep? How do you admit, after twenty-six years of heterosexuality, that you're into something else?

I'll soon find out that what happens in the dark will always come to light.

Printed in Great Britain
by Amazon